Christmas
at the Amish
Bakeshop

Read more Shelley Shepard Gray in

An Amish Second Christmas
Amish Christmas Twins

More from Rachel J. Good

His Unexpected Amish Twins
His Pretend Amish Bride
His Accidental Amish Family
Amish Christmas Twins

More Amish romance from Loree Lough

All He'll Ever Need
Home to Stay
Loving Mrs. Bontrager
Amish Christmas Twins

Christmas *at the* Amish Bakeshop

Shelley Shepard Gray

Rachel J. Good

Loree Lough

www.kensingtonbooks.com

KENSINGTON BOOKS are published by

Kensington Publishing Corp.
119 West 40th Street
New York, NY 10018

ISBN-13: 978-1-4967-3426-6 (ebook)
ISBN-10: 1-4967-3426-2 (ebook)

ISBN-13: 978-1-4967-3424-2
ISBN-10: 1-4967-3424-6

First Kensington Trade Paperback Printing: October 2021

10 9 8 7 6 5 4 3 2 1

Printed in the United States of America

Contents

A Christmas Cake for Rebecca

SHELLEY SHEPARD GRAY

Acknowledgments

What a joy it was to work with Rachel Good and Loree Lough on this collection! I'm also so grateful for the guidance of our editor, Alicia Condon, as well as the entire Kensington team.

Thanks be to God for his gift that is too wonderful for words.

—2 Corinthians 9:15

A successful marriage requires falling in love many times,
always with the same person.

—Amish proverb

Chapter 1

December 1

At last, December had come. She'd made it to her favorite—and the most hectic—month of the year. Though her mother had always told her to stop wishing away the other eleven months, Rebecca Christner had always felt rather justified about her preference for December.

After all, there were a whole lot of reasons to love the month. First of all, everyone, whether he or she was English, Mennonite, or Amish like herself, seemed to be a little bit happier and kinder. The weather was usually crisp, cold, and snowy—but no one was tired of winter yet. Instead, each glorious pure white snowfall seemed to symbolize hope and fresh beginnings.

Then, of course, there was the obvious reason that December was so wonderful. Christmas—the day of Jesus's birth. That was a miracle to be feted and celebrated with cards and baked goods and decorations and gift giving. She had never viewed all the busy-ness as anything but a *wonderful-gut* change from her usual days as the owner of her bakeshop, Rebecca's Porch.

Unfortunately, this December felt a little different. Suddenly, she felt older, was more aware of her single, never-been-married status than usual, and she was already wondering how she was ever going to make one hundred and fifty special-order Christmas cakes this year.

She couldn't believe it had happened.

Almost ten years ago, she'd begun offering fancy three-layer Christmas cakes. The dense cakes covered in fluffy white frosting and topped with a poinsettia made from fondant were her pride and joy. Each not only looked pretty but was also made from the best ingredients she could find. The first time Rebecca had offered the special-order cakes, she'd had two-dozen orders.

They'd been such a hit, the amount ordered every year had grown. Four years ago, feeling overwhelmed, she'd placed a limit on the cakes she would make. The number was firmly capped at one hundred.

Unfortunately, one of the new girls at the shop, not realizing how important the reservation sheet was, made her own. By the time Rebecca realized what had been done, an additional fifty cakes had been ordered.

Now Rebecca had more cakes to bake than ever before and even less time to make them. It was enough to keep her up at night.

Hating to be filled with negative thoughts, she shook off her worries and concentrated on the beautiful morning. After all, the Lord never gave more than He could provide.

It truly was a beautiful morning, too. Instead of being below freezing, it was a rather balmy forty-five degrees. Rebecca was in fine spirits as she ventured out on her morning walk with Goldie, her lovely golden retriever.

With each step, Rebecca felt her usual happiness return. By

the time she was halfway through her walk, she had smiles for everyone. Even the folks who seemed to be in a perpetual state of gloom and grumpiness all year long.

"Morning, Emmitt."

"Morning, Miss Rebecca." The older man nodded, then approached Goldie, who waited patiently for the bow-legged octogenarian to give her his usual morning pet. "Morning, Goldie. You're looking lovely this morning as always."

Goldie wagged her tail. For some reason, Goldie was perpetually intrigued by Emmitt's long gray beard. Her soft brown eyes stared at it with interest when the man reached down to scratch her behind her ears.

"You're a right *gut hund*, for sure and for certain," he murmured before beginning his slow approach back to his house. Goldie wagged her tail in a way that seemed to say she agreed with the statement.

"Have a *gut* day, Emmitt!" Rebecca called out.

He held a hand up in the air without turning around. "You too, missy. Take care now."

"You are a really good dog," she whispered to Goldie as they strode forward, the dog's paws in sync with her own long stride.

"Hiya, Rebecca. How are you doing this morning?" Bethany asked.

"I'm *gut. Danke.*"

"Have you and your girls started baking Christmas cookies yet?"

"Not yet, but I was up early making snowballs and pretzels."

"What about your Christmas cakes? Have you started any of them yet? I put in my order back in September, you know."

Rebecca smiled. "It's a bit early to start those cakes. But I'll begin ordering the ingredients within the week."

"Glad to hear it. Our family's Christmas wouldn't be the

same without one of those cakes in the center of my dining room table."

"*Danke.* Now, don't wait until the end of the month to come in. We've got some special cinnamon tea brewing and all sorts of other treats. You should stop in."

"You know I will," Bethany said with a laugh. "Enjoy your walk, now."

And so it continued. Rebecca walked three miles every morning. Most of the time with Goldie by her side. It was her favorite time of morning. She'd already prayed, baked for two hours in the shop's vast kitchen, and now was taking a well-deserved break before slipping on one of her newer dresses and aprons and helping her staff and customers at the bakeshop. It was a busy life but a good one. Rebecca thrived on routine.

When she spotted an unfamiliar man sitting on the stoop of the Stutzmans' house, she paused. Old Mr. Stutzman was rarely awake this time of morning, and she couldn't remember the last time she'd seen him out to enjoy the day.

And then she got a better look at the man resting on the stoop. Why, it wasn't Mr. Eli Stutzman at all. Her heart started beating faster as her footsteps slowed. Pressing a hand to the center of her chest, she attempted to pull herself together. Surely her wayward heart and forty-two-year-old eyes were playing tricks on her.

But of course they were not. It was *him.*

"Hiya, Rebecca," Aden Raber said easily, just as if he were always sitting on the Stutzmans' stoop. He wasn't. He hadn't been anywhere near her in twenty-five years.

"You're truly a sight for sore eyes," he continued with a grin. "Especially since you look as pretty as ever."

It was all she could do not to glare.

Oh, but he had a lot of nerve to be sitting so calmly! There he was, sipping coffee and looking handsome, fit, and happy.

He was smiling at her, too! Just as if he hadn't broken her heart when she was seventeen.

Though everything in her was crying out to walk right by him without a word, or even turning around, she couldn't. Greeting him in a civilized manner was the right thing to do.

Besides, Goldie was wagging her tail and pulling Rebecca forward, just as if she couldn't wait to see the man.

When Aden's dark brown eyes warmed under his black felt hat, Rebecca realized that he knew he was making her uncomfortable, but instead of attempting to make her feel better, he was merely interested in seeing how she would respond after all this time.

It seemed he hadn't changed much, even after all this time.

Well, Rebecca could show him that she certainly had. No longer was she the naïve girl who'd fallen so hard for him that it had taken months to regroup after he'd broken her heart.

She was tougher now. Well, at the very least, she was tempered by time, like her favorite baking pans.

"Hello, Aden."

He got to his feet. "I was hoping I might see you. Eli told me you walked by here every morning."

Had Aden been waiting out here for her? "I'm afraid you have me at a disadvantage. I didn't know you were in town." And then, because she was determined to guard her heart no matter what, she blurted, "Why are you here?"

Aden didn't seem to be offended by her bluntness. Instead, the lines around his eyes deepened as he spoke again. "I should've known you'd be the same. Still no beating around the bush for you, hmm?" he said lightly.

His comment was embarrassing. As a child and a teenager, she'd always been too outspoken and blunt. Her mother had constantly admonished her for it, claiming that Rebecca would never find a man until she'd learned to be more circumspect.

"I'm merely curious. Nothing more." But still she waited.

"I'm only here on a job." He pointed to the front door. "Eli left after Thanksgiving to spend a month with his daughter and her family in Kentucky. He asked me to do some remodeling work while he was out of the way."

Years ago, owning his own remodeling business had been Aden's dream. Even though she'd never wanted to see him again, Rebecca couldn't deny that she was pleased for him. "You did it," she said before she reminded herself that she should act a bit more aloof.

Walking closer, she noticed that his stomach was still flat and his biceps had gotten bigger. Shame filled her. How could he still look so good? And, more importantly, why couldn't she keep herself from noticing?

Smiling at Goldie, who was practically quivering, she was so eager to be petted, Aden said, "Who's this?"

"My dog. Her name is Goldie."

His hand still hovered. "May I?"

He was being so kind to dear Goldie, Rebecca thawed a little. "If you don't pet her soon, I think she's going to pass out, she's gotten herself in such a tizzy."

He complied, stroking Goldie's neck. The dog closed her eyes in happiness.

Aden laughed. "How old is she?"

"Three. Old enough to stop chewing my shoes but young enough to be good company on my walks."

"I heard you take a lot of walks, too."

She straightened. "It sounds like you've been asking about me."

A new wariness entered his expression. "Only the basics," he said. "I figured that it would be better to know something about you before we met again."

"May I ask why?"

He shrugged. "I wanted to know how you were."

His reply was so honest, so free from judgments or anger, she realized that she wanted to know more about him, too. "Ah."

When she didn't add anything else, he shifted on his feet. "So, um . . . how have you been?"

"Over the last twenty-five years?" She chuckled. "I guess all told, I've been okay."

"Did you ever marry?"

The way he phrased the question, she knew that he knew she wasn't married now. "Nee." She lifted her chin. "I never did. You?"

"*Jah.* Her name was Anna Mae. She died about three years ago."

"I'm sorry for your loss."

"*Danke.* I'm sorry, too." Something appeared in his eyes, something that looked almost like regret but she wasn't sure.

"Did you have children?"

"*Jah.* Three. All girls."

Rebecca couldn't help but smile. Aden was a carpenter, burly, so capable. It amused her to think of him as the lone man in a houseful of girls. "I bet they kept you on your toes."

"They did at that. The eldest is already married, and both of the others have steady beaus. Now they spend their days keeping their men on their toes."

"It sounds like you've had a good life."

His smile faltered. "Why did you never marry, Rebecca?"

Though she knew Aden didn't ask to make her feel bad, she still did.

How could she tell him that she hadn't ever found a man who compared to him? "I don't know. I guess the Lord didn't see fit to send me my match," she murmured. Though to be sure, that was a lie. He had, indeed, given her a perfect mate. The problem had been that Aden hadn't felt the same way.

"I'm sorry for that."

He was sorry? They'd been in love, and he'd left her!

Suddenly, she needed space. It was too hard to stand there with him, thinking about what could have been and what never was. Too hard not to blame him when she'd encouraged him to go in the first place.

Too hard to admit that even though she'd encouraged him to leave, there was a part of her that had always imagined he felt the same way about her that she did about him.

That he would want to rush back to see her because he missed her.

But, of course, that had never happened.

Pasting a smile on her lips, she stepped back a bit. The movement caused Goldie to stand up again. "Well, it's getting rather chilly out here. I need to start moving and warm myself up."

"I suppose so. The cold does creep into one's bones after a time."

"I need to get ready to open the shop, too."

"It's called Rebecca's Porch, *jah*?" After she nodded, he said, "Maybe I'll come in and get coffee or a pastry one day soon. If you don't mind?"

She appreciated his asking that. Appreciated his acknowledgment that he was on her turf, and she wasn't sure how to handle it. But it was time to let the past go—as well as her hard feelings. "I don't mind at all, Aden. Come into the shop whenever you would like."

"I'll do that then."

"Which means that we'll see each other soon." She inclined her head slightly. "Good day."

"*Jah.* Good day to you, Rebecca Christner. And Goldie."

Goldie wagged her tail, causing them both to chuckle. Then, because there wasn't anything more to say, Rebecca lifted a hand. A kind of half-hearted wave before turning away.

Though she didn't look back, Rebecca was fairly sure she could feel his eyes resting on her as she walked down the sidewalk.

Or maybe it was simply hope that he was still thinking about her. If that were the case, then he would finally know how she'd been feeling.

For much, much too long.

Chapter 2

Rebecca Christner was still beautiful.

Shaking his head in exasperation at himself, Aden took a sip of coffee, found it lukewarm, and poured the rest of the cup out. He needed to go back inside and continue pulling out old cabinets—John was waiting for him—but he stood there trying to catch one last glimpse of her before she disappeared around the corner.

Craning his neck, he was successful. He saw one final sway of her navy cloak before she disappeared from sight. How could a woman he hadn't seen in twenty-five years still affect him so?

Because it was Rebecca; that was why.

From the time he'd decided to return to town, Aden had been mentally preparing for their reunion. And, because he couldn't help it, he'd spent many minutes wondering how the years had treated her. He knew from his own experiences that anything could have happened.

She could have gotten bitter or worn out by life. She could have indulged in so many of her sweets that her appearance would be very different from that of the slim girl he used to know.

But instead, Rebecca still seemed to exude something bright and clean. Honestly, she was like a breath of fresh air. She had a bloom in her cheeks, and a smile for her dog.

"How did it go?" his old friend John asked when Aden went back inside the house. "Did she give you the time of day?"

"She did." Of course, not much more than that. "Kind of."

"When are you going to see her again?"

John was far too interested in Aden's reunion with Rebecca. Worried that somehow his friend would share the news with someone who would promptly pass it on to her, Aden took care to keep his answers low-key. "I'll probably stop by her bakeshop one day soon."

But instead of looking disappointed by the casual reply, John grinned. "Will you now?"

His old buddy looked far too entertained. "What does that grin mean?"

"Only that it will be mighty interesting to see you sipping *kaffi* while sitting at one of the girly tables in Rebecca's Porch."

"Girly tables?" Aden rolled his eyes. "You need to advance with the rest of us to the twenty-first century, John. Lots of men drink coffee, and some of them even go into coffee shops to enjoy it."

"You are right. I canna deny that."

Pleased that John was taking his point seriously, Aden added, "I know you think I'm exaggerating things, but it's not just me who thinks this way." He waved a hand, just as if he got paid to advertise coffee shops. "I mean, think about all the Starbucks around. There are just as many men who frequent them as women. I promise that's true."

"Yes, it is. I shouldn't have joked about Rebecca's shop." John looked as if he were going to add something else, but instead picked up his hammer. "Where do you want me, boss?"

"Let's get back to work on those old cabinets. Grab a crowbar and your gloves. Pulling them all out of here is gonna be a tough job."

"It is. They're put on so good, one would think they used Gorilla Glue."

"Gorilla Glue?" Aden knew all about the stuff, but he was pretty shocked to hear John mention it.

"Just keeping up with the times, Aden. You aren't the only one of us who's picked up some new habits over the last twenty-five years."

Aden would've been more inclined to agree if he wasn't so sure that John was pulling his leg. Deciding to play it safe, he said, "Just get to work, *jah*? Eli is expecting a transformation in here, and I aim to make sure he receives it."

"Sure thing." Picking up the crowbar, John got to work.

Aden let him go back to the kitchen on his own. He needed a moment to think about what had just happened and to plan his next steps.

He'd been hopelessly naïve when he'd pictured his reunion with Rebecca. Though he wasn't normally the type of man to be foolishly optimistic, he had imagined their first meeting would have gone better. Back in Ohio, after Eli Stutzman had contacted him about doing the remodel job, Aden had weighed the pros and cons for several days.

On the one hand, there would be a good chance he would be gone for all of December and maybe even Christmas. That meant he would be away from his girls for some time. But just as he'd been ready to refuse Eli's job offer and stay where he was, the girls had reminded him that they'd all made Christmas plans with other people this year. It was Jenna and her husband's turn to go to his parents, Marta was traveling to Florida to see cousins, and Corrine had promised Anna Mae's parents that she'd go to their farm. Of course, all three girls had encouraged him to join them, but he'd refused weeks earlier. None of the places had felt like a good fit.

He'd realized that there was nothing keeping him at home . . . but the dream of what could have been was calling him back to Pennsylvania. Especially after his brother Frank assured him that Rebecca still hadn't married.

Aden was embarrassed to realize that a part of him had thought Rebecca would be so surprised and delighted to see him that she'd be willing to forget how he'd left her with little notice all those years ago.

That she wouldn't remember all the promises he'd made when they'd been alone, sharing their dreams. All those promises he'd broken.

It had been mighty obvious that she hadn't forgotten anything. She might be cordial, but she certainly wasn't going to throw him a welcome-home party.

He needed to back up, rethink things, and come up with a new plan.

Yes, that's what he needed. A December plan. A way to become involved in her favorite month of the year.

No, he needed to be part of one of her favorite things about her favorite month. He had thirty days to do it.

Already imagining all the moonlit walks, sleigh rides, and other assorted activities they could to do together, he smiled. Yes, that's what he would do. They'd get reacquainted during her free time. And maybe—just maybe—by January first, she would be anxious to resume a relationship with him again . . . and maybe even consider eventually moving to Ohio.

It made perfect sense to him.

Chapter 3

Rebecca still felt shaken up, and she didn't appreciate the feeling. It was wreaking havoc with her work, too. All morning she'd been absentminded. She'd even caught Miriam and Sarah—two of her best assistants—exchanging looks of alarm.

She didn't blame them for being confused, either. Miriam had just had to stop her from putting the sour cream pound cake in the oven. It seemed she'd forgotten to add the eggs. Rebecca knew she needed to get back on track and soon, too. If she wasn't careful, she was going to make a bunch of inedible baked goods. Just thinking about the waste made her shudder.

Unfortunately, neither her coworkers' confusion nor the fear of wasting food and money helped her get back on track. All she seemed able to do was daydream. Not that she was doing a very good job! So far, she'd revisited the first time Aden had kissed her, the first time they'd gone to a get-together as an official couple, and the way he'd looked at her when she'd knit him a new navy-blue sweater for Christmas.

He'd looked at her like she'd hung the moon.

"Ah, Rebecca?"

Startled from her reverie, she turned to Sarah. "*Jah?*"

Sarah looked uncomfortable. "Ah, Rebecca, would you like me to finish making that cake for ya?"

"Why do you ask?" Rebecca looked at the mixing bowl. She honestly couldn't remember what she'd been making.

"Because you've put five cups of sugar into the bowl," Sarah said hesitantly. "That's too much for even two chocolate cakes."

Rebecca had been mixing together a chocolate cake? "I'm pretty sure I didn't put five cups of anything in the mixing bowl, dear."

"Sarah isn't wrong," Miriam said. "I'm afraid we've been counting."

Gazing down into the batter, Rebecca realized that the consistency was off. The color, too. Worse, she had no idea of what amounts she'd put in already.

Rebecca made herself admit that she was doing more harm than good at the moment. "I'm sorry, Sarah. It seems you're right. I . . . well, I guess my mind has been drifting today." She forced a laugh that sounded as fake as it felt. "I'm not sure what's been going on with me." Picking up the large stainless-steel bowl, Rebecca said, "I'll get rid of this now."

"Nee, don't do that." Sarah took the bowl away from her. "I can fix it up."

"Are you sure?"

She nodded. "I'll just make three chocolate cakes. No harm there, since they're such good sellers."

On another day Rebecca might have argued with Sarah's suggestion. Chocolate cakes were good sellers, but three extra ones were sure to be difficult to get rid of. However, there was no way Rebecca was going to argue.

"*Danke,* Sarah," she told the eighteen-year-old. "Thank you for looking out for me today." Wiping a hand on her white apron, she shook her head. "I don't know what's happened to me this morning."

"I do," Miriam said. "I heard you saw your old flame."

"What?"

Sarah smiled. "Everyone's been talking about it."

"I didn't realize the people I spoke to on my walks were such a point of interest." Realizing how that sounded, Rebecca cleared her throat. "I mean, if you're referring to Aden, he's just an old friend." An old friend whom she'd once thought she was going to marry.

Sarah covered her mouth as she took over Rebecca's mixing bowl and put in the last of the ingredients.

Miriam, on the other hand, grinned. "Come now, Rebecca. Even you have to admit that your reunion was notable."

"Notable?"

"Well, *jah*. After all, the two of you were out on the street chatting for a good long while. And you even let him pet Goldie."

"Goldie is friendly dog."

"Indeed she is. But this was something more," Miriam said. "At least . . . I heard it was."

Oh! Oh, for heaven's sake. "Aden is an old friend," Rebecca said again. "Once we might have been close, but he moved away to Ohio some twenty years ago." Twenty-five, to be exact.

"He's Levi's older brother, isn't he?" Sarah asked.

Levi was the youngest of all the Raber children. "*Jah.*"

"He's also Frank's, Ruth's, Cal's, Stephen's and Tricia's older brother," Miriam added. "There are seven of them."

Rebecca was stunned. "You sure know a lot about the Raber family."

Sarah piped up again. "Levi is mighty handsome. He told me all about his siblings once."

"I didn't know you knew Levi. And isn't he too old for you?"

"He's twenty-seven," Sarah countered with a slight lift of her chin. "Not too old at all."

"Ah."

"Besides, Levi is just an old friend, you know."

Rebecca pretended not to notice the hint of sarcasm in Sarah's tone. "I see."

Miriam lowered her voice. "Rebecca, don't be mad. You might avoid the Rabers, but most people don't. They're a popular and well-liked family."

"I suppose they are."

"Which means that there's nothing wrong with you being happy to see Aden again. I mean, he's been gone a while. Twenty-five years is a long time."

"That is true," Rebecca murmured before she could stop herself. Noticing Miriam and Sarah exchanging looks again, she decided it was time to get out of the kitchen. "Well, now. Since ah, the two of you seem to have everything in hand, I think I'll go out to see if anyone needs help with the coffee service."

"All right," Sarah said as she picked up a measuring cup. "Don't worry about anything back here. We'll take care of it all."

"*Danke,* girls." After moving out of the kitchen, Rebecca paused for a moment in the small hallway that separated the vast kitchen from the cozy dining room.

Grateful for the privacy, Rebecca placed her hands on her cheeks and made herself take a fortifying breath. Then, in the quiet, she closed her eyes and said a prayer of thanks for Sarah's assistance back in the kitchen. If Sarah hadn't been paying such close attention, Rebecca would have had to throw out all of the batter or, worse, might have unknowingly sold a terrible cake.

When she opened her eyes, she waited for the sense of calm and peace that usually arrived after praying.

It didn't come.

Only then did Rebecca allow herself to admit that the quality of her baked goods was the last thing she was worried about.

How in the world was she going to handle a whole month in Aden's presence? Especially since she now realized that their past seemed to be an open book.

Chapter 4

Late that afternoon, Rebecca knew it was time for a break. After heading up to her apartment, she slipped off her sturdy black loafers and collapsed in her favorite rocking chair with a grateful sigh.

Unfortunately, no sooner had she closed her eyes when Sarah knocked on the door to her living quarters above the shop.

"Rebecca? Rebecca, are you there?"

Goldie lifted her head. Then, after deciding that the arrival didn't require her attention, she rested her head back on her front paws with a low groan.

Rebecca didn't blame Goldie one bit. It was selfish, but all Rebecca wanted to do was ignore the rest of the world. At least for a few hours. She'd even take five minutes.

After contemplating the pros and cons of pretending to be out of earshot, Rebecca got to her feet, walked across the room, and finally opened the door to one of her most eager employees. "Here I am, Sarah," she said, hoping she sounded more upbeat than she felt. "What's going on?"

The girl trotted in the way Goldie used to do when she was a puppy. "I'm sorry to bother you, but I couldn't wait to tell you the news! You just received two more orders for Christmas cakes. Isn't that exciting?"

Sure she wasn't hearing that right, Rebecca leaned slightly forward. "Pardon me?"

"We received two more orders just now! That makes five for the day."

Rebecca was shaking her head before Sarah had even finished speaking. "That canna be right. I already have a hundred and fifty orders for Christmas cakes."

Suddenly looking deflated, Sarah cleared her throat. "I'm sorry, but I believe the count is now at one hundred fifty-five."

"I don't understand how this happened." Folding her arms across her chest, Rebecca said, "Weren't you at the meeting when I announced that we would take no more orders?"

"I might have been." Looking guilty, Sarah mumbled, "I don't exactly remember."

"Oh, Sarah, I canna believe you took five more orders."

"This isn't exactly my fault." She knelt down and petted Goldie. "Plus, some of our customers can be really pushy. They don't like being told no."

"I know they're pushy, dear. However, I only have so many hours in a day. I'm afraid you're going to have to try harder to push back. I really can't make any more."

"You might want to tell that to everyone. You know they won't listen to me."

Sarah was adorable, but she was young. Just eighteen. "I guess I'd better go downstairs and talk to all the staff again." Thinking out loud, Rebecca murmured, "Maybe make a sign, as well."

The girl brightened. "A sign might be a real good idea. You're gonna be so busy!"

Yes, she was. "One hundred and fifty-five cakes." She whistled low. "That's a lot."

"It sure is." Getting to her feet, Sarah ran a hand down her light blue dress. "Some girls are saying that you might set a record this year. Why, Mrs. Hampton told Emma yesterday that she intends to order at least five more for her neighbors."

Mrs. Hampton was a very nice English lady. She'd been a loyal supporter of the bakeshop from practically the first moment Rebecca had opened. So, it was mighty kind of her to say such a thing. But there was no way Rebecca was going to make any more cakes. "Things have gotten out of control," she muttered.

Sarah edged to the door. "I reckon you're right. I'm sorry to be the bearer of bad news, Rebecca."

"Nee, this isn't your fault." She sighed. "I don't think it's anyone's fault."

"I could help you, if you'd like. The chocolate cakes I made this morning have already sold."

"You're a sweet girl, but I make these all myself. If I accepted your help, it wouldn't be the same."

Sarah's brow wrinkled, but after a moment, she nodded. "I guess not. See you downstairs," she said before leaving.

When she was alone again, Rebecca picked up her black tennis shoes and began loosening the ties. Tried to summon the pride she always had presenting a cake that she'd put so much care and effort into.

But now? Now, the problem was that Rebecca could think of a dozen other ways she'd rather spend her time than fulfilling cake orders. Maybe even two dozen.

What was wrong with her? Once, each one of her Christmas cakes had been a huge source of pride. She'd always felt that baking was a nice way to show love and friendship and that the cakes were a fitting symbol of that philosophy. Unfortunately, now they simply felt like a poor substitute for spending time with people she cared about, like her best friend Evie. Or the girls at the bakeshop.

Or Aden.

The knock at the door startled her back to her feet. With a sigh, she threw it open. And then stood there, dumbfounded.

"Aden? Ah, hi." Honestly, it was as if she'd just conjured him up.

"Hiya." He held his hat in his hands. "I decided to stop by this famous shop of yours. When I told the girls that we used to be close friends, one of them said I should come on upstairs to say hello."

"One of the girls just sent you up?"

Looking sheepish, he added, "Sorry, it wasn't quite like that. A couple of them knew my siblings. I think they figured it was safe to do so, but I'm afraid I didn't stop to think that I was probably disturbing you."

"Actually, you came at a good time. Come on in."

When Goldie rushed forward, Aden tossed his hat on the table and knelt down to give the retriever a few pats. "Hi to you too, girl." Looking up at Rebecca, he added, "She's a mighty fine *hund*."

"She is. She's the best."

Feeling a little flustered by his appearance, Rebecca walked to the kitchen. "Did you come into the shop for coffee? If so, I can make you some. Oh! I have some muffins from the batch I made this morning as well. They're dried cherry and white chocolate."

"I didn't come to the bakeshop for food or coffee, Bec."

She stopped and turned back to him. "Oh?"

Aden shook his head. "I think you knew that already."

"If you don't want anything to eat or drink, I'm not sure why you knocked on my door, then. After all, we've already determined that we don't have much to say to each other."

"No, I think *you* were pretending that was the case, but we both knew that was a lie."

Even though they were talking in circles, she couldn't find a way to back down. "I'm not a liar, Aden."

"I know you're not." Sounding more impatient, he blurted, "Rebecca, how about this? I want to discover what you've been doing. I want to know the woman you are now. I want to get to know you, even if I have to act like I never knew you at all."

Those were the kinds of words that used to melt her heart. The type of words that she used to crave from him. That she used to miss so badly, she'd toss and turn all night at the knowledge that she'd likely never see him again.

Afraid to believe him, she blurted, "Why would you want to do that?" She hated to sound so distrustful, but she'd learned the hard way that not every sweet phrase actually meant something.

But Aden didn't wait more than a beat before replying. "Because you're worth it, that's why."

The words were so surprising and sweet, she could only gape. It seemed her mind had just gone blank. By the look that had suddenly appeared on his face, she could tell Aden didn't mind her silence one bit.

Chapter 5

"So, how did it go?" Aden's brother Frank asked when they sat down on Frank and Amanda's enclosed back porch.

Since he needed a moment to think about his reply, Aden stretched his legs and took the time to appreciate his surroundings.

Two of the sides were covered with sliding glass panels that could be locked in place during the winter months. The furniture was made from all-weather wicker, and Amanda had fashioned comfortable cushions out of soft corduroy.

In addition, a small propane heater was on next to the screen door. The warm air mixed with the cool breeze, creating a comfortable climate. It was cool enough that one needed a sweater or jacket but not anywhere near the outside temperature. All in all, it was a very comfortable space to relax.

"I'm not really sure, to tell you the truth," Aden confided when Frank motioned for him to get on with it. "I thought it could have gone better, but it wasn't as bad as it might have been." And that was saying a lot.

"Oh, come now. Rebecca is a nice woman. I canna see her being outright rude to ya."

That was Frank. He had a way of looking on the bright side, even when the situation didn't warrant it. Usually Aden appreciated his brother's gift. But this time? Well, Frank seemed to be missing the point. "She wasn't outright rude," Aden began.

But Frank didn't need to hear another thing. "See?" Looking pleased, Frank leaned back in his chair and propped one booted foot over a knee. "I told ya so. Everything is going to be just fine. She still cares about you."

Just because he admired his brother's optimistic attitude, it didn't mean that he was always going to agree with him. "She didn't say that, Frank. She didn't come anywhere close to saying that."

"But she will. All you have to do is give her time. Women need time."

It was all Aden could do not to roll his eyes. Frank was no more of an expert on the female brain than he was. But instead of debating that point, he got right to what was on his mind. "Speaking of time, did Rebecca ever talk about me much?"

"When?" A line formed between Frank's brows. "Do you mean has Rebecca mentioned you at all during the last two decades?"

"*Jah,*" Aden replied before thinking. Because now he sounded both needy and desperate. "I'm just attempting to figure out where her mind's at."

Seeing that Frank was trying not to laugh, Aden wished he had kept the question to himself. He really was making a cake of himself. He frowned. Was he now going to start thinking of everything in terms of baked goods?

"Well, now. I don't reckon she did." Frank brightened. "But it wasn't like we ever had the opportunity to talk all that much."

"Why was that?"

Frank blinked. "Because of you and our family, of course."

Frank was talking as if he made perfect sense, but Aden was still at a loss. "I'm sorry, but what do you mean?"

"She was upset that you left, you know. And, well, all of us were struggling, too."

"With what?"

"Ah, with you leaving. And other things, of course."

"Such as?"

"Well, our financial situation."

Their family's financial situation had been one of the reasons Aden had left. There had been a lot of mouths to feed, and there was no way he was ever going to make enough money to be able to help if he stayed there. "I thought things got better," he said.

"I know you did, but they didn't."

"Frank, every letter I received from Mamm and Daed said everyone was fine."

"Ah, Aden, I'm sorry to say that they lied to you."

Their parents didn't lie. "You're acting like I was on the other side of the world. I wrote them often and called once a week."

"I realize that, but it doesn't change the fact that they didn't want you to worry about us."

Aden might have been away from his brother for twenty-five years, but it seemed some things never changed. Frank was an expert at making jabs without seeming to do it on purpose. In addition, Frank looked as if he were biting his tongue, which was starting to irritate Aden. "If you have something to say about my leaving, I think you should say it."

"Nothing I can say will change the past. You know that."

Which sounded rather sanctimonious. "So you're just going to keep your thoughts to yourself?"

"It ain't nothing that I haven't been doing already."

If this hadn't been his brother and if he hadn't already been feeling guilty, Aden would've pressed. But there were two things that were working against him. The first was that even as a young boy, Frank had been the most stubborn of all of them, and he was even more stubborn now. The second was that Aden reckoned his brother had a good point.

There really wasn't a single thing he could do to change the past. And he didn't really want to change it, anyway. He'd had a pretty good life. Anna Mae had been a good wife and a good mother. She'd given them three beautiful girls who'd brought them both so much joy.

If she and he hadn't exactly had a passionate, romantic relationship, he'd long ago decided such things weren't necessary for a good marriage. What mattered was compatibility and patience. Kindness and humor. Together, he and Anna Mae had had all of those things.

But Rebecca . . .

"Since it seems we're now going to agree not to delve into the past, why don't you tell me about Rebecca, then?" Aden asked impatiently. "Tell me what you know."

If Frank heard his sarcasm, he didn't let on. "Well, you know she never married."

"Did she have any suitors?"

"I reckon so, though I couldn't say for sure."

"What do you know about Rebecca?"

"That her bakeshop is mighty popular and successful." Frank smiled. "Rumor has it that she might be one of the most successful entrepreneurs in the area."

"Really?" Could one really make so much money from baked goods?

"Oh, for sure." Frank nodded as if to emphasize his point. "Rebecca not only makes all the treats in her bakery case, she does special orders, too. You should see some of the wedding cakes she's made. They're works of art, I tell ya."

Aden didn't know whether to be taken aback or impressed that Frank knew so much about wedding cakes. "Huh."

"Oh, I see your expression. You might think I'm being silly, but it's a fact. She's a gifted baker."

"Since I doubt there are any weddings going on at Christmas, I'll have to take your word for it."

"No need for you to do that," Frank said. "It's Christmas cake season."

Frank was now wearing an almost dreamy expression. "Which is what?" Aden asked.

"Well, you see, Christmas cakes are the bakery's specialty," Frank said. "They're a white cake with cranberries, chopped walnuts, and white chocolate baked inside. The outside has fluffy white icing that tastes like a cross between marshmallows and meringue. Finally, right in the center of the top of each cake, is a magnificent red and green poinsettia made out of some kind of special frosting."

"A magnificent red and green poinsettia?" Aden was trying not to laugh.

"Laugh all you want, but I'm telling you the truth. This cake isn't just good. It's amazing."

"Sorry, but it doesn't sound amazing. It sounds kind of like a fruit cake."

"It's not. It's nothing like that." Frank lowered his voice. "You don't understand. She special orders the cranberries from Maine, the walnuts from California, and gets top-of-the-line white chocolate."

"Frank, you sound like an advertisement."

"I'd happily knock on doors to tell people about these cakes if it meant Rebecca would give me one for free." He frowned. "See, it ain't just the fresh walnuts that make them so special, it's the whole combination. And the secret ingredient."

"What is that?"

"I'm not sure, but Amanda and I think there might be a touch of orange liquor in them."

"Surely not."

"It's just the faintest bit. Whatever she uses, it's magic."

"We need to get you out more, Frank. No one should speak so highly of a cake."

"I'm not the only one who looks forward to it. Rumor has it that they make a hundred every December."

"Every December. She really sells that many cakes?"

"It's an event, I tell ya. They're so popular, one has to make a reservation to get one. Amanda reserved ours back in September."

Aden started laughing. "I know you're exaggerating now!"

"I wouldn't joke about that. I even heard that fights have broken out because people who didn't have a reservation tried to get one. I know for a fact that a woman out in New York offered to pay a thousand dollars for a last-minute cake."

"I hope she got it."

"No one knows," Frank said in an almost reverent tone. "Because Rebecca never told anyone about it, you see."

"Enough about the cakes," Aden said impatiently. "What else do you know about Rebecca, Frank?"

"It's getting late. I'm sorry but I've got to turn in for the night."

"Wait a minute—"

"Besides, if you think about it, Rebecca and those Christmas cakes should tell you everything you've ever needed to know about her." Frank yawned as he stood up. "*Gut* night, Aden. I'll see you in the morning."

"'Night."

When he was alone again, he thought about Frank's cryptic words. Was Rebecca secretly rich because she'd developed some kind of amazing cake that induced people to pay her lots of money? She worked really hard, especially in December, and she was great at keeping secrets.

He never would've thought it, but he was starting to believe that maybe Frank was on to something when he said the Christmas cake was the secret to learning more about Rebecca.

If that was the case, Aden realized now that he had a way to her heart.

He was going to see how he could help with her busiest month.

Chapter 6

It was a snowy, cold morning. A really cold morning. Though Goldie had seemed happy enough about their walk when they first set off, she now kept giving Rebecca a mournful look every few feet. Rebecca had finally taken pity on the dog and increased their pace. Pleased to be trotting in the snow, Goldie let out a happy bark.

"I feel the same way," Rebecca said with a smile. "But not because we're practically running. It will be *gut* to get home. This morning's walk has been chilly, indeed."

Though her eyes were watering and her nose was likely bright red from the wind, she tried to feel more optimistic. After all, if the morning had been seventy degrees and sunny, it wouldn't feel like December. And she really needed to be in a holiday mood because she had hours and hours of holiday baking ahead of her.

It was just too bad she didn't feel all that motivated at the moment.

No, all she really felt like doing was sipping hot chocolate, reading a book, and daydreaming about Aden.

He'd been so kind to her yesterday. And he'd looked at her so intently that she'd felt like a young girl again. The way Aden focused on her was one of the things she'd liked best about him. Before he'd returned to town, Rebecca had wondered if she'd exaggerated his mannerisms over the years. But she hadn't. Aden really did look at a person as if there weren't anyone else in the world who mattered. Back when they were teenagers, she'd fooled herself into thinking that for Aden no one really had mattered but her.

Now she was far smarter. If Aden had such focus, it wasn't because the person he was talking to actually mattered to him all that much. No, it was that he had developed a special skill and learned to use it to his advantage.

Immediately, she was ashamed of her thoughts. That wasn't kind, and she sounded cynical and bitter. Those were definitely not traits she'd ever hoped to possess.

"Goldie, I need to adopt a new, far more Christmassy attitude," she said.

Goldie looked up at her and wagged her tail.

Deciding to take that as a vote of approval, Rebecca increased their pace. The exercise would do them both a world of good.

"Rebecca, do you always walk as if you're being chased?"

She turned to face Aden. "Do you always yell at women walking at six in the morning?"

"Only pretty brunettes walking golden retrievers."

"It must be my lucky day then . . . or not," she teased.

He laughed. "Honestly, I'm glad I caught you," he said as he sidled up next to her. "I was starting to worry that I missed your walk this morning."

"Why were you looking for me?" Oh, she hoped she didn't sound as hopeful as her heart was.

"I was looking for you because I learned something last night that I wanted to talk to you about."

"What was that?"

He smiled at her. "I learned you're some kind of Christmas cake master chef."

She chuckled at the description. "Hardly that."

"Nee, I mean it, Rebecca," he added. "Actually, *mei bruder* Frank told me about your special cakes. He said they were worth every penny and quite in demand."

"That was nice of him to say." At least, she thought it was. Of course, she really wanted to ask why Aden had been discussing her cakes with his brother in the first place. That seemed a rather odd thing for them to care about.

"It wasn't nice at all. He acted as if I were the last person on earth to know about your special cakes." Lowering his voice, he added, "Frank told me there are cranberries, walnuts, and white chocolate in the cake batter."

She grinned, enjoying their silly conversation. "That is true."

"I told him that it sounded like a fruit cake, which he claimed was a sign of my ignorance."

"I'm liking Frank more and more with every minute."

"He also said you had a secret ingredient that may or may not be orange liquor. . . . Care to tell me?"

"Nee, I would not." Especially since it *was* orange liquor.

"He also said you only make them in December."

"That's true again. You certainly found out a lot, Aden."

"I'm guessing that you don't get much sleep in December?"

"Not much." Not much at all.

"How do you handle it?" Looking at her intently again, he added, "I'm not being snarky; I am genuinely interested."

"I do a lot of prep work ahead of time."

"Like what?"

"Well, I special order all the extra ingredients and prep them ahead of time." Seeing that he was looking at her intently, she added, "For example, each cake has a cup and a half of chopped walnuts. I order really good, fresh walnuts, but I don't pay to have them chopped, so the walnuts arrive whole. We spend a long time cracking the shells, pulling out the fruit, chopping the nuts, and then measuring out the correct amount and putting them into individual snack bags."

"For every cake?"

She nodded. "*Jah.* See, then all I have to do when it's time to bake a cake is pull out one baggie for each cake. It saves a lot of time when I start baking twenty or thirty cakes at a time."

"It sounds like a lot of work."

"Oh, it is. But all the special ingredients are worth it. A few years ago, I made two cakes for my girls so we could do a taste test."

"Your girls?"

"The girls who work for me," she explained. "Anyway, I made one cake with all my special-ordered ingredients, and one with ingredients that one can find on a regular grocery shelf."

"What did you discover?"

"The regular cake tasted just fine . . . but the special cake, well, it was just a whole lot better."

"I see." Aden sounded agreeable, but he was looking at her as if she were a stranger, which was a bit alarming.

"You're looking at me funny. What did I say?"

A line formed between his brows. "Nothing. I mean, nothing really." When she kept staring at him, he looked sheepish. "I'm simply trying to come to terms with the fact that the girl I once knew has become such a successful businesswoman."

"I'm hardly that." However, she did like that he thought so. She'd worked so hard to make Rebecca's Porch something to be proud of.

"I beg to disagree. Everyone talks about your talents in the kitchen. I think it's wonderful that you've become such a success, too, though I fear you might be doing too much. Maybe you should let the other ladies help you make those cakes."

"My staff does bake other things. However, I fear you're right. When it comes to my Christmas cakes, I am full of pride. I feel I'm the only one who can make them exactly right."

"You do have a way in the kitchen, Rebecca."

She laughed. "I hope so. I spend the majority of my time there!" But though her words were modest, she couldn't stop her cheeks from heating with pleasure. She had worked hard, and she was pleased to have a thriving business to show for it. But that said, she knew that having a successful business didn't mean one had a successful life. There were areas where she still needed to grow when it came to being well-rounded.

"Anyway, I thought maybe I could help you."

"Do what? Bake?" She was joking, of course. After all, why in the world would Aden want to spend a day in her hot kitchen?

"*Jah.* Or, I don't know . . . maybe other things. Make those prep bags."

His offer meant the world to her. It meant that he valued her job and that he appreciated it enough to try to help. But what if he was just saying the words? After so long, it was hard for her to believe that anything he said was from the heart.

So she decided to give him a way out. "When are you going to do all that? In the middle of the night when you aren't sleeping?" she joked.

"Someone told me a while back that people make time for the things that matter to them. I want to make time for you."

She was touched. Her heart felt as if it were clenching. She wanted to believe him, wanted to depend on him. But when Aden left again—and she knew he would—she'd have to be prepared to pick up the pieces.

"No one has ever told me this, but maybe they should have," she said softly. "If people make time for what matters to them, then perhaps people should also say yes for no other reason than because they want to."

"Is that your roundabout way of saying that you want to say yes?"

"It is." She smiled at him. "Yes, Aden. *Danke.* I would love your help."

She *would* love it, too. She just hoped her heart would still be in one piece when he was gone.

Chapter 7

Rebecca had never married, and she'd never had children. But she had made a lot of friends. They were from many corners of her life—her church community, the many women at work, the customers in her shop, and even the dozen or so men and women she and Goldie visited with almost every day.

She also had Evie.

Evie had been just a girl when Rebecca's heart had been broken by Aden's departure. Now the young woman was in her twenties and lived in the city of Lancaster. She had dark brown hair that she delighted in wearing all sorts of ways. She also had hazel eyes, freckles, and a fondness for old jeans and flannel shirts. Evie was the receptionist and sometime office manager of a family-practice physician.

In a lot of ways, Evie was everything Rebecca had never been. She was social and vocal and constantly on the go. She sometimes spoke her mind when she should listen and sometimes took chances when it would have been safer to be more thoughtful.

Rebecca was the opposite. After Aden's departure, she'd

started keeping her feelings and opinions to herself. Then, after stewing on things too long, she'd erupt, which always came as a surprise to whomever was in the vicinity.

Evie was also as English as a girl could be. She hadn't been raised Amish, didn't want to be Amish, and didn't secretly covet Amish things. Instead of their differences creating a barrier between Evie and Rebecca, they pointed out the things that mattered most.

When she knocked on Rebecca's door that evening at a quarter after six, she held a giant bag of Chinese takeout.

As Rebecca took it from her, she reckoned it had to weigh close to three pounds. "Evie, what in the world? I thought you were going to pick up an order of beef and broccoli."

"Oh, I did get that," Evie said after she kissed Rebecca on the cheek and tossed her cute tangerine wool coat on a side chair. "But I also got fried rice and an order of lo mein noodles and some egg rolls, too."

"So, what you're saying is that you bought enough food for a large family."

Evie raised a shoulder, looking unconcerned. "Yeah, probably. But whatev. You need to eat something, Rebecca, and I do, too."

Walking into her small kitchen, Rebecca pulled out two plates and two bowls. "It smells really good."

"Since it's from Top Wok, it *is* going to be really good. I love that place."

Unable to help herself, Rebecca smiled at Evie's hairstyle. Today Evie had arranged her hair in four braids and had pinned them all up in some kind of complicated bun. "I love Top Wok, too. Have I even thanked you for going to so much trouble to feed me?"

Looking put-upon, Evie shook her head. "Nope. So far, all you've done is complain about how much food I brought over."

Her friend might have been joking, but Rebecca was pretty sure her assessment was accurate. Busying herself with the cartons, she said, "Thanks for taking care of me, Ev. If there was ever a night when I needed to pig out on Chinese food, this is it."

Evie, who'd been washing her hands, stilled. "That sounds ominous. What's happened?"

Rebecca took a deep breath. "Aden Raber came over to see me."

Evie gaped. "Aden the-one-who-got-away Raber?"

"It was actually more like Aden the-one-who-*ran*-away-Raber. But yes."

Evie scowled as she started digging through Rebecca's drawers for a pair of serving spoons. "I hope you told him to turn around and start walking the other way." When Rebecca stayed silent, Evie frowned. "You didn't do that, did you?"

What could she say? "Nope."

"Why?"

What could she say? "I don't know."

"Yeah, right." Evie started piling food on her plate and then sat down at the table.

Feeling as if she were a wayward teenager about to get a talking to, Rebecca followed suit. "Shall we pray?" she asked as soon as she sat down.

"Of course." Evie bent her head and closed her eyes.

Closing her own eyes, Rebecca gave thanks for her food, the hands that prepared it, for Evie, and her family and friends . . . and then, because she couldn't help it, she added a prayer for Aden, too.

When she opened her eyes, she noticed Evie staring at her. "What?"

"You know what. I have a feeling that you were praying for Aden."

"He was one of the people I prayed for, yes." Rebecca lifted her chin. "And there isn't anything wrong with that."

"I didn't say there was."

"Evelyn, I can practically feel the disapproval wafting off you."

Evie had just taken a bite of rice. She hastily covered her mouth with her hand as she giggled. "Wafting? That's quite the description."

"It fits." Rebecca raised an eyebrow. "Or does it not?"

"You tell me if I'm wrong. Should I not be worried about you becoming smitten with him again? Or are you two just friends now? What was he like?"

Rebecca paused for a moment to pet Goldie, who had come to the table with a hopeful look in her brown eyes. Even though Rebecca knew better than to give her any scraps, she still slipped the dog a piece of chicken.

"Aden is the same yet different," she said at last.

"Which is as clear as mud."

Rebecca had to agree. "I suppose, but it's clear to me, I guess." Thinking about him for a moment, Rebecca said, "Aden is still blond and personable, just like he always used to be."

"But?"

"But he also seems to be more aware of me now."

Evie put down her fork. "What do you mean by that?"

That was Evie for you. She always pushed Rebecca to think about things more deeply. "Well, Aden kind of watches me every time I speak. It's as if he's memorizing everything I say."

"And you like that?"

"I think I do," she said after a moment. "Most of the time when we were growing up, Aden was very focused. But then, just a few months before he moved, he seemed more restless."

"Which worried you?"

"Looking back on it, I guess it did, though I realize now that he was preparing to leave."

"But now?"

"Now?" Rebecca thought for a moment. "Well, now Aden seems to look at me like he doesn't want to be anywhere else. It's nice." It was also disconcerting.

"That sounds positive. . . ."

Rebecca nodded before scooping up another forkful of rice. "He offered to help me make the Christmas cakes."

"Really? He's a baker?"

"Nee, not at all." Remembering the conversation, she said, "Aden asked how I prepare everything for my big baking month, so I told him how I spend time cracking open walnuts and chopping chocolate and other ingredients and how I place the measured amounts in plastic bags. He offered to chop the walnuts, measure them, and put them in the bags for me."

"That would make you so happy."

"It would." She really hated everything about those walnuts—except how delicious the fresh nuts made her cake. She held up a hand. "I'm hardly going to know what to do with myself if I don't have sore, torn up fingers on New Year's Day."

Evie frowned as she gazed at Rebecca's hands. "Your fingers are usually in such bad shape I wonder how you manage to pin your dress together."

"Very carefully," she joked. When she noticed that Evie didn't crack a smile, Rebecca backpedaled. "Usually, my hands aren't that bad." Although they had been before she made herself limit the number of cakes.

Evie put her fork down. "I feel terrible, Rebecca."

"For what?"

"All this time, I've known that you enjoyed making the cakes yourself. Actually, you insisted on making them."

"*Jah,* that is true. So why do you feel bad about it?"

"Because it never occurred to me that I could have helped you in other ways. Aden's offer of helping with all the prep work was ingenious." She shook her head. "I should have done that years ago."

"Don't feel bad. I never thought about it either, and I'm the one who was doing the work."

"So, you said he offered. Did you take him up on it?"

"Oh, I took him up on it, for sure. He didn't even have to ask me twice."

"I'm surprised."

"You shouldn't be. I might be stubborn, but I'm no fool. Especially when it comes to my sore fingers."

Evie smiled but didn't comment. She munched on an egg roll instead. Rebecca followed suit but felt a little off, most likely because it was obvious that Evie was attempting to hold her tongue, and the young woman never did that.

When they were just about finished eating, Rebecca couldn't take it anymore. "What are you thinking?"

"Uh, that this food is really good and I was smart to pick it up?"

"Nee, I'm serious. I'm half surprised your mouth isn't bloody from biting your tongue."

Evie wrinkled her nose. "Way to make the end of a meal appetizing, Bec."

"Come on, I really want to know."

"Fine." After looking as if she were mentally practicing a speech, Evie said, "Rebecca, I think it's nice that Aden offered to help you chop walnuts. I even think it's kind of neat that you're going to see him through the holidays."

She leaned forward. "But . . . ?"

"But what's the point of it all? Is he only here to make himself feel better? Are you only being friendly with him because you don't like being on bad terms with him? Or . . . is it something else?"

"Such as?"

"Even though you already sound irritated with me, I'm going to go ahead and ask you the question that's been running through my mind. Rebecca, how are you going to feel when he leaves again? Because that's what he's going to do, right?"

Against her will, Rebecca nodded.

"Well?"

"I don't know," she said at last.

A look of sadness reached Evie's eyes, making her seem far older than her years. Or maybe age had nothing to do with it. Maybe it was that she knew what Rebecca hadn't wanted to accept in her heart. Without a doubt, Aden was going to leave again, she wasn't going to follow him, and she would be crushed.

All over again.

Chapter 8

They'd made a date to meet at the shop at three o'clock on Tuesday afternoon. Aden had gotten up at dawn and started working at the house by seven that morning. By two in the afternoon, he and the rest of the men had put in more than an honest day's work. After making plans to meet with a plumber at the house the next day, he'd gone back to his room at Frank's house to shower and eat a quick lunch.

And to mentally prepare for the most important part of his day.

At three o'clock, he arrived at the bakeshop, just in time to greet a group of ten women who had obviously been enjoying some kind of Christmas get-together. He knew a few slightly, which was enough to trap him into a conversation with a few of the ladies about Christmas plans.

When they finally wandered out the door with a buzz of laughter, Aden turned to Sarah. "Is Rebecca in the back?"

"She is." She chuckled. "No doubt she's been working especially quietly back there."

"Because?" He would have thought a bakery full of customers would've made Rebecca very happy.

"Oh, you know. Our Rebecca is *gut* with small numbers of people. Big groups? Not so much." Wiping down a table with a cloth she'd tucked into her apron, she continued. "Everyone understands though. Well, at least they do in December."

"Let me guess the reason: Christmas cakes."

"*Jah.* Christmas cake season is nuts, for sure and for certain. Which means it's a blessing that you're here to help with those walnuts."

He rolled his eyes at the pun. "Indeed."

"Would you like a cup of *kaffi* and maybe a cookie? It's all fresh, you know."

"I don't want to make you do any more work."

"Bringing you a cup of coffee and a treat won't take but a minute or two.

"Then, *danke*. I would like that very much."

"You want any sort of cookie in particular?" She gestured to the filled glass display case.

There had to be at least ten different types of cookies in it. Every one of them looked amazing. "Anything but chocolate." He thought again. "Or raisin. I'm not a big fan of raisin cookies."

Sarah looked bemused. "Is anyone?"

"I'll have to ask Rebecca," he joked as he walked back into the kitchen.

Rebecca looked up at him from the stool she was perched on in the back corner of the vast space. "Ask Rebecca about what?" she said.

"If anyone is a fan of raisin cookies. Are they?"

"Oatmeal raisin, *jah*. Plain raisin? Not so much."

"I should've known that you would take my question seriously."

She smiled. "I don't joke about baked goods, Aden."

"Good to know. So, are you ready for some help?"

"I am. I was just looking at the list of orders. There was a mix-up in the paperwork. Someone lost track of a sheet. It's been found again, but there are twenty-five more cakes ordered than I planned on."

"So, you'll be making one hundred and seventy-five cakes?"

"*Jah.* Whatever you do, don't let me get talked into even one more."

"Don't worry." He looked around and then whistled low when he saw a grocer's-sized box of walnuts. "Where would you like me to work on these?"

"Right here is fine." She pointed to a nutcracker that was attached to the counter, so all he would have to do was pull a lever. "Here's your cracker. There's a tool to get the meat out, and here's a cutting board and knife to chop them." Finally she pointed to a pair of stainless-steel measuring cups. "Each cake contains one and a half cups of chopped nuts. Put them in a bag and then number the bag."

"Surely you don't have to number them?"

"I do." When she spied his frown, she propped a hand on one of her hips. "Aden, no offense, but I wouldn't go into your home remodels and show you a better way to do your work. Unless you'd like my advice?"

"I would not. And I get your point."

Just as he was about to sit down and roll up his sleeves, she called out, "*Halt!*"

He jumped back. "What?"

"Aden, you must wash your hands first. And then put on gloves."

"Really?"

"We're a commercial kitchen. Of course, really." She looked as if she were about to say something else, but Sarah came in with a tray holding two steaming mugs of coffee and a plate of cookies.

After thanking Sarah, Aden held a cup out to Rebecca. "It looks like we need some sustenance first."

She smiled at him as she held the ceramic mug between her hands. "Indeed."

He held up his mug. "Cheers, Rebecca. Here's to a productive afternoon."

Looking bemused and as pretty as ever, she clicked her mug lightly with his and then took a sip. He did the same, then picked up a cookie and bit into it. When Rebecca saw what he'd picked, she burst out laughing. "Of course you picked the oatmeal raisin cookie, Aden."

"Of course." Even as he was tempted to spit that bite out, he smiled at her. He still didn't care for raisins, but that didn't mean he wasn't enjoying the moment. Actually, he thought he might not have ever been so happy.

Well, at least not in quite a long time.

Three hours later, he swore he was going to add walnuts to his list of un-favorite foods. Each one of the shells was as hard as a rock, and getting all of the walnut pieces out was aggravating. Especially since Rebecca kept checking and making him take out each smidgen of edible nut.

The metal tool that she encouraged him to use did help, but it reminded him an awful lot of something on a tray at the dentist's office.

Then, when he finally had one or two cups of walnuts shelled, it was time to chop them into small bits before finally carefully measuring out a cup and a half and depositing the pieces in a bag. Oh, and he couldn't forget to number the bag, either. Now he had ten bags. Only a hundred and sixty-five to go.

"Rebecca, are you sure you don't want to switch to using better tools?"

She was putting portions of white chocolate and dried cranberries into similar pouches. "What sort?"

"A food processor, maybe? Or even a blender?"

Her lips tilted up. "Those would be rather difficult to use, since this is an Amish kitchen, Aden."

"I know that, but perhaps someone can find you one of those gadgets that run on batteries or gas." He snapped his fingers. "Oh, I know! I've seen some choppers that are hand-powered. You put whatever you want to chop in the plastic container, screw on the lid tightly, and then press a lever."

"I've seen those, too."

"Well, what do you think?" He was ready to go find one for her that afternoon.

"I think by the time I put everything in the gadget, chop it well enough to go in a cake, then scoop it all out again, I might as well have just done what you are doing now and chopped it with a knife."

"You might be right." He knew he sounded doubtful, but he was shocked at how particular Rebecca was being.

"Sorry, but I know I am. And, before you start telling me to begin buying chopped walnuts, I have to tell ya that's not how I want to do things."

"I hear ya."

Compassion filled her gaze. "I know it's a tedious chore. You can stop anytime you want, you know."

"And leave this for you to do all by yourself?"

"*Jah.*"

"Rebecca, I'm not going to do that." He was actually a little offended that she'd think he would abandon her.

"I don't see why not. I do this every year."

"You make too many of them every year."

"You don't understand. These cakes are a labor of love for me. I like making them myself because I think it shows my customers how much I care about them. Even if they never realize how I actually make them, *I* know, and that's what matters to me."

"I know, and I understand. I feel that way about my work."

She smiled softly. "But just because I do it my way, it doesn't mean you have to do it, too. I promise, I realize shelling walnuts is an arduous task."

"I'm not going to give up."

"Want to trade chores for a bit?"

"Nee." But still he found himself sighing like a child with a list full of chores.

She giggled again. "I do appreciate your help, Aden. You are making the time go by fast."

"I am enjoying our time together as well." He wasn't lying, either. He found being with her relaxing. Plus, the more they chatted, the closer he felt to her. Little by little, it was as if all the years and heartache between them were falling away.

"I have an idea," she said after a few minutes. "How about you tell me some stories?"

"About what?"

"Tell me something about your *kinner,* Aden. Tell me about your life."

He usually loved talking about his kids and his carpentry job, but, sitting across from Rebecca, he felt as if his stories were going to widen the breach between them. "I'm not sure where to start, Bec."

"Start with how everything is now. Then we'll work backward."

"I can do that."

She smiled at him sweetly. "*Gut.* Now begin."

Because it was Rebecca, he cracked another walnut and started talking. And she was right—before he knew it, another hour had passed.

Chapter 9

It was crunch time. Another batch of cakes were scheduled to be picked up tomorrow. Forty of them. Even though she was achy and didn't feel her best, Rebecca had gotten up at four that morning. For hours, she ignored her headache and sore throat and concentrated on baking layer after layer of cake.

When Sarah and Katie, another one of her assistants, arrived, they helped as much as she would allow. Sarah made the icing and took care to carefully remove the cake from each pan and set it on a wire rack. Katie washed dishes, scrubbed pans, softened butter, and cut out the fondant poinsettia petals that would eventually grace the next group of finished cakes.

The girls lifted her spirits and made the remainder of the day fly by. At four o'clock, they were staring at forty finished cakes.

"I hate that all I ever remember about this is how pretty all the cakes look, lined up like they are," Katie said.

Rebecca nodded. "I'm guilty of the same thing." Now that the last batch of cakes was out of the oven, she felt as if she could breathe a little easier. "I, for one, must have forgotten just how sore my neck and shoulders get."

"Are you sure you aren't coming down with something?" Sarah asked. "You've complained more than once about aches and pains today."

"I think I'm just getting old."

"Since I'm two years older than you, that's worse news for me," Aden called out as he entered the kitchen.

Chuckling, Rebecca winked at Katie. "I'm afraid that canna be helped, Aden. I'm feeling old, but you actually *are* old."

He raised his eyebrows at her but then whistled softly. "Now, look at that. Ain't that a sight to see?"

"It is, isn't it?" Rebecca loved seeing the cakes lined up on the counter. "Don't they look *wunderbaar*?"

"They do, indeed. What happens next?"

Katie pointed to a stack of white boxes. "Next, we need to put the boxes together, carefully place a cake in each, tape them up, and write the name and order number on each." She looked at the clock. "Hopefully, we'll get done before five."

Rebecca knew that Katie had been putting in extra hours at the bakery, as well as taking care of her baby, and crocheting two stuffed toys for the babe in the evening. "Aden, would you mind helping me with this? If you are able, I can send Katie home."

"I can help," he said.

Katie's eyes widened. "Nee, there's no need for that."

"You'll only be leaving an hour early, and I won't take it off your time."

"But that ain't right. There's so much to do."

"I will be fine. You've been working so hard, practically like a whirling dervish, what with the shop so busy and all these cakes." Rebecca made a shooing motion with her hands. "Go on, now. Go rest or play with Annie or crochet . . . or take care of one of the ten other things on your list for the day."

After looking from Rebecca to Aden, Katie nodded. "All right. *Danke.*" Less than five minutes later, her apron was hanging on a hook and she was out the door.

Aden chuckled. "You just made Katie mighty happy."

"If I did, I'm glad. But have I just made you upset with me?"

"Not at all. I can put together boxes with the best of them," he said easily. "How about I unfold them, you put the cakes in, and then I tape them shut?"

Liking his plan, she nodded. "After we finish, we can write down the names and numbers."

After taking off his jacket, he rolled up his sleeves, washed his hands, and then got to work. "One," he said when he handed her a complete box.

"*Danke.*" Her eyes widened when she saw a jagged line on his forearm. "Aden, you're hurt!"

"Hmm?"

"Your arm. Look."

He looked down at his forearm, then shrugged as he put together another box. "That? I'm fine. It's just a scratch."

"How did it happen?"

"I was pulling out some old boards and my arm got caught in the shuffle. I'm fine."

"It doesn't look fine. I bet it hurts. Or at least it did."

He chuckled as he rested yet another folded box on the counter. "It's nothing to worry about, Rebecca. Start putting those cakes in boxes. As soon as we are finished, I'm taking you out of here."

"That's not necessary."

"It is. I'm taking you out to supper."

"Is that right? And where are we going?"

"To Jerry's Mexican. We're going to sit down, have a hot supper, and then take Goldie for a walk."

"You've planned the whole evening," she said as she slid one cake into a box, then immediately slid in another.

"I have to, otherwise I reckon there's a real good chance you won't ever leave this building."

She felt her cheeks warm because that was likely true. Before Aden had arrived, all she'd been thinking about doing was taking a bath, putting on old pajamas, and falling into bed.

After sliding in another cake—she'd now boxed eight cakes—she joked, "I didn't know you were so bossy, Aden."

"It's not bossy if I'm trying to take care of you."

"Well, I don't know if Anna Mae liked being told what to do, but I'm not sure I like it all that much. I'm not used to it, either."

"Noted."

Rebecca literally felt as if the room's temperature had just dropped ten degrees. Of course, the moment she said the words, she had wished she could take them back. "Aden, I'm sorry. I . . . I shouldn't have said that."

"It's your kitchen. You can say whatever you want." His voice sounded brittle. "And, just for the record, Anna Mae didn't enjoy being bossed around much either." His voice hardened. "Though she never complained about my caring about her."

Now Rebecca felt even worse. "Like I said, the words just slipped out. Please forgive me."

"There isn't anything to forgive if you're saying what is on your mind."

"I was just making a joke. Can't we forget about it?" She was desperate for him to forgive her.

"How about instead we talk about Anna Mae? You've asked me about my job and my *kinner* but not about her. Why is that?"

Because it hurt too much to think of him with another woman. Because it reminded her that after Aden had left her, he'd gone on to have a full and rich life while she had struggled for so long. Because it was a reminder that he'd loved Anna Mae enough to marry her, but he'd never written Rebecca a note in twenty years. After slipping a couple more cakes into boxes, she said, "I don't know."

He gave her a long look from across the kitchen. "I had a good marriage with Anna Mae."

"Okay," she said quickly. "I'm glad."

"Hold on, now. I'm not done." Taking a deep breath, he continued. "We raised our children and did our best to have a good family. I did my best by her. I loved her, too. However, that said, our life together wasn't perfect."

Rebecca couldn't help but look up at him.

His voice lowered. "See, Anne Mae and me? We were a lot alike, which some people might have thought would be good, but it wasn't always good. She never pushed me or startled me or made me wonder how I could be better."

Rebecca felt terrible that he felt forced to tell her so much. "Aden, really—"

"*Nee,* let me finish," he said as he folded the last of the forty boxes. "I fear I took her for granted. I was anxious to prove myself and start a business. She did a lot of things with the children without me. It was very apparent after she died that I might have loved my children, but I didn't really know them. That was on me, not her."

Rebecca's head was spinning from the information. Realizing that he was waiting for some kind of response, she chose her words with care. "Aden, obviously I've never been married. So, I don't think I'm the best person to comment on your story."

"But if you were?"

"But if I was . . ." She paused, choosing each word with care. "Since I know you and I know the man you are now, I feel that you probably don't have anything to apologize for. The Lord gives us lots of days to live because we make mistakes and work through them. Whatever mistakes you've made, it sounds like you've worked to correct them."

"What about you? Do you ever wish you had married? Did you ever come close?"

Her heart started beating faster as she attempted to build up the courage to answer.

Chapter 10

He'd caught Rebecca off guard, and Aden almost felt bad about it. But only almost. Truth be told, Aden wanted to know more about her, more about the many years they'd spent apart. She'd been suspiciously silent though. Almost as if she feared giving him too much information, which baffled him. What could have happened that she was so reluctant to talk about?

After a full minute passed, Rebecca tucked her head. "Sorry," she mumbled. "I guess you're wondering how such a simple question could be so difficult for me to answer."

"I don't think it's simple at all." Sharing their pasts wasn't easy. It brought up old memories and a wealth of feelings that had been buried so deep it almost physically hurt to pull them into fresh light.

"Really?" she asked, her brown eyes looking both hopeful and wary.

"We have a lot of time and pain between us," she went on. "I know you hurt me when you left . . . and I know that my not understanding your reasons for leaving didn't make things better for you. That's a lot to get over."

"It is, but I thought we'd gotten through that." What more did they need to say? Feeling sorry for her, he gave her an out. "You don't have to share everything. Just share what you want."

"All right. I can do that." She took a deep breath. "The short answer is no, I never fell in love again. I never even came close."

"Why? Did I hurt you that badly?"

"I don't know if it was your leaving, or if my absence of feelings had more to do with me than you."

"With you? Rebecca, no matter what is between us now, I can promise you that I never thought you lacked feelings. I always felt cared for by you." No, he'd felt adored by her. So much, he almost hadn't left.

She picked up a couple Baggies and rearranged them. "Back when we were younger, when we both still lived at home, things were complicated for me. You had your big family and all of your financial burdens. But I, well, I just had my parents. It was just the three of us, you know."

He nodded. "Of course. I remember Landon and Charity well."

"If you remember them well, then you probably remember that my parents were rather rigid." She chuckled. "They liked things just so and for me to fulfill their high expectations."

He didn't remember that . . . or maybe he'd simply forgotten? "I remember that you didn't complain about your parents," he said slowly. "You always seemed to take everything they did in stride."

She sighed. "*Jah*, I got really good at that. But to be honest, I kept a lot of things from you."

"Why? I feel like I told you everything."

"You did." Looking bemused, she said, "Maybe that's why I kept so much to myself. You needed someone to listen and help you shoulder your burdens. I wanted to be that person for you."

Rebecca was essentially saying that he'd been self-centered. The thought shamed him—especially since he feared she was right. "You didn't think I had time for you, Bec?"

"Oh, I know you did. But I didn't want to be just another thing for you to worry about." She shook her head, as if to clear the air. "What I'm trying to tell you is that, when you left and I was alone, my parents weren't very happy with me."

"With you? But you didn't do anything wrong."

"They didn't feel that way. They made me doubt myself, doubt my ability to be in a relationship. Maybe even doubt my ability to love. They said that if you had truly loved me, then you would have asked me to go with you when you left."

"What? That isn't true at all. I had to leave. I . . . Rebecca, I had to stop being a burden to my parents and start helping them financially."

"I know you said that." But she still sounded doubtful.

"It was true. I didn't make up stories."

"I didn't think you had." She swallowed. "But my parents felt that given the way you left, there had to be more to it than you let on."

He couldn't believe it. He opened his mouth to speak but shut it again quickly. How in the world could he say what was on his mind without sounding critical of her parents? "Rebecca, I . . . well, I'm sorry for that. You're right. I guess I should've explained more to you."

To his surprise, she smiled. "I'd rather hear what you are really thinking instead of hearing an apology."

"In that case, I'll say this—I wasn't even twenty, and you were barely seventeen."

"I know."

"I had about a hundred dollars to my name."

"I had less than that."

"If any of my children had left that young . . . *nee,* if my girls had ever dreamed of following their boyfriends when they were so young . . ." He took a deep breath. "I would've put a stop to it."

"I know," she said again. "I'm not saying I agreed with them. I'm trying to tell you that they didn't think we were in love."

"We were." Realizing that this was the first time he'd ever actually said that he'd loved her, either to her or to himself, a lump formed in his throat. Back when they were teenagers, he'd been very fond of her. He'd also taken her for granted. She'd been the pretty girl from the well-off family who had been easy to be with and had offered him a respite from all his worries at home.

He felt his cheeks heat with embarrassment. "Even though I don't regret leaving, I wish I had left things with you in a different way. I'll always regret that."

"The path I took wasn't a bad one, Aden. I was young when you left. Too young to know what I wanted. When I realized that the future I had imagined with you wasn't going to take place and that I was never going to please my parents, I began to have other dreams."

"This shop."

She chuckled. "Eventually, yes. But before that I dreamed of being a really good baker. I worked at another shop and learned beside some really talented cooks."

"And now you have a thriving business."

She nodded. "I do. It's thriving; it's a product of my hard work, and I've made a nice life for myself. I have friends, and I'm part of the community. I'm happy."

Aden realized that Rebecca wasn't making that up or exaggerating so he would feel better. No, she really was happy. "Now all you have to do is make a bunch more Christmas cakes tomorrow . . . after I take you to dinner tonight."

Her smile brightened. "Put that way? Well, it's not much at all."

Aden couldn't disagree.

Chapter 11

On the morning of December twenty-third, Rebecca woke up feeling as if she'd been hit by a train. Every bit of her body hurt. She had a blinding headache and a terribly sore throat. When she started feeling both hot and cold at the same time, she gave in and took her temperature. It was one hundred and two.

Seeing the numbers on the thermometer hit home in a way that all the rest of her aches and pains hadn't. She couldn't deny the obvious anymore. She was sick. Really sick. And she still had another forty cakes to finish, the last of which were supposed to be picked up by ten in the morning on Christmas Eve.

But what could she do? She couldn't go into the bakery and risk infecting other people.

Taking two ibuprofen, she wrapped herself in a blanket and huddled on the couch, trying desperately to think of what she should do. She couldn't risk infecting the other girls, but she couldn't disappoint her customers either. They looked forward to her Christmas cakes all year. Oh, what was she to do?

The knock at her door sounded like machine gun fire. She winced as she got to her feet and answered it, then stepped back several paces. "Hiya, Evie." As usual, Evie looked adorable. Today her dark hair was arranged in two low braids under a fleece navy cap. She had on jeans, boots, and what looked like a red and white sweater under her jaunty hunter green coat.

In comparison, Rebecca felt like a faded dishrag.

Evie's smile was bright. "Hey, Bec! I stopped by to see if you wanted— Wait." Her whole expression turned to one of concern. "Rebecca, sorry, but you look terrible."

"I know." She tried to stand up straighter but even doing that hurt. "I'm kind of sick."

"Um, no offense, but you look much worse than that."

"I don't think you're supposed to say such things out loud," she chided. "It isn't polite, you know."

Evie didn't even crack a smile at her joke. "Well, I don't think you're supposed to be out of bed, Bec." Gesturing toward the other room, she said, "Go on. Back to your bedroom."

Even though she was feeling dizzy and weak, Rebecca resisted. "Hold on, now. I canna do that. I've got to figure out how to get my cakes made."

"In your current condition? I don't think so." Still studying her, Evie added, "You really do look like you're about to fall over. You've got dark circles under your eyes and your lips are chapped. You have a fever, don't you?"

On any other day, Rebecca would have argued with Evie about her appearance. It couldn't be that bad. But she had too many other things on her mind to focus on. Namely, dozens of Christmas cakes that needed to be made. "You don't understand, Evie."

"And why is that?"

"Because Christmas is almost here."

"Don't you see? That is exactly why you shouldn't be working right now. You could get worse." She softened her bossy tone. "You need to get better by Christmas Day."

At the moment, the only thing that Christmas Day meant to Rebecca was that the cakes would be done, the shop would be closed, and she could sleep all day. "You don't understand. I have forty more cakes to make. I don't know what to do!" And yes, she was now whining in a rather unattractive tone.

Evie rolled her eyes. "Of course you don't, Rebecca. Because you are too stubborn and prideful to let anyone else make them."

"People have paid for *me* to make the cakes. I'm not going to let them down."

Evie put her hands on her hips. "Rebecca, I'm going to be as blunt with you as I possibly can. People are not going to want a cake baked by you right now. Even the thought of eating something that you touched makes me shudder."

Tears sprang to Rebecca's eyes. "That's not very nice."

"No, it's not. But sometimes the truth hurts. Ain't so?"

Rebecca usually hated when Evie threw Amish words and phrases at her, but at the moment, she couldn't deny her friend spoke the truth. "*Jah.*"

Looking her over, Evie seemed to come to a decision. "Where is the cake recipe? Is it around?"

"The Christmas cake recipe? Why?"

"Oh, stop sounding like I want to steal your secrets. I don't want to make it, but there are a lot of very capable women downstairs who can. Where is it?"

Rebecca realized that, all those years ago, when Aden had informed her that he needed to leave, she'd known she didn't have a choice. The Lord was giving her another one of those moments. "Sarah or Katie knows where the recipe is."

"All right then. Now go get in bed and get some sleep. I'll put everyone into motion."

"You?"

"I may not be an amazing Amish baker, but I'm extremely good at ordering people around."

"I noticed," she grumbled.

"I'm so thankful for your faith in me, Rebecca," Evie retorted sarcastically. "It really means a lot."

"I'm sorry. I'm not at my best right now. I simply can't believe that I've gotten so sick. I don't know what happened."

"Life happened. Now, please try not to be so hard on yourself. You're human. I'll be back in a couple of hours. If you aren't in bed resting when I come to check on you, I'm going to load you in my car and take you to the doctor."

"You wouldn't." Rebecca really hated the doctor.

"You know I would. And I'd do it with a smile on my face, too."

"Evie, you're acting like a bully."

"Can you say abscessed tooth?"

The mention of Evie's awful tooth problem from two years ago brought Rebecca up short. Evie had come over with a swollen cheek and a pocketful of denials about how much pain she was in. Rebecca had threatened to drive Evie's car herself to the dentist if the girl didn't do it on her own. But then Evie had waited another twenty-four hours. A day after that Evie had been admitted to the hospital. "Fine."

Looking delighted, Evie smiled as she guided Rebecca back to bed. "I thought you might see it my way. Get some rest and stop fretting, dear. You're sick, and there are lots of cakes to prepare, but Christmas Day is near. Which means that miracles can happen when you least expect them."

On that note, Evie walked out of the room. A few seconds later, Rebecca heard the door shut and Evie's footsteps trotting down the stairs.

Rebecca tried to worry. She even tried to feel guilty about what was about to happen . . . but at the moment, all she cared about was that her head was now resting on a pillow and the headache that she'd been fighting for hours had finally abated.

The room was dark, Goldie had hopped up on the bed next to her, and someone else was in charge for a couple of hours.

Evie was right. Miracles really did happen when one least expected them.

That was a blessing, indeed.

Chapter 12

Aden was half inside a cabinet under a sink when Sarah found him.

"Aden? Aden, is that you?"

"It is." He would know her sweet, singsong-y voice anywhere, so he called out, "Do you need something, Sarah?"

"Well, um, I'm sorry but I need to talk to you."

He had a wrench in one hand and was double-checking a connection for the kitchen sink. He wasn't exactly a small guy, which meant it hadn't been easy to wedge himself into place. "I'm kind of in the middle of something." He tried not to sound as impatient as he felt. "Can it wait a few minutes? Or how about I come find you at Rebecca's Porch later this afternoon?"

"I'm sorry, but I can't wait, Aden. This is important."

Taken off guard by her change in tone, he started easing his way out of the cupboard.

"I'll finish that up if you'd like," John called out.

"Okay, but mind the copper fittings. I fear one of 'em is loose."

"I'll check them right away."

Trying to ignore the fact that he now had at least two people watching him wiggle backward out of the cabinet, Aden focused on not hitting his head.

When he ended up sitting on the paper-covered wooden floor, he peered up at Sarah. "All right, I'm out of there at last. Now, what's going on?"

"Rebecca is terribly ill, Aden. So much so, Evie asked me to fetch you."

All thoughts about water pressure, leaking, and faucets fled his mind as he scrambled to his feet. "What happened? Is she hurt?"

"*Nee,* just sick. But she's really sick."

"Has someone taken her to the doctor?" John asked.

"I don't believe so." Sarah shifted impatiently. "I haven't thought to ask."

After exchanging a confused look with John, Aden said, "Talk to me. What do you think? Does Rebecca need to go to the hospital? Should I find a driver?"

"I don't think so." Looking more flustered, she added, "I mean, I really hope not. Aden, I just need you to come over to the bakeshop."

"To the bakeshop?" The girl was talking in circles and not making a lick of sense. "Ah, don't you mean her apartment above it?"

"*Nee.* I mean the bakeshop." Looking even more impatient, she raised her voice. "Aden, I wouldn't have come here to fetch you if it wasn't important, and it's really important. Now, wouldja please, please come with me? Everyone is waiting."

Who was everyone? "Of course." Worried and more than a little bit confused, Aden exchanged another look with John.

"Go on. We've got this," John said. "Besides, you know no one's working again until the twenty-seventh. We've got time."

John's reminder put everything in perspective. His buddy

was correct. Most people were taking a few days off to celebrate Christ's birthday. Aden could do the same.

On the flipside, he also realized that Rebecca had been counting down her cakes, and he was very aware that she had more cakes to get done before the next day.

"I'll walk over with ya, Sarah," he said as he grabbed his jacket and knit cap. "*Danke,* John," he called out.

"No worries."

"I'll be in touch," he added before following Sarah out the door. The blast of snow and cold was jarring after the warm confines where he'd spent the last hour.

Aden didn't speak as he walked by Sarah's side down the three blocks from the Stutzmans' house to Rebecca's Porch. It was now evident that his questions weren't going to get any answers and that Sarah was too anxious to give him any kind of reasonable reply anyway.

When they got to the café, he noticed that it was packed as always—but there were also a couple of women standing at the counter arguing with one of the gals.

He recognized one of them. Meg Beachy had been in school with him. She'd been difficult as a teenager, and she didn't seem to have relaxed much in the years since.

When she spied him, she gestured him over. "Aden Raber, I've heard that you and Rebecca have reunited. Maybe you could help me."

"We're friends, but I don't work here."

"I know that." Looking impatient, she raised her voice. "All I need you to do is intervene for me."

"About what?"

Miriam, who was standing behind the counter, rested her hands on the top of it. "There is nothing to intervene about, Meg. You may not get your Christmas cake before ten tomorrow morning. Come back then."

Meg rolled her eyes. "Tomorrow is Christmas Eve. I'm going to be far too busy to come back here to pick it up." She smiled. "Couldn't you make an exception just for me?"

"And us, as well?" one of the ladies standing in line asked. "I hate how all our cakes are being held hostage in the back because of some silly rules."

Aden was gaping at the women when Sarah nudged him. Realizing that she wasn't trying to get his help but move him into the kitchen, he gave Miriam a sympathetic smile and followed.

When the kitchen door closed behind him, he found Katie near tears and Rebecca's friend Evie striding toward him.

"Aden, we need your help."

"Do you need me to sit with Rebecca?" He really hoped that was the case because he was worried sick about her.

"No, I need you to help make forty cakes. Actually, we only need thirty-six more now," Evie muttered as she examined the clipboard.

"Pardon me?"

Evie lowered her voice. "Did you see those women out there?"

"If you're talking about the ones who are demanding cakes now, then yes, I did. They were hard to miss."

"Good. If you saw them, then I think you understand how serious this is. They are already being pushy. So pushy, Miriam is about to close up the shop early. We have to get these cakes done. There is no other option or choice. And Rebecca cannot make them. Rebecca cannot even step in this kitchen!"

"I understand, but I don't see what I can do."

"You can grab a mixing bowl and start making a cake."

"I don't know what to do." Yes, he sounded helpless, but what did they expect? He felt like a third-string baseball player being told to suit up and hit a home run.

Sarah pointed to a recipe on the counter. "If you can build a house, you can follow this recipe. We need someone to make cakes and put them into pans. Miriam and I will decorate them with the poinsettias and Katie is going to handle monitoring them in the oven and the frosting."

"What are you doing?" he asked Evie.

"I'm going to get all of you everything you need, box up cakes, double check lists, and wait on Rebecca so she doesn't infect the kitchen."

"I see." Leaning against the counter, he said, "Well, I guess—"

Evie cut him off. "Aden, we don't have time to chat. Go wash your hands, put on an apron and gloves, and get to work. We're going to be here for hours as it is."

There was a time for talking and a time for doing. This was obviously a time for the latter. Walking to the sink, he washed his hands thoroughly. Next, he slipped on the gloves, pulled the largest white apron from a hook, and said a quick prayer, both for guidance and of thanks, since the apron was plain and white and not frilly and pink.

Reminding himself that Sarah was right—he was good at following directions—he walked over to the mixing bowl. "I'm ready."

Handing him a bar of butter, Sarah smiled at him. "*Gut.* Here you go."

Chapter 13

Eight hours later, Aden was leaning against one of the kitchen's stainless-steel countertops and smiling at the sight in front of him. He'd done it. He'd mixed up the batter for thirty-six three-layer cakes. Then, because there was no way he was going to leave the young women while they did the rest of the work, he'd learned the art of professionally icing cakes. It seemed applying a base layer of icing was the key to avoiding a crumby topping.

After conquering cake batter, he'd taken the next lesson in stride. The girls had giggled when he'd compared the process to spackling a piece of drywall.

While he'd been painstakingly smoothing the base layers of frosting, Katie, Miriam, and Sarah had applied the fancy, fluffy layer of icing and finally the fondant poinsettia on the top of each cake. The cakes were now lined up like proud school children along the counters. Evie had asked if she could take a picture of them before the boxing. They'd all thought that was a fine idea, so they'd spent the time cleaning until Evie came downstairs from checking on Rebecca.

Sarah smiled at him. "Aden, you look like the cat who got the last plate of cream."

"I feel like it. Never again will I take your jobs for granted. Baking is hard work."

"It is hard," Miriam agreed, "But then again, every day is not like this."

Katie pressed her hands together and looked up to the ceiling. "Please God, don't give us a night like this ever again. Or at least until I recover from tonight."

"Amen to that," Aden said.

They all turned when Evie came back into the room. She held up her hands as if she were a surgeon. "Before you ask, I already washed my hands in the washroom down the hall. I'm as clean as I can be."

"How is Rebecca?" Sarah asked.

"I think she's improving. Her fever has broken, and she's sleeping again. If she's still fever free next time she wakes up, I'll help her take a shower."

Aden exhaled a breath he hadn't even realized he'd been holding. "Praise God. She sounded so sick, I've kept doubting myself. I've been wondering if I should've taken her to the hospital after all."

"I thought the same thing," Miriam said, "But *mei mamm* reminded me that the flu just has to run its course. Since she raised five of us, I figured she knew what she was talking about."

Evie took out her cell phone and snapped a bunch of pictures of the cakes, taking care not to capture any people in the photographs. "These look amazing! As pretty as any of Rebecca's cakes."

Eyeing them critically, Katie tilted her head to one side. "I wouldn't say *as* pretty, but they do look good enough to eat." She wrinkled her nose. "If I had a mind to eat a slice."

"You don't want a piece?"

Even Aden shuddered. "At the moment, I canna even think about eating a bite until next year."

"Well, let's get the cakes boxed and labeled and try to get a few hours of sleep before the line forms to pick them up," Evie said.

Now that they had done so much, boxing, labeling, and checking off the names took no time at all.

Then Aden noticed one unfrosted cake in the back corner. "What about that cake?" he asked Miriam. "Did we forget one?"

"Hmm? Oh, that's an extra one." She pointed to two small bowls next to it. "It sounds silly now, but I had put it aside thinking maybe Rebecca would enjoy decorating it. But she's sleeping now, so I doubt that will happen."

"May I finish it?" he asked.

Sarah looked at him curiously. "You mean do all the icing and the fondant?"

"I do. I'd like to finish it myself and take it up to Rebecca tomorrow morning." When he noticed they were all looking at him strangely, he added, "I know it won't be very good, but I'm all right with that."

"You know what? I can do that for you," Miriam said.

"I know you could, but I'd like to finish it myself. I mean, if I can mix up a cake and even put on the base coat of icing, I think I can figure out the rest."

"Are you going to do it right now?" Sarah asked.

"I think so, but you don't need to stay. I've got this." Remembering that it was very late, he added, "But first, I'll walk you ladies home."

Evie rested a hand on his shoulder. "You stay here and finish Rebecca's cake. I'll drive the girls home. Thanks for your help today, Aden."

"*Nee,* thank all of you. Sarah, I'm glad you came to get me."

"I am, too," she replied. "*Gut* luck with the cake. Um, slow and sure is the way to frost and decorate it."

"I'll do my best. Good night. Oh, and Happy Christmas Eve."

Miriam brightened. "It is after midnight now, isn't it? Happy Christmas Eve to you, too!" After another round of good-byes and good wishes, the kitchen door closed. Minutes later he saw Evie's SUV drive down the street.

He was now alone in the kitchen, thinking about Rebecca, who did so much but never made much of a fuss about it. Picking up a spatula, he dipped it into the icing and scooped up a good amount, then started the swirls that Katie and Sarah seemed to do without any effort at all. Five minutes later, he realized that to make a good icing swirl took a lot of practice and maybe an eye for design that he didn't possess. His finished cake looked like an edible abominable snowman.

A very lopsided one.

Realizing it was close to one in the morning, he looked at the plate of red and green fondant. To his dismay, the flower petals and green leaves weren't already cut out. Instincts told him to wait until morning to get Sarah to help him. Because she had such a steady hand, she'd cut out and arranged most of the fondant. But he didn't want to wait. Plus, there was something about making this cake on his own that was calling to him.

He wanted to show Rebecca how much he cared.

After taking one more look at the design, he picked up the sharp knife and got to work. Even though it was soon apparent that he was even worse at decorating than he was at icing, he continued.

When he was done, he looked at the cake with a critical eye.

The flower petals weren't evenly spaced and the green leaves had gotten lost in the mess. "It looks like an injured snowman," he said with a sigh. Although he was tempted to remove the design and start again, Aden knew he had no option but to leave it alone. He was no expert cook, but even he realized that he wasn't going to be able to accomplish anything better until morning.

He needed to go home, get some sleep, and then hope and pray that Rebecca would be well enough to receive visitors the next morning. Then, perhaps he could find a way to tell her how much he cared about her . . . and give her the cake, too.

Hopefully she would realize that even if his skills were terrible, his heart was in the right place. That had to count for something, surely?

He really wanted her to know how much he cared about her.

Turning off the bright battery-powered lamp, he locked the door behind him and headed home. There was a light coating of snow on the ground, and several houses that he passed had twinkling lights out front.

Feeling prouder of himself than he had in years, he started whistling softly. His heart was full, his body was tired, and tomorrow was Christmas Day.

Aden doubted he'd ever felt as much joy in his heart. At least, not in a very long time.

Chapter 14

She'd showered, put on a clean, brick-red dress, eaten some cinnamon toast, and sipped a pot of hot tea. Looking in the small mirror in her bathroom, Rebecca decided that she almost felt like herself again. An exhausted, drained, and rather weak version of herself, but still much improved.

Turning to Goldie, she said, "I bet you'd like to take a small walk outside, hmm?"

Goldie barked and trotted to her leash.

Slipping on her navy cloak, Rebecca took Goldie out, leaned against the front of the building while the dog did her business and half-heartedly tried to chase a squirrel, then took her back into her rooms.

As Rebecca carefully made her way to the kitchen, she heard several bright voices inside.

"Hello," she called out as she opened the swinging door.

Miriam, Evie, Sarah, and Katie were huddled together, giggling at something on the back counter. Practically in unison, they turned around to face Rebecca at the sound of her voice.

"Rebecca, you're up and dressed!" Miriam said as she rushed to her side. The other women followed suit.

"I am. I couldn't laze about in bed for two days." Looking around the room, she paused in confusion. "I would have thought you all would be as busy as bees right now. Where are all the cakes?"

"We carried them into the dining room a few minutes ago," Evie said. "I put them in alphabetical order, so hopefully we'll be able to distribute them in no time at all as soon as ten o'clock arrives."

Rebecca was impressed. "I never thought of alphabetizing the boxes."

Evie shrugged. "I'm good at organizing things."

Reaching out, Rebecca squeezed Evie's hand. "You're also *wonderful-gut* at taking care of friends. I don't know what I would have done without you yesterday," she said with a fond smile. Looking at the other girls, she felt tears form in her eyes. "Without all of you. You saved the day. Thank you so much."

"You're welcome, but don't start thinking of getting sick next year!" Miriam teased.

"Even if I did, I wouldn't worry about a thing. It seems you all handled everything just fine."

"We did, but we didn't do it alone. We had Aden," Sarah said.

That was surprising. "What did Aden do?"

"Quite a bit," Evie said with a secret smile.

"Such as?"

Sarah answered. "For starters, he made all the batter for the cakes."

"Really? He measured and everything?"

"He did . . . and even included the secret ingredient," she whispered.

Rebecca wasn't even going to touch that. "And?"

Miriam grinned. "Once he finished with the batter, we taught him how to put the base layer of frosting on the cakes."

"Once I reminded him to go slowly, he did a good job," Katie said.

Rebecca was starting to wonder if maybe she shouldn't have been so quick to feel relieved. "Should I take a peek at the cakes? You know, just to make sure they look okay?"

"*Nee,*" said Aden as he entered the kitchen. "I can promise you that I kept to the jobs that didn't take too much skill. Plus these ladies checked and double-checked my work."

"Almost all of it," Miriam teased. "I think we might have left you alone too long last night."

"What do you mean?"

"That," Sarah said, pointing to something on the back counter.

Aden's voice turned concerned. "Wait a minute. Are you speaking of my cake? What's wrong with it?"

"Sorry, but not much is right," Miriam teased.

"Does it really look that bad?" Before any of the girls could answer, he trotted to the back counter.

Feeling left out and more than a little confused, Rebecca followed Aden to the back of the kitchen. And then stood staring at the cake on the platter. It was one of the Christmas cakes, of course. But it looked rather like a blob . . . with a terrible injury. "Oh my," she blurted.

"Oh, wow," said Aden. "I knew it didn't look good . . . but I didn't think it looked this bad."

"What is it?" Rebecca asked as soon as she could find her voice.

Just then they heard a chime, followed by several knocks.

"Oh, my word!" Katie exclaimed. "It's five minutes to ten. Our customers have arrived."

Rebecca turned on her heel. "I'll start distributing the cakes."

"*Nee!*" Evie, Sarah, Katie, and Miriam said in unison.

"We'll take care of this," Evie said. "You sit down and talk to Aden."

Before Rebecca could argue, the ladies left, leaving the two of them alone. "So, the cake?"

Aden's cheeks flushed. "Perhaps you should sit down."

She pulled out the small wooden chair next to her desk and sat. It just happened to be very close to the cake, which might or might not have been a good thing. She wasn't sure, but Rebecca had a feeling that Aden had used double the usual amount of icing on it.

And, as for the poinsettia? Well, she reckoned it looked a bit like a gaping wound, especially since the dye had started to run in rivulets down the side of the cake. She couldn't seem to stop staring at it.

"Bec, turn the other way, wouldja? I don't want to watch you stare at it anymore."

He sounded really upset! "Aden, what's wrong? Talk to me."

"Well, it's like this—after boxing all the cakes, we had an extra one, and I wanted to decorate it for you."

"Why?"

"Because you do so much for everyone else. I wanted you to have a special cake for yourself. And, I guess around one last night, I decided that it would be a good way to show my love."

"Love?"

He nodded. "I realized last night that creating something special for other people is a way of showing love. That's why you try to make your cakes so perfect and special. So all of your customers will know how much you care about them. And I wanted to do the same thing for you."

"You wanted to show you cared?" Needing to be closer, she got to her feet again.

"*Nee.* I wanted to show you my love." While she stared at him, he added, "You were right, Rebecca. I did love you all those years ago. And this month? Well, it took no time at all to realize that my feelings for you have returned tenfold. I love you again. I love you very much."

"You love me enough to spend a whole night making cakes."

"*Jah*. But please don't worry. I promise the others look better than this one."

Her insides felt like mush. "I loved you long ago and I love you today as well," she whispered.

He stepped forward and took her hands. "One day, we'll look back on this and laugh. But for now, maybe I could give you a hug?"

She nodded just seconds before he enfolded her in his arms and held her close.

She felt him kiss her temple. "I can't be away from you again, Rebecca. I'm not going to go another year without you by my side."

They had a lot to get through, but, over the last week, she'd learned something very important. She did love her shop, but it wasn't everything. She loved her friends and her longtime workers and neighbors, too. But they weren't enough. "Aden, maybe after the new year, we could talk about my moving to Ohio."

"You'd move for me?"

She nodded. "It might be difficult, but I could find a place to stay and start over. I can make cakes anywhere."

"Even though your offer means the world to me, I've already decided that I'm going to move back here. I have some remodeling job offers already, and my siblings are here. Plus, I can't leave you. I'm not going to make you leave Rebecca's Porch, either."

"Are you sure?"

"More than sure. Even my girls agree with me. I'm staying, Rebecca."

It took a second or two, but slowly Aden's words sank in. "You're not going to leave."

He shook his head. "I can't." Taking a deep breath, he said, "Rebecca, all those years ago, I really thought my leaving was for the best . . . for both of us. My future was so uncertain; I had no idea how long it was going to take for me to get on my feet. And it did take a long time. Years."

"I would've waited for you."

"That didn't seem right. I didn't want to make you wait years for an uncertain future with me." He lowered his voice. "And then, by the time I was doing all right, I didn't know how to reach out to you. I felt like I'd waited too long."

When she continued to stare at him, slowly processing his words, he lowered his voice. "I was just a scared kid when I left, Rebecca. If I had known that everything was going to turn out the way it did, I would've made different choices."

She reached for his hand. "You don't need to explain any more. I was a scared kid back then, too. I'd like to imagine that I would've been just fine by your side, but I don't know if that's the truth. All I do know is that the Lord was with both of us and He brought us back together at this point in our lives."

"And?"

She smiled. "And I have to say that His timing is perfect. Right now, at this moment, I wouldn't change a thing."

Aden's expression softened. "Right now, at this moment, I don't want to be anywhere except where you are. I love you and I want to marry you, Rebecca. Please say yes." Looking at the cake sheepishly, he added, "I promise, I won't bake you any more cakes."

She looked at the cake and realized she'd never seen anything more perfect. "I don't think I've ever been given a more perfect cake in my life. I love it."

"Oh, Bec. It rather looks like roadkill."

"I think it looks like love." Smiling at him, she added, "Tomorrow, I'm going to eat my slice."

"How about we share it?" he asked. "It might be your cake, but I did put my heart into it."

Her laughter rang through the building, under the swinging door, and into the dining room where at least fifty people were lined up waiting to pick up their special cakes.

"Is that Rebecca Christner laughing?" one of the ladies asked Evie when she stepped up to pay.

"It sure sounds like it," Evie said as she ran the woman's credit card.

"I wonder what she's so happy about?" the customer asked as she signed the receipt and then took hold of her cake, now securely nestled in a large paper bag with handles.

Sarah shared a smile with Evie, then spoke. "I reckon she's happy because Christmas is tomorrow and she has a Christmas cake to eat for dessert."

"If she has a cake of her own, then she'll have a wonderful Christmas, that's true."

Sarah nodded. "Christmas is the most wonderful day of the year, you know." Smiling at the other girls, she added softly, "At least, it is around here."

Best Christmas Present Ever

Rachel J. Good

With many thanks to my Amish beta readers

Chapter 1

"Lizzie!"

Her boss's sharp voice jerked Lizzie Bontrager away from her concerns and back to Kallis Diner. Coffee cascaded over the sides of the mug and sloshed onto the counter.

Lizzie set down the pot and swished a damp rag over the Formica to wipe up the spill. She couldn't serve this cup to a customer, so she set it in the nearby pan of dirty dishes. After pouring a fresh cup, she headed for one of the cracked, fake-leather booths.

She had to keep her mind on her job, but the letter she'd received on Saturday worried her. A neighbor had written to say Lizzie's *aenti* in Lancaster seemed to be losing track of reality. The neighbor offered to help when she could. As much as Lizzie wanted to be there, she couldn't take time off so close to Christmas.

Partway across the room, Lizzie tripped on a chipped corner of the linoleum. By grabbing the edge of one of the metal-legged tables, she righted herself. Coffee splashed over the rim of the cup and puddled in the saucer. She pulled out the towel she kept tucked in her apron waistband and wiped the cup and saucer.

Behind her, Eleni huffed loudly. Of course, the boss's eagle eyes had noticed Lizzie's near-accident.

The day only went downhill from there. Lizzie squirted ketchup on a man's business suit while she tried to unclog the container, tipped salad with dressing into a woman's lap, and mixed up two orders.

Plus, she spent too much time with customers. She tried so hard not to get involved, but she got sidetracked by people's needs. When she found out it was a little boy's birthday, she took him one of the animal cupcakes she made for the restaurant, paid for it from yesterday's tips, and sang to him.

When she turned around, she met Eleni's glare.

Mamm had always warned Lizzie to rein in her bubbly, exuberant personality. But harnessing her high spirits proved as difficult as taming her wiry red curls. No matter how tightly she wound the rolls at the side of her head and confined them into the bob at the back of her neck, wrapped the bun in netting, and covered it with her *kapp*, springy little curls popped out as she rushed around.

She finished off her day by dropping a trayful of dishes on the way to the kitchen. Right in front of her boss.

As Lizzie cleaned up the smashed dishes, Eleni grasped her arm. "Meet me in the kitchen the minute you're finished here."

When Lizzie entered, Eleni stood, scowling, near the swinging door, drumming her fingertips on the edge of the counter. Lizzie's stomach knotted. All day long, Eleni had rushed through the diner like a whirlwind. She never stood this still. And despite her busyness, she never once made any mistakes. Unlike Lizzie.

Through clenched teeth, Eleni issued her ultimatum. "One more accident. One more cold meal. One more customer complaint, and you're out of here. Do you understand?"

I can't lose this job. I just can't. "I'm sorry."

Eleni's face remained rigid and icy. "Do you understand? Yes or no?"

Lizzie stared down at her sneakers and nodded.

When she woke the next morning, Lizzie determined to turn over a new leaf. She'd pay attention to her work, ignore her instincts to help people, and do her best to avoid accidents. The morning started well. Without catching any customers' eyes, she took the orders from her assigned tables. So far, so good.

A short while later, she bustled away from the counter with four breakfast plates. The first went to an elderly woman sitting alone at a table, staring off into the distance, her eyes sad. She didn't look up as Lizzie set the eggs and toast down.

Despite her internal warnings, Lizzie couldn't ignore this hurting woman. "Are you all right?"

The *Englischer* looked up with dull eyes. "I buried my husband last week."

"I'm so sorry." Lizzie shifted the tray to one side and laid a hand over the woman's gnarled fingers.

Tears slipped down the lady's cheeks. "We never had children. It was only the two of us."

"That must be so hard."

"Lizzie!"

At Eleni's sharp rebuke, Lizzie straightened, tipping the serving tray.

Nooo!

She grabbed for it. Caught the edge of the tray. Two plates slipped. *Crash!* White crockery shattered. Poached eggs slithered to the floor. Yolks broke in a yellow liquid mess. Cranberry juice splattered her skirt and dripped down her calves.

Lizzie squeezed her eyes shut. Eleni's furious face floated before Lizzie's eyes. She'd done it again.

"I'm so sorry," she whispered to the woman. "I'll be right back." Juice and egg yolk dotted the woman's orthopedic shoes.

Gripping the last plate tightly, Lizzie hurried to the next table to set it in front of the customer.

"I'm not eating cold pancakes." His voice boomed around the restaurant. "And is that mess the rest of our meals?" He pointed to the shattered dishes.

Eleni, her jaw tight, hurried to the table. "I apologize. I'll have the kitchen rush fresh meals to all of you. On the house."

The man glanced at his watch. "We don't have time to wait. I'll be sure to tell everyone about your poor service." He shoved back his chair and stalked to the exit, his colleagues following him.

Christmas bells in the garland above the door jangled loudly as he yanked open the door. "If I were you," he yelled over his shoulder, "I'd fire that incompetent Amish girl."

"Lizzie . . ." Eleni growled. "I'm not sending the busboy to clean up that mess. You do it. I'm reassigning your tables to the other servers until you're done."

"I'm so sorry."

"I've heard that one time too many."

Eleni headed to the elderly woman's table. "Please forgive us for the mess. Your meal will be on the house."

"No need. I'll gladly pay. And I disagree with that man. That girl's a gem. She has a good heart."

The supportive words soothed Lizzie's embarrassment, but she doubted Eleni believed kindness could make up for this disaster. Lizzie scurried off before her boss caught her eavesdropping.

Her hands full of cleaning supplies, Lizzie hurried back to the table and passed Eleni, grumbling under her breath. Lizzie whispered, for what felt like the hundredth time, "I'm sorry."

"Sorry doesn't pay for messes and lost customers."

Lizzie cringed. She'd been warned. One more careless mistake and she'd be fired.

As she knelt to wipe the elderly woman's shoes, Lizzie repeated her apology.

"Don't worry about it, dear. Wet shoes and messy floors are easily fixed. Broken hearts are not." The woman reached out and put a small roll of bills in Lizzie's hand. "God gave you the gift of caring. Use it well."

"I can't take this."

"You can and you will." The woman pressed Lizzie's fingers closed over the money. "God used that spill to teach me a lesson." She set more bills on the table and hobbled to the door.

Lizzie tucked the rolled-up money into her pocket, cleaned the floor, settled the woman's bill, stuffed the extra change into the tip jar, and headed to the kitchen to return the cleaning supplies.

Eleni brushed past her. "We're shorthanded today. Get your orders out to the tables so everyone else isn't stuck covering for you. We'll talk later. I want to see you in my office at the end of your shift."

At least Eleni hadn't fired Lizzie on the spot. She could work the rest of the day. She needed the money.

Whatever it took, she'd be a model employee. She didn't have long to prove herself, but she'd give it her all.

She double-checked all her orders. She slow-walked all the meals to her tables. And she kept her eyes averted so she wouldn't be tempted to comfort anyone or start a conversation.

The day zipped by. Other than a few minor mishaps—knocking over a saltshaker as she filled it, forgetting to bring silverware to one table, and not filling water glasses promptly—Lizzie had her best day ever.

Maybe Eleni might change her mind.

Eleni folded her hands on the desk. "Let's start with the positive. You're very friendly and personable, and you have a beautiful smile. You also care about people. Most customers really seem to love you." She paused. "But you spend too much time talking with people and neglect your other customers."

Lizzie wanted to say she'd try harder, but she didn't want to act as if she expected to keep her job. And even if she stayed, she couldn't promise to do better because whenever she sensed how people were feeling, she couldn't help trying to cheer them up or encouraging them to talk about their problems.

"We might be able to overlook that on occasion," Eleni continued, "but not every day. The holidays are the busiest time of year, and it's not fair to the other servers to make them pick up your slack."

Lizzie bowed her head. She hadn't meant to make more work for the others.

"That's not the worst of it." Eleni passed Lizzie a three-page list. "These are the expenses we've incurred since you started working here."

Broken dishes, spilled food and drinks, carpet cleaning, suit cleaning, free meals to pacify irate customers . . .

Eleni sighed. "And that doesn't include the wasted coffee and two dry-cleaning bills for yesterday, or the broken plates, ruined meals, and lost customers today. I'm sure you can see that you're more of a liability than an asset to this restaurant."

"I-I didn't mean to be. I'll try harder." Lizzie hadn't meant for that last sentence to slip out.

"No, I'm sorry, but we can't keep you on. We've given you several chances to improve, and it hasn't gotten any better."

Lizzie clenched her hands in her lap. She was fired. She grasped at one last possibility. "What about the cupcakes?" Children loved the animal-shaped ones she decorated, and women begged for boxes of her flower-topped cupcakes for their teas and parties.

"You're a gifted decorator, but I'm afraid the money that brings in doesn't outweigh those costs." Eleni waved a hand toward the list. "In fact, my husband and I discussed it. We've decided to deduct these costs from your paycheck. He thinks we should have been doing that all along."

"But they total more than my paycheck."

"I know. Thanos wanted to charge you for all of it, but it's almost Christmas. Consider it a gift."

A gift? Eleni considered Lizzie's losing her paycheck a gift?

As Lizzie stared at the long list, she had to admit, from the Kallises' viewpoint, they'd given her a lot.

"What about the apartment?"

Eleni grimaced. "That was conditioned on your employment. Since you'll no longer be working here . . ."

Neh. She'd not only lost her job, she'd lost the roof over her head. She and Mamm had lived in the apartment over the restaurant for years. Eleni had been kind enough to let Lizzie stay after Mamm died last year. Lizzie only paid for utilities, although that took most of her meager paychecks. Tips in this small diner had barely covered those expenses and her food. She had no savings.

"It's not hard to get employment over the holidays," Eleni said soothingly. "And we'll give you until January to find a new place."

"*Danke*," Lizzie said in a small voice as she stood. She forced herself to add, "That's kind of you."

If she had someplace to go, she'd pack up and be out the door this minute. But not only could she not afford to rent another place, she also wouldn't be getting a paycheck to buy food. What would she do? No home and no job so close to Christmas.

Chapter 2

Christian Yoder bottled up the fear tangling his insides, pasted on a smile, and slapped a card down on the rollaway tray over his daughter's hospital bed.

"Dutch!" seven-year-old Johanna crowed.

Faking a sheepish expression, he reached for the card. He'd done it to distract her, and it had worked.

A slight smile tilted the corner of her lips, as he lifted the card from the wrong place. Meanwhile, she placed a card on one of the stacks, rapidly depleting her blitz pile.

He shrugged. "I got mixed up."

"But it's supposed to be a girl." Johanna's exasperation seemed as fake as his ploy.

As they finished their game of Dutch Blitz, both of them avoided talking about tomorrow. But even five fast-paced games had provided only a brief distraction.

"Blitz!" With a triumphant smile, Johanna snapped her final card onto a stack. Her eyes glowing, she glanced up at him.

He sighed. "You beat me again."

"It's all right." She patted his hand. "Maybe you'll win next time."

Her small warm hand on his, her grown-up response, and the glare of the overhead fluorescent lights stung his eyes. Christian attempted a rueful smile, but his throat had closed, and he couldn't force out a lighthearted comeback.

Her eyes grave, Johanna studied him.

Christian worried his forced smile might dampen her happiness. But before he could read her expression, she ducked her head and scooped up her favorite deck—the one with the red carriage. Tapping the cards to align them, she evaded his gaze.

The tight pressure in his chest increased until his ribs ached. What would he do if she didn't survive?

Please, God, I can't bear to lose her too.

His wife's passing had left an aching hollowness inside. In the five years since, Christian had gotten through the days by devoting all his time outside work hours to Johanna. They'd formed a deep, unbreakable bond. A bond that could only be severed by death.

He couldn't think about that. Especially not now. Not tonight. With shaky hands he gathered the blue cards, while Johanna picked up the yellow deck.

His cell phone rang, startling both of them. He'd gotten the phone because of Johanna's health. Only a few people had his number—the hospital and medical personnel and his boss.

Christian gazed down at the display. His boss. Christian had requested today and tomorrow off. Why was Merle calling now?

He debated about answering, but when it rang once more, he picked it up.

"We need you to come in. Joseph got hurt, and they're calling for a blizzard tomorrow. We need to get the house under roof tonight." Merle spoke so fast, he barely drew in a breath.

"I can't. I'm at the hospital."

"She doesn't have surgery 'til tomorrow, right?"

"*Jah*, but—"

"Then get over here now. I need everyone right away. I'm getting floodlights delivered so we can work late into the night if we need to."

"I need to be with my daughter tonight."

"Look. You have two choices. Either you get over here now, or I'll hire someone else. If I do that, don't bother coming back. I'll turn your job over to the new hire."

"That's blackmail."

"No, it's business. I can't afford to let snow mess up this job. I'll give you half an hour to get here. If you don't make it by then, I'm calling in someone else." Merle hung up.

Christian sat with the dead phone in his hands. What was he going to do? If he didn't go, he'd lose his job. How would he pay the hospital bills and provide a home for Johanna? But if he went . . .

"Don't leave me, Daed." Johanna clung to his hand, breaking his heart.

How could he leave Johanna here alone? For the millionth time, he wished his wife were still alive. For so many different reasons. Right now, she could keep their daughter company.

He squeezed Johanna's hand gently and kissed her forehead, then he stood. "I have to feed Sampson and do some work, but I'll be back later tonight." He had no idea how much later. She'd be sound asleep by the time he returned.

Tears glimmered in her eyes. "I miss Sampson. I want him here."

"I know." Although Christian had explained hospitals wouldn't allow dogs, Johanna often begged for Sampson to visit.

"I don't want you to go."

Her breathless little voice tore him apart inside. "I wish I didn't have to, but the nurses will take good care of you until I come back.

"I'm scared."

Christian almost threw his job to the wind. His daughter needed him. Wasn't that more important than roofing a mansion? Of course it was. But finding another construction job before spring would be impossible.

He sat on the bed beside Johanna and wrapped an arm around her, drawing her close. "Let's pray about it."

Her words barely a whisper, Johanna pleaded, "Dear Jesus, please help me not to be scared while Daed is gone."

Christian added his prayers to hers along with a silent request that God would keep her safe and guide the doctors tomorrow. When he lifted his head, he gave her a squeeze. "I'll be back to spend the night."

"Promise?"

"*Jah*, I promise." Christian planned to spend every night with her, but tonight he'd be awake all night, praying over her.

He walked out of the room, then paused in the doorway to wave and reassure her. "Remember, Jesus is with you."

Johanna bit her lip. "I want to be as brave as Daniel in the lion's den, but it's hard."

Christian choked back the lump blocking his throat. He couldn't answer. He could only nod. Was it fair to expect a seven-year-old to have that much courage? She'd been through so much in her short life—losing her *mamm*, her grandparents, and now dealing with a brain tumor.

His voice husky, he managed to say, "You've faced many lions already."

She leaned back against the pillow. "I'm tired."

Tired of facing lions? Of fighting the disease? Or both?

"Take a little nap. It'll make the time pass quickly."

"I'm too big for naps."

Not anymore. Your body needs all the rest it can get.

Her eyes drifted shut before he reached the door.

Lord, please keep her safe. Let her sleep for a long time. And please, please heal her.

How could he handle it if he lost her?

Lizzie trudged upstairs to the apartment. *Lord, what am I going to do*?

She could stay here in the apartment until January, but she'd have to find another job and a place to live. And she also had to figure out what to do about her aunt.

Sinking into a chair at the kitchen table, she picked up the letter she'd dropped there yesterday. She'd deciphered the sloppy scrawled letters already, and she reread the brief message for the fourth time:

> *I'm worried about your aenti. Miriam hasn't been doing well. Her memory is failing, and she keeps asking for your mamm. She doesn't have a firm grip on reality sometimes, so she really needs someone to care for her.*

This morning, Lizzie had pulled out her checkbook and all her bills. She'd paid them, hoping she could send the remaining balance to care for her *aenti*. Actually, Miriam was Mamm's *aenti*, and she was in her eighties. But after the bills were paid, Lizzie barely had enough for groceries for the next week or two.

She pulled the tip from her pocket. Fifteen dollars! When the servers had divided up the money from the tip jar tonight, she'd slipped away, leaving her portion for Eleni. Her boss had nodded, acknowledging the payment, and even managed a small smile.

With these three fives and what was in her account, Lizzie could buy food. Or she could spend the money on bus tickets.

She and Mamm had gone to Lancaster from Fort Plain a few times. She'd need to get a ride to Fonda, then a bus to Albany. The worst part was heading from Albany to New York City. All the traffic and crowds and waiting made her nervous. And this time she wouldn't have Mamm for company. Once Lizzie walked to the station and boarded the bus to Lancaster, she could relax. All in all, the trip took more than ten hours with the waiting times between switching buses.

Next came deciding what to pack. The furniture and household goods belonged to the Kallises. The Bible, Mamm's worn copy of *Martyrs Mirror*, and several other books went into the suitcase, followed by Lizzie's few dresses, aprons, and toiletries. After she emptied the other garments from her dresser and wrapped her dress shoes and sneakers in plastic bags, she shut the case and scrubbed at the cranberry juice stains and assorted other splotches on her dress and apron. Then she hung them near the radiator to dry.

Her heart heavy, she walked through the apartment as memories of Mamm flooded her mind. They'd had many special times together in this small apartment. Lizzie ached at the thought of leaving the place she'd called home for the past sixteen years.

Only two more things to do. She slipped downstairs to the kitchen. First, she mixed up huge batches of cake batter and filled the ovens with cupcakes. While they baked, she arranged her bus tickets and transportation to the station.

After the cupcakes cooled, Lizzie decorated all of them. She created the customers' favorite flowers, animals, and snowmen. By two thirty in the morning, she'd filled the bakery cases and stored the extras in the walk-in cooler. At least the cupcake sales might pay back a little of what she owed Eleni and

Thanos. Perhaps, once she could afford it, she'd send them money.

When she got in bed, Lizzie tossed and turned until dawn. She rose, put on her still slightly damp dress, tugged her bonnet over her *kapp*, slid her feet into winter boots, and shrugged into her winter coat. Before she slipped out the side entrance and locked up, she set an apology note for her bosses on the counter. They'd be able to rent the apartment for extra money too.

Exhausted and freezing, she settled into the seat of the hired car, grateful for the warmth. As they pulled away from the curb, Lizzie turned to watch the diner disappear into the distance. A few tears trickled down her cheeks. Life as she'd known it had come to an end. Riding away from the home she'd shared with Mamm left an emptiness in Lizzie's heart.

By the time she reached Lancaster, hungry and tired and lonely after the grueling, eleven-hour trip, Lizzie struggled to put on a cheerful face. She called from the bus station to let Miriam's neighbor, Mrs. Heise, know she'd be coming, but nobody answered. Lizzie hoped her *aenti* would be happy to see her.

She'd head to the neighbor's house first to thank Mrs. Heise for looking after Miriam. If Mrs. Heise still wasn't home, Lizzie would head to her *aenti*'s house. After the huge snowdrifts in Fort Plain, Lancaster's six inches seemed to barely cover the lawns. In many places, it had turned to slush. Cars splashed through it, throwing the gray, melting snow from their tires onto her legs.

She took out the envelope to double-check Mrs. Heise's address. *18 . . . 22 . . . 24*. This should be the house. She mounted the steps to the porch and knocked.

An old lady who looked vaguely familiar opened the door and pressed a hand to her heart. "Lizzie? Well, my goodness. Do you ever look like your mother as a young bride."

Lizzie winced. The long trip had reminded her so much of times she and Mamm had traveled together, and Mrs. Heise's words stabbed those fresh wounds. Lizzie forced a smile to cover her pain.

"Come in, come in, and get out of the cold. I didn't expect you to come so quickly."

"I didn't have any way to let you know before I left." She couldn't have made a long-distance call on the diner phone. "I tried calling from the station."

"I heard the phone ringing, but by the time I got to it, it had stopped."

"I hope my *aenti* will be all right with my showing up like this." Once again, she'd made an impulsive decision.

Mrs. Heise's face clouded. "I don't know that it'll make much difference to Miriam one way or the other, but she does need someone to watch her. She doesn't know who people are most of the time."

"You think she'll recognize me?" Mrs. Heise's letters had hinted that Miriam had some memory loss, but this sounded as if it were more than forgetfulness.

"I really can't say." Sadness filled Mrs. Heise's eyes. "Some days she's better than others, but her memory's slipping. Let me get my coat and take you over there. Miriam's used to me dropping in, but she doesn't always remember me." She pulled on a coat and boots.

When they reached Miriam's porch, Mrs. Heise reached out and patted Lizzie's shoulder, though she had to reach up to do it. "Now don't get your feelings hurt if your aunt doesn't recognize you. Like I said, she has good days and bad days."

"I understand."

"Oh, and don't be shocked at the condition of the house. People from her church often stop by and offer to clean or cook, but Miriam refuses to let them in. I've been doing what I can, when she lets me, but she dislikes people touching her things."

After Mrs. Heise had knocked several times without getting an answer, she turned the knob and walked in. "Miriam? Tilda here. I've brought you a visitor."

No answer.

They traipsed through the downstairs and reached the kitchen. Once again, Mrs. Heise's hand fluttered to her heart. "Oh, my stars. Miriam, how many times have I told you not to cook dinner? I'll bring over meals."

Miriam stood in front of the stove, happily tossing raw ground beef in the air. The kitchen was a disaster. Flour coated the floor. Half-opened containers dotted the counters, amid spills of various ingredients. A jumbled pile of cans and boxes lay scattered on the pantry floor. Miriam's *kapp* was askew, and her dress had more stains than Lizzie's did after a day of working at the restaurant.

The only positive things Lizzie could find in the scene: the stove was off, and her *aenti* appeared cheerful.

Lizzie's heart sank. She hadn't realized her *aenti* needed this much care.

"How long has she been like this?" Lizzie whispered.

"The past few weeks it's gotten much worse. That's why I wrote to you. I do my best to keep an eye on her, but—"

With a sympathetic glance, Mrs. Heise rushed from the kitchen. "I need to get home to take the meatloaf out of the oven, but I'll be back with dinner shortly. Then I'll help you clean up."

"No need to make us dinner." Lizzie gestured to all the cans of soup and stew on the pantry floor. She could also cook the meat if any still remained in the pan.

Mrs. Heise shook her head. "Don't eat anything from the pantry unless you check the dates. Many of those cans and boxes expired several years ago. And smell the meat. No telling how old that is."

"*Ach!* I'll have to clean out the pantry then."

"Yes, we can do that, but"—Mrs. Heise leaned closer to whisper—"you can't do it while Miriam's watching, or she'll dig the cans out of the trash."

"I heard that, Tilda." For a moment, her *aenti* seemed to know her neighbor.

Mrs. Heise turned to face the stove. "I'm making meatloaf, Miriam. I'll bring it over."

"*Neh*, I'm making hamburgers." Miriam tossed another spoonful in the air. Half of it landed in the frying pan, but the rest splattered on the stove.

Miriam frowned at her neighbor and spotted Lizzie. She waved the spoon. "Anna Grace!" She rushed over and hugged Lizzie, squishing slimy, rotten-smelling ground beef against the back of Lizzie's dress.

Lizzie's eyes filled with tears. Her *aenti* had mistaken her for Mamm.

Chapter 3

Christian could barely keep his mind on the roofing. Johanna filled his every thought.

"Hey, can you hand me another one?" Pete, one of Christian's *Englisch* coworkers, pointed to the bundles of shingles beside Christian.

"Huh?" Christian stared at the place Pete had indicated for a second. They'd started with equal piles, but Pete had already finished all of his. Christian still had several stacks to go.

"Christian? You all right?" Pete's brow creased with concern.

"What?" *Neh*, he wasn't all right, and he wouldn't be until tomorrow afternoon when he knew for certain Johanna had made it safely through surgery.

"Hey!" Pete waved a hand in front of Christian's face. "The shingles?"

Christian handed over two stacks, determined to beat his coworker in laying the next two bundles.

Pete took the shingles but didn't return to work. Instead, he studied the small section Christian had completed. "What's with you tonight? You're usually twice as fast as the rest of us."

"Sorry. A lot on my mind."

"Wait a minute. Weren't you supposed to have off today? What are you doing here? Is today the day your daughter—?" He stopped, with a sympathetic look.

"Tomorrow," Christian mumbled.

"I can't believe Merle made you come in. He's a slave driver."

Christian didn't answer, although inside he rather agreed with Pete. He'd made up his mind that, if Merle insisted Christian had to work tomorrow, he'd quit. Even if he didn't have another job to go to. He should be with Johanna right this minute.

"Go back to the hospital," Pete said. "I'll lay your shingles once I've finished mine."

"But you'll be here most of the night."

"I don't mind. It's not like I have anyone to go home to."

Patting the stacks of shingles beside him, Christian nodded. "*Danke*. I'll finish these first, then go down and bring up some more." Knowing that as soon as he completed these he'd get to leave, Christian whipped through his piles before Pete finished his two.

As Christian carried more up the ladder, he thanked God for his friend's kindness. "I owe you," he told Pete before climbing down and hurrying to his buggy.

By the time he reached the hospital, Johanna was sound asleep. He brushed her tangled blond curls from her face. They'd be shaving off some of her beautiful hair in the operating room. The idea of her having bald patches made his eyes well with moisture.

Then he shook himself. There were much worse things than losing hair. And he might have to face those tomorrow.

* * *

After her long trip to Lancaster and then an evening spent cleaning Miriam's kitchen, Lizzie had fallen into bed, drained and disoriented. It had been years since she and Mamm had visited Miriam. To see her lively, friendly *aenti* in this condition broke Lizzie's heart. Worst of all, Miriam kept mistaking Lizzie for Mamm despite Mrs. Heise's attempts to correct her.

Now, Lizzie lay in bed daunted by all the work she'd face today. She rose at dawn to make breakfast before her *aenti* decided to cook. Then she'd start on the house, one room at a time. The accumulated dust, dirt, and junk might take weeks to get in order. Although the cleaning seemed overwhelming, she loved feeling useful and helping people. Now she could do that for her *aenti*. If Miriam would let her.

On her way to the kitchen, she peeked into the dining room. Papers had been piled high on all the surfaces and strewn across the floor. Many of them seemed to be bills. She'd check through those after breakfast to be sure everything had been paid.

Miriam shuffled into the kitchen twenty minutes later, still wearing the stained dress from yesterday. Had she worn it to bed? Lizzie would have to make sure her *aenti* bathed and changed, but first they'd eat. Mrs. Heise had brought over a few groceries last night, but they'd need to go to the market.

Her *aenti* glanced at the scrambled eggs Lizzie was dishing onto their plates. "I wanted to make breakfast."

Lizzie couldn't help feeling sorry for Miriam as she sat at the table, looking dispirited. "I know you're a good cook." At least, she had been.

Miriam brightened. "*Danke*. I'll wait until your *daed* comes down to make pancakes. They're his favorite."

Lizzie bit her lip. Did Miriam mean Lizzie's *daed* or Mamm's *daed*? Either way, they'd both been gone for more than a decade.

She set a plate of eggs and toast in front of Miriam, and her *aenti* smiled. "This looks good."

When they bowed their heads for silent prayer, Lizzie asked God for wisdom in helping Miriam. Less than an hour later, Lizzie was praying for patience.

Miriam insisted on doing the dishes. First, she squirted half a bottle of dish detergent into the sink, but forgot to put in the stopper. After Lizzie inserted it, Miriam let the sink overflow. While Lizzie cleaned that up, a wet plate slipped from her *aenti*'s hands and shattered.

Lizzie half-laughed and half-cried as she swept up the shards. She'd had plenty of practice cleaning up spills. Was that why God had given her the job at the diner? To prepare her for caring for Miriam?

Finally, Lizzie settled her *aenti* in a rocking chair in the living room. Several gardening magazines and glossy photo books of flowers, trees, and animals had been stacked on a chest that served as a coffee table. Lizzie suspected Mrs. Heise had left them.

Miriam selected a book of flowers and spent hours alternating between admiring the flowers and staring out the window at buggies, cars, and people. Lizzie thanked God for the busy street and Mrs. Heise's kindness.

With her *aenti* facing away from the archway into the dining room, Lizzie tackled the papers. She tossed unimportant papers, flyers, and advertisements into a recycling bin. That reduced the clutter by two thirds.

Then she opened all envelopes. The stack of bills from the past several months, each one with a higher balance and penalties for nonpayment, grew higher and higher. Lizzie discarded all but the most recent ones. The gas bill had a notice that it would be shut off in thirty days unless they paid in full or contacted the company about a payment plan.

Near the bottom of the stack, she discovered that property taxes hadn't been paid in June, when they were due. The notice showed a penalty had been added. Lizzie gulped at the huge amount. Even more worrisome, Miriam only had until December 31 before the bill moved to delinquent status.

Lizzie rooted through the unsorted papers and dug through drawers crammed with junk to find a checkbook. She unearthed one in the last drawer she opened. The last entry had been in early June. And if the balance was correct, Lizzie could pay most of these overdue bills, but not the tax bill.

In a frenzy, Lizzie tore open bank statements until she came to the most recent one. The balance on that statement matched the one in the checkbook. She buried her head in her hands. If only she had money to take care of this debt. Would Miriam lose her house if they didn't pay the real estate taxes?

Lizzie had no idea. But one thing she did know for sure. She needed a job right away.

"Yoo-hoo!" Mrs. Heise walked through the front door, carrying a large bowl with a foil-wrapped package balanced on top. "Thought you might need some lunch. Then afterward, I'll watch Miriam so you can grocery shop."

Lizzie stretched and leaned forward to see the battery-powered clock on the kitchen wall. Had she been working that long?

As they ate, Lizzie whispered her concerns to Miriam. "I need to get a job, but I'm worried about leaving my *aenti* here alone."

Mrs. Heise patted her arm. "All my children are grown and gone. I have plenty of time on my hands. I'd be happy to check in on Miriam while you're working. I've been doing that already."

"*Danke*. That would be *wunderbar*."

While Mrs. Heise and Miriam cleaned the kitchen together, Lizzie headed out toward the small area of stores she'd seen on her way into the neighborhood. With no buggy, she'd need to find a job within walking distance.

At shop after shop, the owners repeated the same answer. "Sorry, no openings."

Lizzie's toes stung and so did her eyes. She'd already walked more than a mile. Could she walk this far in the middle of a winter snowstorm? She'd have to. She had no choice. She had no money to pay a driver.

Please, God, help me to find someplace to work.

A small voice inside urged her on. Two more *neh*s almost made her turn around, but then a cute little building up ahead drew her attention. *Rebecca's Porch*, the sign read. A gift shop, perhaps?

As she approached, cakes tucked into the display window lightened her spirits. When she stepped inside, the bakery enveloped her with its warmth and coziness. Lovely floral cloths in different patterns covered small café tables. Vanilla and cinnamon perfumed the air. Lizzie inhaled deeply. Several girls rushed around refilling coffee cups or carrying in baked goods from the kitchen to put in the display case.

A middle-aged Amish woman stood behind the counter. "Can I help you?"

"I hope so. This is such a lovely shop, so warm and homey." Lizzie babbled on, "I like the tablecloths, and the smells . . ." She took in another deep breath.

The woman's eyes lit up. "*Danke*. The aroma makes me happy too. I'm so grateful to spend my days in this shop. It was my dream."

"You're the owner?"

"*Jah*, I'm Rebecca."

The door behind Lizzie opened, and gust of icy wind blew across her back.

"Aden." The woman's eyes softened. "You're here early."

The man's loving eyes rested on Rebecca, filling Lizzie with longing. She doubted anyone would ever look at her that way. Her unruly red hair, her tendency to accidents, her haphazard housekeeping, her . . .

"I didn't mean to keep you from ordering." The man stepped back and motioned for Lizzie to step up to the counter.

"I, um, I'm looking for a job."

Rebecca's regretful look signaled she'd be Lizzie's next rejection. "I'm sorry."

Aden interrupted. "Rebecca, you could use some help. Even if this girl only cleans and greases pans, sweeps up, clears dishes, takes coffee to the customers—" A teasing smile curved his lips. "She could also help shell walnuts."

"Are you trying to get out of that?'

Mirth in his eyes, Aden placed a hand on his heart. "Why would I do that?"

Lizzie broke in. "I'm happy to shell walnuts. And I can decorate cakes. I worked in a diner in Fort Plain, but now I'm living in Lancaster to take care of my *aenti*, and I have to make money because . . ." She stuttered to a stop. How unprofessional. And what would she do if they asked for references? How could she explain being fired?

A serious expression on his face, Aden glanced from Lizzie to Rebecca. "Maybe this is the answer to my prayers." He grinned. "I've been hoping to spend less time with walnuts and more time with you."

Rebecca's eyes glittered with tears. "I'd like that. And we are swamped with orders." She turned to Lizzie. "You can decorate?"

Lizzie nodded. "I did specialty cupcakes for the diner. Flowers. And animals. And lots of holiday designs."

"Can you do poinsettias?" Rebecca pointed to the display case. "On cakes?"

"Of course." The ones in the case were cut from fondant. She could do that.

"Trying to keep up with all the orders has tired me out lately."

"You work too hard." Aden's sympathetic look revealed his deep love.

Would he convince Rebecca to say yes? A frisson of excitement exploded inside Lizzie. She liked the atmosphere and this sweet couple.

Please, Lord, I'd love to work here with these two. Help them to take me.

"All right," Rebecca said finally. "When can you start?"

"Now." The word shot out of Lizzie's mouth before she could stop it.

Rebecca blinked.

Behind Lizzie, Aden laughed. "An enthusiastic worker is a gift from God, don't you think?"

"*Jah*, well, how about tomorrow?" Rebecca seemed a bit hesitant. "Can you come in at eight?"

"I'll be here. And *danke*, *danke*, *danke!*" Lizzie tamped down the rest of her exuberance until she had exited and was out of sight of the window. Then she shouted, "Hallelujah! *Danke*, Lord!" She couldn't help skipping a little.

The walk home didn't seem as long or cold as it had earlier. She had a job!

Chapter 4

Mrs. Heise showed up at seven. "I wanted to give you extra time to get to work."

Lizzie thanked her several times before hurrying out the door. She tried to slow her steps. She didn't want to arrive too early and appear overeager. But the whole way there, her heart sang.

How lucky could she be? This must be divine intervention. An Amish bakery with a kind boss. God had not only answered her prayers, He'd given her even more than she could ask or think.

Now it was up to her to make the most of it. Pay attention. Be careful. No accidents. No mistakes.

She vowed to be the best employee ever.

Her resolve lasted through the first hour. Rebecca assigned Sarah, one of the other Amish girls, to show Lizzie around and teach her the duties she'd be expected to perform.

"The most important thing to remember," Sarah explained, "is that Rebecca wants us to show God's love to every customer who comes through the door."

Lizzie's heart swelled. With a philosophy like that, she'd love working here. But she promised herself she wouldn't get so involved with customers that she'd forget her other jobs.

"Rebecca's great to work for. And it's nice to be in a place where all the employees are kind, caring, helpful, honest—" Sarah broke off. "Just a minute." She raced over to the door and opened it for a mother struggling to enter with a baby stroller.

When she returned, she showed Lizzie how to operate the cash register, introduced her to the other employees, and then went with her to take cinnamon tea and pastries to a table of ladies.

"Looks like you already know how to do all this." Sarah appeared impressed.

"I used to work in a diner, and I decorated cupcakes for them."

"You know how to decorate? That'll be a big help, although Rebecca insists on doing her special poinsettia cakes herself." Sarah pointed to a list several pages long. "People put their orders in months ahead."

Lizzie's eyes widened. "She'll do all of those herself?"

"She has every year." Flashing Lizzie a smile, Sarah headed to the kitchen. "If you need help, holler. Otherwise, we'll all be in the kitchen baking."

One of the cinnamon-tea women came up to the counter. "I need to order one of Rebecca's poinsettia Christmas cakes."

Lizzie fetched the list and thumbed through it. Every line was filled. She rummaged through the drawer below the cash register. *Gut*. Office supplies lay neatly in divided trays. She pulled out paper and a pen, and took down the information.

Several other ladies rushed the counter. "You're taking Christmas cake orders?"

Soon Lizzie had two-dozen new orders because they requested extra cakes for relatives or neighbors. After they'd all paid their bills, she stapled the sheet to the back of the list. Then she cleared their table.

She removed the last two plates and headed for the plastic bin of dirty dishes. Her foot caught on a chair leg. One plate went flying. *Crash!*

Rebecca rushed from the kitchen, followed by the other girls.

Lizzie burst into tears. "I'm so sorry," she blubbered. "You can take it out of my pay."

"Are you hurt?" Rebecca's alarmed expression turned to one of concern.

Lizzie gulped back a sob and shook her head.

"Please don't worry. It's only a plate. Plates can be replaced. People can't."

Rebecca's soft, reassuring voice made Lizzie feel worse. She didn't want to cause Rebecca or her business any problems. She hurried for the broom.

How different this bakery was from the diner! Rebecca's kindness warmed Lizzie all the way through. She wanted to do her best, but would she make the same mistakes?

Walking beside his baby girl as they wheeled her down the hall on a stretcher was one of the hardest things Christian had ever done. And then he had to let them transfer his sleeping daughter into the operating room, knowing it might be the last time he'd ever see her alive.

He clenched his fists at his side and clamped his jaw shut. He wanted to command them to stop the surgery. Tell them he'd made a mistake. Removing a brain tumor was a delicate operation. Even if Johanna lived, the consent forms he'd signed had listed so many possible complications. All of them scrolled through his mind.

The nurse, wearing a Mennonite prayer covering, touched his arm. "Let's pray for your little girl." She bowed her head and asked God's blessing on the surgeon and the medical team and for Johanna's full recovery.

Christian swallowed the lump in his throat. "*Danke*," he said when she raised her eyes.

She patted his arm. "She's in God's hands now. You look exhausted. Why don't you go home and get some sleep? They'll call you when she's out of surgery."

How could he leave until he was positive Johanna was out of danger? He headed up to her room, but the emptiness made him more distraught. He paced the hallway, but kept having to move to one side for nurses and visitors and stretchers and wheelchairs.

The chapel. He'd go to the small, quiet room to pray. He knelt and prayed for almost an hour before peace descended. *Lord, not my will, but Yours.*

With those words, he rose. He needed to go home and shower. He'd gone straight to the hospital after finishing the roofing job. And he had to walk and feed Sampson.

The storm Merle had warned about began as Christian and Sampson left the house. A sporadic spritz of wet snow fell, and he slid along behind Johanna's exuberant Westie, whose fluffy white coat hid the icy flakes.

Those chores kept him busy, but couldn't still his racing thoughts. Every few minutes, he sent up another plea for Johanna and for the doctors. For wisdom. For skill. For steady hands.

Once he'd finished walking the dog and taken care of his horses, Christian headed back out. Freezing winds whipped his face, jolting him awake after his sleepless night. The slippery roads could be treacherous, so he appreciated his horse's steady footing. He took back roads to the hospital to delay his arrival.

Up ahead, Rebecca's Porch called to him. Coffee would keep him awake. He pulled his horse into the shelter provided for Amish customers and rushed through the bone-chilling cold and light snow to the entrance.

The aroma of warm pastries and freshly brewed coffee drew him in. He sank into a chair near the window where he could watch snowflakes dust the fields. If the snow grew heavier, he'd leave for the hospital.

But as long as the snow held off, sitting here was better than being surrounded by hospital sounds and smells. Here, his mind could relax for a minute, and he had some peace to pray. Two more hours to wait . . . or maybe six hours or longer? He couldn't occupy this spot for hours, but several tables remained empty, so maybe they wouldn't mind if he stayed awhile.

"You must be freezing. But isn't the snow beautiful?" A bubbly redhead with a generous smile stood by his side. "Would you like some coffee?"

Christian blinked. He'd stopped in here from time to time, but he'd never seen this Amish girl before. "You're new?"

Her eyes sparkled, and her lips stretched even wider. "*Jah*. This is my first day, and I'm so excited to be working here."

Despite his gloom, Christian couldn't help returning her enthusiastic grin. Not one of the fake smiles servers gave hoping for extra tips, but a genuine one that matched the caring in her eyes.

"Coffee would be good, but I can get it myself." They had a self-serve coffee and tea counter.

"*Neh, neh*." She laid a gentle hand on his shoulder. "Sit and thaw out. I'll bring it. How do you like it?"

"Two sugars and two creams."

"I'll be right back." But the girl detoured off to help an elderly man totter to the counter and then stopped to pick up a child's empty milk cup. "More milk?" she asked with that gorgeous smile.

The gentleness in her expression eased some of the loneliness in his heart.

* * *

Returning with the milk for the small girl, Lizzie passed the man who'd wanted coffee. He stared out the window morosely. *Ach! I forgot his coffee.*

She rushed to fill the cup and hurried over. A little coffee sloshed over the sides. With the cloth she kept tucked in the waistband of her black dress apron, she wiped away the spill and set the cup in front of him.

"*Danke.*" His words were polite, but he didn't even look at her as he took a sip of his coffee. He seemed wrapped in sadness.

He choked and grimaced. Then he pulled the cup away to stare into it. "Black?" He sounded bewildered. "Didn't I ask for two sugars and two creams?"

Lizzie wished she could disappear through the floor. How could she have made that mistake? She'd planned to have a perfect first day.

"I'm so sorry. Let me get you another cup." She reached out to take it, and her hand bumped his. Hot coffee cascaded over his hand.

He sucked in a sharp breath, shook his hand, and blew on his fingers.

"I'm so sorry." Lizzie yanked out the cloth and dabbed at his fingers. "I'll get some ice."

"It's all right," he assured her.

But she felt awful. That had to hurt. She took his hand in hers to examine the reddened skin. The strong, callused hand of a hard worker. Hands that made her heart flip over.

He cleared his throat, looking uncomfortable. Could he tell the direction of her thoughts?

She dropped his hand. Then she wiped up the spill on the table. "I'll get you another cup right away."

"No need. I can put sugar and creamer into this one." He pushed back his chair.

Did he not trust her to get those for him? Not that she blamed him. So far, she'd forgotten his order, brought him the wrong coffee, and spilled it all over, burning him in the process. But she needed to do something to make it up to him.

"Let me get them for you. I promise not to make another mistake." She bit her lip, waiting for his answer.

"Don't worry about it. It is your first day, after all."

"*Danke* for being so understanding. I'll be right back." *Two sugars, two creamers*, she chanted as she headed to the coffee station, as if she might forget.

She forced herself to ignore all the other customers on the way there and back. When she reached the table, he was mopping the coffee from the saucer with her cloth. *Ach!* She should have done that.

"I'm sorry," she said again as she collected the stained and sopping wet rag. She held up his creamers, sugars, and a stirrer.

With a grateful smile, he took them from her.

A quick pang shot through her. He didn't want her to put them in. But Lizzie couldn't help noticing the level of coffee in the cup. "At least you have enough room for the creamer now."

He glanced up at her with a startled expression. Then a slow smile blossomed across his face, making him breathtakingly handsome. And making her aware of his beard. She concentrated on the tabletop.

"Do you always look on the bright side?" he asked.

Her breath caught in her throat. Lizzie could barely get out an answer. "I try to."

She forced herself to look away from his searching gaze. While she'd been talking, five people had gathered at the register, around the room water glasses and coffee cups waited for refills, and a tray of fresh baked goods waited behind the counter to be put in the display case.

"*Ach*, I'd better go help those people."

Sarah popped out of the kitchen with a tray of breakfast muffins. "My goodness, Lizzie, why didn't you call us?"

She set down the muffins and scurried to the cash register, leaving Lizzie free to refill drinks, take orders, and clear empty tables. Each time Lizzie passed the man's table, her heart went out to him. Distress etched deep lines into his forehead and around his eyes and mouth. And he stared off into the distance as if visualizing something terrible.

If only she could ask what was wrong. But she had too many customers to handle. After the rush died down, she filled the cases with baked goods.

The man's empty, staring eyes called to her. Sarah had said Rebecca wanted them to show God's love to the customers, which Lizzie already felt drawn to doing.

Unsure how to start the conversation, Lizzie offered to refill his coffee.

He looked up, surprised, and her cheeks heated. He'd barely taken a few sips.

"I, um, thought maybe you'd like it warmed up. Or maybe the coffee doesn't taste right? I could make a fresh pot." She rattled on to cover her embarrassment. "Or I could bring you a different flavor?"

"It's not the coffee." The heaviness of his words made Lizzie want to reach out and put her hands over his clenched fists. But his beard told her he was married.

As she rushed from one task to the next, her heart burdened, Lizzie wished she could do more to lift the man's spirits. He looked so tired, so hungry, so sad.

Sarah brought out hot cinnamon rolls.

Jah, cinnamon rolls were warm and soothing treats. Lizzie would give him one.

After checking out another customer and putting the rolls in the display case, she selected the largest one with bakery tissue, set it on a plate, and carried it over.

"What's this? I didn't order anything."

"I know. My treat. I find cinnamon rolls very comforting." She hoped he would too.

"That's very thoughtful of you. But I can pay."

"No need. I can see you're feeling down and, well, I kind of hoped it might cheer you up a little."

He stared at her a moment, his eyes dazed, but still lost. "*Danke*."

Ignoring the warning message inside, she set her hand over his. "I can tell one pastry isn't enough to heal what's hurting, but I'll be praying."

One corner of his mouth lifted to create a half-happy, half-sad smile. "You're a special person, Lizzie."

She took a step back. How did he know her name?

Christian hadn't meant to frighten her. "Don't look so worried. I overheard Sarah say your name. And my name's Christian." He hoped he sounded friendly and not like a stalker or something. If his mind hadn't been so filled with Johanna, he might not have let her name slip out.

"Oh." She breathed out a small sigh of relief, and her cheerful expression returned. At least until she gazed at him. Then her eyes crinkled in sympathy. "If there's anything I can do to help . . ."

"You've done plenty already."

Her brow furrowed. "You mean mixing up your order, spilling your coffee, and burning your hand? I'm sorry."

"*Neh*." He gestured to the roll. The tang of cinnamon tantalized him. And she was right. Cinnamon rolls were comforting. "You seem to have a knack for healing hurting hearts. I'm afraid my hurt is too big for a cinnamon bun to heal." Now why had he confessed that?

"But God can help with anything."

"*Jah*, and I've been praying nonstop all night."

"If you don't mind sharing, I'll pray too." When he hesitated, her words rushed out, "I didn't mean to pry. I only meant . . . well, never mind. I can pray for you without knowing anything."

Now Christian felt sorry for her. "Wait, Lizzie. I didn't mean to make you think you were nosy. It's kind of you to ask. It's just that it's hard for me to talk about."

She opened her mouth as if to apologize again, but he stopped her.

"I'd be glad for your prayers. My daughter, Johanna, is in surgery right now. They're taking out a brain tumor. I don't know if she'll live, and, if she does, if she'll be herself afterward."

"That must be hard." Sympathy gushed from Lizzie. She looked as if she wanted to reach out and hug him. Then she quickly dropped her hands to her sides. "I'll definitely pray for her. And you. And the doctors, of course."

For some reason, her abrupt movement left him disappointed. He hadn't been hoping for a hug from a restaurant server. And a stranger, at that. Or had he? His loneliness was doing strange things to his insides.

He calmed himself enough to say in a neutral tone. "I'm grateful for the prayers." It meant a lot to him to know a stranger was lifting Johanna up to the Lord.

Lizzie's whole face lit up. "I'm happy to do it. I'm sure God can heal Johanna."

Christian loved the way Johanna's name flowed from Lizzie's lips. Her voice exuded love and caring, and her eyes shone with compassion. He could tell Lizzie's words were genuine. She really would pray.

"I'm sure your daughter's a special girl," she said softly.

"She is." Johanna's courage flashed through Christian's mind. "She's braver than I am." He told Lizzie what his daughter had said about Daniel and the lion's den. "I wish I had her simple faith."

"I think that's why the Bible says to 'become as little children.' They're so trusting. When we get older, we let doubts get in the way of believing."

Lizzie had spoken the truth. He'd let doubts and fears get in the way of his faith. If only he could trust in God's healing with a childlike faith.

The door opened, letting in a cold gust of air and a flurry of snowflakes. Since he'd entered the bakery several inches of snow had fallen. He'd better leave soon.

"I have to go." Lizzie waved toward the entering customers. "But I won't forget your daughter."

And Christian wouldn't forget this server who'd gone out of her way to be kind and caring. He couldn't keep his eyes off her as he nibbled the cinnamon roll she'd brought.

If he hadn't been so worried about Johanna, he'd have enjoyed following her movements even more. She reminded him of a bird in flight. Swooping here, then there. Landing lightly with a stunning smile. Flitting off to another table. Spreading joy wherever she went.

She brushed past his table with a pot of hot coffee, filled his cup three-quarters full, and dropped two sugars and two creamers on his table. And left with a smile that warmed him more than the coffee.

Chapter 5

Lizzie wished she could do something more for Christian than top off his coffee cup. She prayed, of course, but his mention of Daniel gave her an idea.

Because of the pending storm, few customers entered, and those who did grabbed their orders and hurried out. Several workers from local shops braved the freezing weather, but as business dwindled, Lizzie popped her head through the kitchen door.

"Sarah, can I ask a favor? Could you watch the cash register for a short while?"

"Sure. You want to take your break now?"

"*Jah*." She needed to ask more favors. Taking a deep breath, she faced Rebecca, who was folding white chocolate and cranberries into her cake batter.

Rebecca took one look at Lizzie's face. "Is everything all right?"

"A customer's daughter is in surgery right now, and I'd like to make a special cupcake for the little girl. Could I have a cupcake without icing and use some of the pastry bags and tips? I'll pay for all of it."

"No need to pay. Take whatever you need."

Lizzie intended to pay for this and the cinnamon roll. She didn't want to take advantage of Rebecca's generosity. "I'm doing this on my break."

"If you're doing something for a customer, then you can still take a break."

"*Danke*."

"I'm the one who should be thanking you. I love it when we can brighten people's days. Lizzie, I'm so glad we hired you."

"So am I." Aden wriggled his fingers in the air. "I hope you're coming to shell walnuts."

"I can do that, if you'd like."

"Aden," Rebecca said with mock sternness, "you volunteered. Now get back to work. Lizzie already has a job to do."

How could Lizzie have been so lucky to get this job? God couldn't have brought her to a better place to work.

She selected a cupcake from the cooling rack. "Katie, do we have marshmallows?"

"Check the storage room shelves." Katie waved to one of the doors off the kitchen.

Lizzie took three marshmallows from a bag and twisted it shut. Then she used fast-drying royal icing to anchor two rounded sides down beside each other on top of the cupcake. Then, with more icing, she glued the third marshmallow on top at the far end.

Katie stopped squirting buttercream icing in swirls atop the other cupcakes and eyed Lizzie's creation. "What are you doing?"

"Making a foundation for my lion." She tapped the top marshmallow. "This'll be the head. And the bottom two will form the body."

"I can't wait to see this." Katie still looked puzzled.

Lizzie chose a round tip with the largest opening, slid it over the lower part of the coupler on a small pastry bag of chocolate icing, and screwed the plastic ring into place. Then she twisted the bag closed and fitted it into her palm.

After squeezing out a test blob to check for air bubbles, she built smooth rounded shapes around the marshmallows. She could have done this with marzipan or fondant, but she loved the weight of a pastry bag in her hand. The perfect push and squeeze to keep the icing flowing smoothly. Once the main shape was built, she pushed out paws to make a sitting lion.

With yellowish icing and the grass tip, she squeezed out icing strands to make a mane. The u-shaped tip made perfect curved ears. Eyes, nose, mouth, whiskers, and lines on the paws flowed from a small round tip. Then she curved a long, thin tail around the body. One quick press of the grass tip added fluff at the tip of the tail.

Katie watched, open-mouthed. "That's adorable. Rebecca, you've got to see this," she called.

As Lizzie pulled the tip straight up to create yellowish grasses around the lion, everyone crowded around.

Rebecca looked at Lizzie in astonishment. "Is that what you meant when you said you make animal cupcakes?"

Embarrassed by all the staring eyes, Lizzie ducked her head. "*Jah.*"

"What else can you make?"

Lizzie shrugged. "I made snowmen, Santas, angels, Christmas trees, reindeer and other animals, and flowers. I can make them in marzipan or fondant too."

Rebecca set a hand on her shoulder. "We can't waste your talent. Tomorrow when you come in, I want you to report to the kitchen to make samples of your cupcakes. We'll put them in the display case to see what people order."

"Really?" Lizzie clasped her hands together. She'd get to decorate cupcakes. Not squeezed in between other duties or after hours, but during paid work time.

"*Jah*, really." Rebecca smiled at Lizzie's excitement.

"*Danke*. For this." Lizzie motioned toward the cupcake. "And this." She waved a hand around the kitchen. "For letting me decorate cupcakes. And for giving me this job." She could have hugged Rebecca.

To calm her excitement, Lizzie headed for the swinging doors that led into the bakery. *Gut*. Christian still sat at the table, nursing his second cup of coffee.

Before heading to his table, she picked up one of the individual cupcake boxes. She wanted to rush to his table to show him, but she forced herself to walk slowly, her gaze on the ground, scanning for any hazards that might trip her up.

When she set the box on the table, he studied it a second. "What's that for?" Then he glanced up. Up to the cupcake Lizzie held facing him. He gaped. "A lion?"

"It's for Johanna." Lizzie set the lion on the bottom of the box and folded up the sides.

"You made that?" He searched her face for the truth. "Johanna will . . ." His words faltered. "If she's all right, she'll love it."

Maybe I shouldn't have done this. What if something happens to his daughter? *And he has to look at the lion*?

Christian couldn't believe Lizzie had taken the time during her busy day to make a special cupcake for a child she didn't even know. His eyes stung just thinking of her kindness.

"How much is it?" He reached for his wallet.

"It's a gift."

"*Neh*, I'll pay for everything." He indicated the empty coffee cup, the plate that once held the cinnamon bun, and the lion cupcake.

His phone buzzed. The hospital.

"Mr. Yoder? Your daughter came through the operation fine, and she's in recovery. The surgeon would like to speak with you."

"I'll be right there." Christian jumped up and headed for the door with the cupcake box. Lizzie would be thrilled. Wait, he'd forgotten to pay. He patted his pockets. Where was his wallet? Oh, no. He'd forgotten to take it out of his pocket when he'd changed clothes.

"Good news?" Lizzie called. "Just go. I'll take care of your bill."

"I can't let you." But he had to. He had no money. "I'll be back," he promised. And he meant to keep that promise.

Right now, though, he had to hurry.

His heart singing, Christian raced to the hospital as fast as he could without overtiring his horse. The coffee, cinnamon bun, and Lizzie had raised his spirits. She'd brought a warmth into his life that he hadn't experienced since . . . well, he didn't know when. He'd have to stop by the bakery to pay her back. Why did that thought bring him so much pleasure?

Best of all, Johanna had survived surgery. Even if she might never be herself again, even if she had any, or all, of those terrible complications, he'd still love her and care for her. The only thing that mattered was that she was alive. *Danke*, Lord.

By the time he'd stabled his horse at a friend's house and sprinted toward the hospital, the blizzard Merle mentioned had begun. Christian raced through the lobby and dashed into an elevator as the doors were closing. He couldn't wait to see Johanna. But first, he needed to hear what the doctor had to say.

The nurse who'd prayed with him asked him to sit while she notified the surgeon. "God is good, isn't He? Your little girl made it through."

Still in his scrubs, the surgeon came out to meet Christian with a clipboard in hand and a smile on his face. "Surgery went well. We got it out cleanly, but we may recommend chemo to get rid of any traces."

"Will Johanna be all right?"

"Her prognosis is good."

All the tension in Christian's body melted away, leaving him limp and drained. "When can she go home?"

The surgeon made some notes on his clipboard. "I expect we'll keep her here for anywhere from six to ten days, depending on her recovery."

As he thanked the surgeon, Christian tried not to let his disappointment show. Johanna might be in the hospital for Christmas. Then he shook himself. He needed to be like Lizzie and focus on the positive. Johanna had made it through the operation.

Danke, Lord, *for miracles. Please help Johanna to heal completely*.

He continued to pray as he sat with her in the recovery room and went with her to the PICU. All the abbreviations they used jumbled in his brain, but one kind nurse explained PICU was the pediatric ICU.

Although he'd been told what to expect, at the sight of Johanna, Christian swallowed down the nausea sliding up and burning the inside of his chest. This was his little girl. The one with the big bandage on her head. Pale, drawn, and groggy, she looked too small and fragile to be hooked up to all this machinery.

Her eyes fluttered open. "Daed?" Her lips barely moved, and the word came out on a whisper. Then her eyelids closed.

Christian restrained himself from scooping her into his arms and hugging her. He placed the cupcake box on the bedside table and sat next to her, holding her hand as she drifted in and out of consciousness. A small spark of recognition sometimes flared in her eyes when they opened.

But as suppertime approached, her breathing slowed, and her eyes stayed shut.

"Is she all right?" he asked the nurse who checked Johanna's vitals every fifteen minutes.

"She's doing fine. I expect she'll sleep through the night now, and she may be drowsy for much of tomorrow. That's not unusual after anesthesia."

Christian's stomach growled. He hadn't eaten since the cinnamon bun that morning, but he didn't want to leave his daughter.

"Hey, Dad," the nurse said, "a bit of advice. You look like you could use a break. Take care of yourself. Eat, sleep, exercise. You need to be healthy."

"But what if she wakes?"

"We're here to care for her. And like I said, she's probably down for the night. Take a little time off. You'll come back refreshed."

Although he hated to leave Johanna, in his rush, he'd not only forgotten his wallet, he'd also neglected to give his neighbor the house key. Friends from church lived next door, and they'd be taking care of his horses, and their young son had begged to feed and walk Sampson. But he couldn't do it if they didn't have the key.

Christian would hurry back. Heavy traffic on the main roads forced him to take a roundabout way. Less-traveled streets also might be safer in the snow—if they'd been plowed. To avoid a traffic backup because of a fender bender, he took another winding detour.

He didn't admit, even to himself, that the direction he'd chosen went right by Rebecca's Porch. Not until he passed it. And then his spirits plunged to see it was already closed. What had he expected?

He'd been foolish to come this way. Even if the bakery were

open, he had no money. He already owed Lizzie. Besides, these smaller roads had not been well plowed, and night had already fallen. His battery-powered lights illuminated the figure of a woman walking in the road ahead—an Amish woman, judging from the silhouette of her coat and long dress.

Why had she chosen to walk in the street in such dangerous weather? The small shops in this area had all closed, and many sidewalks were still unshoveled. Maybe he should offer her a ride home. He slowed his horse.

As he neared, he slid open his door to call out, "Can I take you somewhere? It's too cold to be out here."

The woman turned. Lizzie?

"Christian?" She appeared as surprised to see him as he was to see her. "What are you doing here? I thought you'd be at the hospital."

"It's freezing outside. Hop in and I'll explain while I take you home."

"I don't think . . ."

"Please don't argue, or we'll both freeze."

When she opened her mouth to protest, a puff of white floated out.

He spoke first. "I promise not to hurt you or kidnap you."

"It's not that. I don't want to take you out of your way."

Christian couldn't believe it. She'd walk in twenty-degree temperatures to avoid inconveniencing others?

"Lizzie, please? You're making my teeth chatter just looking at you." Maybe if he made her feel sorry for him, she'd relent.

It worked. She rounded the buggy and got in. He breathed a sigh of relief.

He shut his door. "We lost some of the heat with the door open, but it should warm up soon. There's a blanket on the seat behind you if you need it."

"Is Johanna all right?" She asked the question hesitantly as if worried she'd upset him.

"The surgeon said he thinks they got it all, but he wants her to have chemotherapy to be safe."

"I'm glad she made it through the operation. Isn't God wonderful?"

"*Jah*, He is." As much as Christian rejoiced over Johanna, his heart also rejoiced at the chance to spend more time with Lizzie.

Lizzie had stayed until closing, her mind focused on Christian and Johanna. When Christian had rushed out the door, he'd looked hopeful. She'd prayed he'd had good news. All day, she'd sent up prayers for the little girl. It thrilled her to know God had answered her prayers and Johanna had made it safely through.

Christian's question interrupted her thoughts. "Where do you live?"

"I don't want to take you out of your way."

"I'm not going to leave you outside in the cold and snow."

"But don't you have to head to the hospital? That's in the opposite direction."

"I need to feed and walk the dog and gather some supplies for spending the night with Johanna."

"You're staying overnight at the hospital?" *What a dedicated father.*

"Johanna doesn't like being alone at night, and I feel guilty leaving her."

"I can imagine, but I'm sure her *mamm* will keep her company while you're gone."

Christian's shoulders slumped, and he mumbled, "My wife died just before Johanna turned two."

"I'm so sorry." Lizzie clapped a hand over her mouth. How many times had she said that to him today? But this time, her blunder was worse than spilled coffee. She'd hit a deep wound.

"You didn't know. But that's why I don't want to leave Johanna alone, even for a minute. I plan to hurry back."

"And I'm taking up your time."

"*Neh*, you aren't. I was heading this way already."

"You're sure?"

Instead of answering, Christian straightened his shoulders and changed the subject. "When I left, Johanna was sleeping, so I haven't had a chance to show her the lion cupcake. I can't wait to see her eyes light up. She'll be so excited."

"I'm glad." Lizzie wished she could see the small girl enjoy the cupcake. "I hope you'll remind her how brave she's been."

"I certainly will. And I'll tell her how kind you are."

"I didn't do anything special."

"You've done a lot more than you realize. For me and for Johanna." The look Christian directed Lizzie's way set her heart thumping.

Most likely, she was misinterpreting his gaze. But, since she'd just learned he was a widower, she couldn't help hoping.

Christian made the mistake of turning to look at Lizzie, and her bright smile twisted his insides. He needed to get the conversation back into neutral territory.

"What about you? Why are you walking in this weather? Did your buggy get a flat tire?"

She laughed. "*Neh*, I moved here from New York State to take care of my *aenti*, but she doesn't have a buggy." And Lizzie had no money to pay for a driver.

"You walk every day?"

"It's only my first day, but I guess I will be."

He'd forgotten she'd told him it was her first day. When he finally pulled up at her *aenti*'s house, the smile she gave him more than made up for the extra distance he'd driven. "Do you work tomorrow?"

She nodded. "Rebecca wants me to make cupcakes." Lizzie got out of the buggy. "*Danke* for the ride. I'll keep praying for Johanna." With a quick wave, she whirled around and disappeared into the house, taking her bright, sunny smile with her.

Dropping Lizzie off had taken him far out of his way, but he'd never let her know that. Tomorrow, he'd head this way again so he could pick her up. She'd been so kind to him, he could help her out. And he'd pay his bill.

Once he got home, he took care of Sampson and the horses before he bathed, dressed in fresh clothes, and put his wallet in his pocket. After he packed clean clothes for tomorrow, he dropped the key at his neighbor's house.

Before heading back to the hospital, Christian checked the PICU rules—four visitors over age twelve—and contacted his sister to let her know the surgery had gone well. His sister would stop by the hospital around ten with her two oldest daughters.

Christian regretted being away so long. He could have cut the time almost in half by not driving by Rebecca's Porch and not taking Lizzie home, but he couldn't have let her walk home on those slippery, dark roads.

He checked with the nurses, who assured him Johanna hadn't woken. But as he settled into the chair beside the bed, he bumped the railing and startled her. She cried out.

"It's all right." He took her hand. "It's only me."

"Daed?" She struggled to focus her eyes. In a tired voice, she asked, "What's that?" She squinted at the white bakery box on the bedside table illuminated by the bright hall lights.

"A surprise for you." Christian folded down the box sides so she could see the lion.

"For me?"

"*Jah*, because you've been so brave."

"*Neh*, I wasn't. I was so scared inside." Her whisper dropped even lower. "I still am."

Christian set down the lion and took her hand. "I am too, but the worst is over." He tried not to think of the chemo. "The doctor said he took out the tumor."

"But I still feel sick."

"That's probably from the medicine that put you to sleep. It'll go away soon." At least, he hoped so.

Christian reached out to smooth back her hair, the way he always did to soothe her, and his hand stopped in midair. He'd almost forgotten they'd bandaged her head, and half of her hair had been shaved. And how could he touch her with all the tubes and machines? Swallowing hard, he lowered his hand to her shoulder.

"What's wrong, Daed?" she asked weakly.

"Nothing," he lied. He couldn't tell her what she looked like. They'd warned him her face might be swollen and bruised, her eyes puffy, so he'd been expecting it. But no explanations had prepared him to see his daughter looking like this.

"Would you like to try a bite of cupcake?" As soon as he said it, he realized his mistake. They'd given her a little water earlier to test her swallow reflex, but he had no idea when she could have solid food.

Johanna surprised him. "*Neh.*"

He'd never known her to turn down a sweet treat. Maybe once the effects of the anesthesia wore off, she'd regain her appetite. But he'd check with the hospital to see when she could eat it.

"It's cute," she murmured before drifting off again.

Nurses came and went during the night to check on her, startling Christian from dreams of Lizzie. He jolted awake when a cart full of breakfast trays rattled in the hall. If he didn't leave soon, he'd miss Lizzie walking to work.

He freshened up and changed his clothes, then he bent over Johanna before realizing he couldn't kiss her head or forehead. Would it hurt if he kissed her on her bruised face? He straightened up and settled on patting her shoulder. "I have to run out for a while, but I'll be back soon."

"Sampson?" she asked in a small, tired voice. Then she closed her eyes again before he could answer.

He should tell her the truth, but her deep, even breathing indicated she'd fallen back to sleep. Should he ask forgiveness for misleading her? He'd misled Lizzie too.

Please forgive me, Lord.

Chapter 6

Forty minutes later, Christian sat drumming his fingers on his knee, the reins held loosely in his other hand. An accident had snarled both lanes of traffic in his direction, and the median strip prevented anyone from turning around.

As he always did whenever he heard of an accident, he prayed for those involved. Then he prayed for Johanna and everyone else he knew, including Lizzie. Not only had he missed picking her up, but Johanna also must be wondering why he'd been gone so long.

After another half-hour wait, one lane of traffic began moving, but cars and trucks refused to let Christian move over. He didn't blame them. Nobody wanted to be stuck behind a buggy after they got through the traffic jam. He sat and sat until an elderly lady in a huge antique car with tail fins motioned for him to go in front of her.

Should he go to Rebecca's Porch, or turn around and go straight back to the hospital? He'd come all this way, he may as well settle his bill. Then he'd rush back. By now, though, Johanna would have her cousins for company.

When Christian entered, the bakery employees were in a tizzy, all flocking around Lizzie, who sat on a stool behind the counter, her head in her hands.

"Aden's hitching up the horse," Rebecca said soothingly. "He can take you to the hospital."

Had she been hurt? Christian pushed through the gawking crowd. "Lizzie, are you all right?"

She blinked at him, but didn't answer.

Sarah placed a hand on Lizzie's shoulder. "Her *aenti* took a tumble and may have broken some bones. Lizzie needs to get to the hospital."

"My buggy's ready to go, and I'm headed to the hospital. I can take her."

A relieved smile crossed Rebecca's face. "That would be *wunderbar*. I could use Aden's help here."

"Come, Lizzie." Christian waved toward the exit.

Her eyes dazed, she followed him outside. Sarah ran after her with a coat. "You forgot this. I'll let Aden know."

Lizzie nodded her thanks.

"I'm sorry about your *aenti*," he said as he pulled out of the parking lot. He wished he could do something to erase the worry lines on her forehead. She'd comforted him yesterday. He wanted to do the same for her. "I'll pray."

She turned grateful eyes in his direction. "*Danke*. I hope she'll be all right. Mrs. Heise said they took her in an ambulance. I hope it's not her hip."

"She'll be fine. My brother used to volunteer as an EMT, and he took many older people to the hospital for broken hips. They all recovered."

"Good to know." Lizzie's watery smile did little to lessen the concern in her eyes. "I hope my *aenti* will heal well too." She twisted part of her apron into small pleats. "But I'm also worried about my job. I've been nothing but trouble for Rebecca since I started."

"I'm sure Rebecca won't hold your *aenti*'s accident against you. She has a very kind heart." He pulled up to the hospital entrance. "You go in. I'll park."

With a quick *danke*, she rushed inside, and Christian drove several blocks away. One of the men he worked with had turned his garage into a temporary stable for Christian's horse and buggy while Johanna was recovering. As Christian cared for his horse, his phone rang.

Seeing Merle's number, Christian answered with an impatient, "Hello?"

Merle never bothered with pleasantries, so he snapped back, "Where are you? The owner is paying extra to get this done a month ahead of schedule. Get over here now."

"I'm supposed to have today off." He'd already given up one of his vacation days. Only partially, thanks to Pete.

"If you're not here in twenty minutes, you can forget this job."

Even if Christian left now, he couldn't make it there that fast. Plus, if Johanna did well, she'd be transferred out of the PICU later today. He wanted to be there for that. "I can't—"

Merle exploded before Christian could finish. "Never mind. I need someone more dependable. I understand Pete did most of your roofing job the other night." Without a good-bye, Merle abruptly ended the call.

Although Christian appreciated having uninterrupted time with Johanna, what would he do about a job? He had enough savings to cover him for a month or two, but even with the church's help, he'd struggle to pay hospital bills.

Lord, I'm going to trust this is Your will. Please help me to find a job in Your perfect timing.

Perhaps God had given him more time with Johanna. Christian sprinted back to the hospital to find Lizzie talking with a nervous *Englischer*.

"Call me when you're ready to come back, dear," the woman

said. "I'm sorry to leave you, but I need to deliver Meals on Wheels."

"I'll be fine," Lizzie assured her.

Christian didn't want to abandon her too. "I can stay with you."

"My *aenti* is getting X-rays, and I'll be fine. Johanna needs you."

"My sister and her twin daughters are visiting Johanna, so she has company. But I should let them know where I am." He didn't want to leave Lizzie alone. "Would you like to go upstairs with me to meet Johanna while they're doing your *aenti*'s X-rays?"

Lizzie's eyes lit up. "I can't stay long."

"I'll give the desk my cell number so you'll know when she's finished."

After Christian returned, Lizzie accompanied him to the elevator. "Johanna still has tubes and monitors. She also looks kind of beat-up. I don't want you to be shocked."

He needn't have worried. Lizzie was her usual friendly self. She greeted everyone with a sunny smile.

Johanna's puffy eyes narrowed.

"I'm sorry I took so long," Christian apologized. "I thought you might like to meet the lady who made your cupcake. This is Lizzie."

"You must be Johanna." Lizzie's sweet voice soothed away Johanna's frown. "Your *daed* has told me how brave you are."

His daughter's face relaxed. Her eyes drifted shut again. "I'm sick, so I can't eat," she mumbled. "But I like looking at it."

"We offered to eat it for her," one of the twins said.

"But she wouldn't let us." The other one shot a pleading look at Johanna.

"That's enough, girls," their mother warned.

Christian introduced Lizzie to everyone and explained that her *aenti* was getting X-rays.

"I hope she's all right," his sister said. "I'll pray for her."

"*Danke.*" Lizzie turned to Christian. "I should get back downstairs."

"I'll go with you."

Lizzie shook her head. "You should stay here with Johanna and your company. I'll be fine. Mrs. Heise will pick us up. But thank you for bringing me."

He pinched his lips shut before he blurted out, *it was a pleasure*. He took a deep breath to slow his racing pulse before he answered, "You're welcome."

With a tender glance at Johanna—a glance Christian wished had also been directed at him—Lizzie left the room, leaving it colder and drabber without her colorful presence.

Lizzie fell into bed that night exhausted. Miriam's injury turned out to be a broken leg rather than a broken hip, which the doctor assured Lizzie would heal more quickly. Mrs. Heise drove them home, helped Lizzie set up a downstairs bedroom in the parlor, and brought them takeout for dinner. But Miriam was so unsteady on crutches, it worried Lizzie and Mrs. Heise.

"I have a portable wheelchair somewhere in the attic that my husband used years ago. If you don't mind crawling around in all the junk up there," Mrs. Heise said, "it might be just the thing for your aunt."

So, Lizzie ventured into the dim, cobwebby attic next door to dig out the chair. Then she dusted it off and brought it over to the house.

Miriam seemed to like sitting in the wheelchair, and because she didn't have enough strength to move it herself, Lizzie relaxed, knowing her *aenti* couldn't get into too much trouble. With the next day being an off-Sunday, the rest of the weekend passed uneventfully.

On Monday, Lizzie rose long before dawn. Most bakers came in at five to get a head start on the day's work. By going in before six, Lizzie hoped to make up some of the time she'd missed on Saturday.

As she picked her way through the dark, slippery streets, she pretended she was riding in Christian's buggy. Their fake, but lively, conversation kept her mind off the stinging snow pellets whipped into her face by the icy winds. Talking to Christian also made the walk seem shorter.

Rebecca answered Lizzie's knock on the kitchen door. "Lizzie, what are you doing here so early?" She didn't sound upset, only curious.

"I came to make up the time I missed." She followed Rebecca into the toasty warm kitchen. Lizzie's toes stung, and she flexed her stiff, freezing fingers.

"Well, we're glad you're here. You won't believe all the orders we have for you." Rebecca took down several sheets of paper thumbtacked to the corkboard in the hallway.

Lizzie skimmed the list. At least thirty names, followed by cupcake flavor, design, and number. Thirty snowmen, fifty poinsettias, twenty-five Christmas trees, two-dozen reindeer . . . the list went on and on. She read the orders under her breath.

Sarah smiled. "Quite a few of those are for birthday and Christmas parties. The flowers are for a women's church luncheon."

Hundreds of cupcakes. How would she ever decorate all of them?

At a little after seven, Christian drove back and forth from Lizzie's house to the bakery twice without catching a glimpse of her. Fresh snow had fallen overnight, covering black ice underneath, so he worried about her walking to work. And he still needed to pay her.

She'd told him she started at eight. If so, she should have left by now. Either she'd overslept, or she'd gone in early.

Although darkness shuttered the shop, lights shone from the back of the building. Christian turned into the narrow alley running past the bakery parking lot. His buggy wheels rattled down the rutted dirt lane beside the bakery. Feeling like a creeper, he struggled to peek inside the large kitchen windows. All he wanted to do was make sure she was safe.

Rebecca stirred a huge bowl. A man, his head bowed, grimaced as his arm moved up and down. Sarah carried a tray of cupcakes across the room . . . to Lizzie! The overhead lights reflected off her red hair as she leaned over with a white bag in her hand.

The man glanced toward the alley, and Christian flicked the reins to get his horse moving. He wished he could stay to watch Lizzie decorate cupcakes. But Rebecca's Porch didn't open until ten. He'd stop by later to pay her and find out about her *aenti*.

Right now, he needed to get back to the hospital before Johanna woke. The cold, dark weather and loss of his job increased his feeling of isolation as he drove on deserted, unlit roads. Until now, caring for Johanna had kept him too busy to think about another relationship, but Lizzie's kindness set off a yearning for something more, something to fill what he'd been missing in life. Longing and loneliness stayed with him as he navigated the back roads to the hospital.

Lizzie worked as fast as she could on the orders. She alternated between decorating, working at the counter, serving and refilling coffee, and answering the phone. The old black wall phone rang so often, Lizzie held the receiver between her ear and shoulder to listen while she decorated another cupcake.

Most of the calls were requests for poinsettia Christmas

cakes or her cupcakes. She had to start extra sheets to record orders for both.

Poor Rebecca looked so pale and worn out, but she soldiered on, making cake after cake. As Lizzie headed back to the kitchen for another tray of cupcakes and more icing, she overheard Sarah and Rebecca talking about Christmas cakes.

Lizzie only caught the tail end of Rebecca's comment.

"No more orders." She sounded frustrated and overwhelmed. "I told everyone at the staff meeting to limit the cake orders to one hundred."

Sarah's distressed voice carried. "I think we have around one hundred and fifty."

Ach! Lizzie hadn't been at the staff meeting, and she'd taken most of those extra fifty orders. So far, she'd been nothing but a liability for the bakery. Soon, she'd have a multi-page list of mistakes that rivaled the disasters at Kallis Diner.

The phone rang again. Instead of rushing to answer it, Lizzie busied herself with squeezing out carrot noses for the snowmen. It took a precise amount of pressure to start thick and pull the orange icing to a perfect point. If she wiggled the tip back and forth slightly as she did it, it created little ridges, making it look like a real carrot.

Sarah sighed and left the kitchen. "Lizzie, it's for you," she called. "She says it's an emergency."

Not again. It must be Mrs. Heise. What had happened to Lizzie's *aenti* this time?

Mrs. Heise's voice quivered. "I'm sorry to bother you at work, but my daughter in California is expecting twins. She's gone into labor a month early. I hope they'll be all right."

Lizzie hoped so too. "I'll pray for them."

"Thank you, dear. I don't want to leave your aunt alone, not while she's in the wheelchair, but I need to take care of my other grandchildren."

Lizzie's mind raced. What could she do?

"Are you all right?" Rebecca put an arm around her. "You look like you're about to faint."

"My *aenti* . . ." Lizzie struggled to explain.

Rebecca's brows drew together in concern. "The one who got hurt on Saturday?"

Lizzie nodded. "The woman who's caring for her needs to leave."

Mrs. Heise's voice came through the phone. "My flight leaves in three hours."

"In three hours?" Lizzie regretted the shrillness of her tone.

She's leaving that soon? Rebecca mouthed.

"*Jah*."

"You're welcome to bring your *aenti* here," Rebecca suggested. "Or if you'd rather go home, we'll find someone to cover your shift."

Again? She'd left them shorthanded on Saturday while she went to the hospital. If she did it again, would she even have a job?

"Do you mind if she's here?" Lizzie was desperate to keep working. "Her wheelchair could fit between the picture window and the shelving unit." She might block a few baskets, but nobody would buy the souvenirs in them during the middle of winter.

"That's fine with me. But will she be bored?"

"Not at all. She's losing her memory, but she loves watching people."

Rebecca's lips curved into a smile. "This sounds like the perfect solution."

Lizzie fought back tears. She couldn't believe Rebecca's generosity.

"Are you there? Lizzie? Answer me," Mrs. Heise squawked into the phone.

"I'm here. Can you drop off my *aenti* on your way to the airport?"

"At the bakery?" Mrs. Heise sounded incredulous.

"My boss said it's all right."

"If you're sure?"

Rebecca's nod confirmed the answer.

Still overcome by Rebecca's kindness, Lizzie barely managed to get out a "*danke*."

"The man across the street is shoveling snow," Mrs. Heise said. "I'll ask him to help me get Miriam into the car."

Lizzie raced to finish as many cupcakes as she could before her *aenti* arrived.

And when Mrs. Heise pulled in forty minutes later, Aden rushed outside, lifted Miriam into her wheelchair, set a stack of magazines in her lap, and pushed her into the bakery. Rebecca sent Sarah upstairs for an afghan to wrap around Miriam. "We don't want her catching a chill."

Lizzie angled Miriam's chair so she could see the customers but also watch the traffic on the street outside the window. The magazines fit on the window ledge beside her. As Lizzie draped the afghan over Miriam's lap, her *aenti* released a sigh and rested back in her chair.

All the workers introduced themselves to Miriam, who stared at them blankly and didn't respond. Since her accident, she'd retreated into her shell. No more trying to cook, no more repeating the same story over and over. Perhaps being around people might spur her to talk.

The other girls went out of their way to keep an eye on Miriam, bringing her treats or a cup of warm tea, pointing out interesting sights out the window, or admiring flowers in the magazines. Once again, Lizzie thanked the Lord for her job and her caring boss and coworkers.

In addition to all those blessings, she had Christian's

thoughtfulness in driving her home and to the hospital. Lancaster had started to feel like home.

After Rebecca lowered the blinds at the end of the day, Lizzie helped Miriam into her coat. Then she took her *aenti* outside before Rebecca locked up. Lizzie wanted to avoid having people see her push the wheelchair home through the snow.

Knowing Rebecca, she'd ask Aden to drive them home, and Lizzie didn't want to trouble him. They'd done so much for her already. But she hadn't counted on running into Christian.

He drove slowly along the street, scanning for Lizzie. A figure up ahead seemed hunched over. That didn't remind him of Lizzie's walk, but as his lights crawled across the ground, the metal of a wheelchair gleamed.

What in the world? She was pushing her *aenti* through ice and snow?

He pulled beside her. "Lizzie, what are you doing?"

"Going home."

"In the snow with a wheelchair? What if you slip and break your leg? How will you take care of your *aenti*?"

As soon as he said it, Christian wished he could take it back. Lizzie couldn't help that she had no buggy. He jumped out and took the wheelchair handles to steer it toward the passenger door.

"I try not to think about negative things like that." Lizzie's half-hearted laugh held a trace of worry. "As you said, I try to look on the bright side."

"What's the bright side about pushing a wheelchair through snowdrifts?" He motioned for Lizzie to crawl into the back seat. Then he gently lifted her *aenti* up and onto the front seat and tucked the afghan around her before stowing her wheelchair.

"I don't go through snowdrifts. Most of the roads get plowed and—"

"And I'm sure the brisk air is good for your health, you need exercise, and you're grateful to have a job." He chuckled. Was he starting to think like Lizzie?

"You're right." She tossed her head indignantly. "All of those are benefits."

"But what if your *aenti* gets pneumonia from the cold?"

"Are you purposely trying to worry me?"

"*Neh*, I'm just pointing out some concerns. You always find the best in things, but I'm a realist. A problem-solver."

"So, you have a solution?"

"I do." He loved the way her eyes lit up as she turned to him eagerly. He hoped she'd like his idea. "I could drive you to and from work every day."

Her face fell. "*Neh*, I don't want to take you out of your way."

"Tell me something. You went out of your way to help me the morning of Johanna's operation. You even took time from your work to make her a special cupcake. Did that bother you?"

"Of course not. I'm happy to help."

"That's how I feel now."

"But I can't let you do that. Not when I can't do anything in return."

"Oh, I'll expect payment."

Her tense shoulders relaxed. "How much do you want?"

Christian could tell she wouldn't agree to let him do it for free. "Here's the deal. One cinnamon roll for me. One lion cupcake for Johanna. Every day. And your cheerful, upbeat conversation to lift my mood."

"That's not payment. I'd happily give you all of those."

"And I'd happily give you rides." His lips curved up into a slow, lazy smile, allowing time for his point to sink in.

"Oh, you." She made a fist and gave his arm a powder-puff punch.

"Please, Lizzie? I really do like having company." His throat tightened. More than he'd ever imagined.

Chapter 7

Christian sounded serious, making Lizzie tongue-tied. And she hadn't been fair to her *aenti*. Miriam shouldn't be riding in the wheelchair through the snow-covered roads in freezing temperatures.

"All right," she agreed. But she'd find some way to pay him back in addition to cinnamon rolls and cupcakes.

His face softened into a relieved grin. "Since you like looking on the bright side, I thought of one more payback. I won't have to worry about you and your aunt getting stuck in a blizzard."

Lizzie stuck out her tongue, then regretted the childish gesture. But Christian laughed heartily.

"You remind me of another redheaded Lizzie I used to know. She was from around here, not from New York, but she was the liveliest little girl ever. Always daring me to do things that got us both in trouble."

Lizzie sat stock-still. *That's impossible. It can't be.* "Wh-what was her name?"

"Lizzie Bontrager."

"I'm Lizzie Bontrager."

"You are? What a coincidence. But it's a pretty common name in Amish country."

"*Neh*, you don't understand. I'm that Lizzie Bontrager. I used to live here."

He slowed the horse and stared at her. "Where?"

"Around the block from my *aenti*. And I had a friend named Christian. We did everything together."

"Lizzie?" This time he pulled over. "I thought you were from New York."

"After *Daed* died, we moved to Fort Plain to stay with Mamm's parents. They've both passed on, but we stayed."

"You were ten when you left?"

She nodded.

"I never knew where you went. Mamm told me you'd gone to live with your grandparents, and when I begged to visit, she said you lived too far away. But she never mentioned where you went. And she insisted I find other friends who were not, um, troublemakers."

Lizzie giggled. "I was a troublemaker, wasn't I?"

"I didn't mind. Everything you suggested sounded like fun. Crawling out on our roofs after our parents went to bed to look at the stars. Going to the pond to catch tadpoles, hoping to see them turn into frogs."

"Except you fell in."

"And you laughed so hard, I pulled you in too."

They'd both gotten scolded. And Christian's *mamm* had forbade him to play with Lizzie for two weeks.

His eyes faraway, Christian's expression grew tender. "After you left, I never had fun like that again. I missed you so much. Even though you were two years younger and a girl, you were my best friend in the whole world."

"And you were mine. My best and only friend."

* * *

The sober timbre of her voice struck Christian. "I can't believe that. Everyone at school liked you and wanted to play with you."

"*Jah*, here. In Fort Plain, everyone had been at school together since they were six. I had a hard time fitting in. Besides, I had to go to work with Mamm at the diner."

Her words sounded so small and tight, Christian wanted to reach out to her, to hold hands the way they used to.

"Eleni, one of the owners, fixed me a desk in the windowless office. I brought books to read and kept quiet until Mamm's shift ended."

It hurt Christian to think of boisterous Lizzie cooped up in a dark room with no one to talk to.

"That's probably why I chatter to everyone I see now." Lizzie said it with a biting humor that didn't hide her pain.

He couldn't bear the thought of Lizzie—his Lizzie, his best friend—being so lonely. He'd known loneliness, but his could not compare to hers.

For once, Lizzie struggled to find words. Christian had meant so much to her when she was young. She hadn't said so, but he was the main reason she hadn't made friends in New York. She'd pined so much for him, and nobody she met had been as much fun.

Instead, she'd retreated into herself. She'd rather walk around the playground pretending to talk to him, much like she'd done on her recent walk. Then, when Mamm started working at the restaurant, Lizzie had welcomed the isolation. She read books, but she also daydreamed about Christian. Over time, her memories faded, and she'd thought about him less and less. But meeting him again had awakened all those old feelings, and being around him stirred new ones.

His protectiveness toward her and his gentleness with Johanna and Miriam strummed harmonious chords on her heartstrings. As the buggy started up again, Lizzie scooted over slightly on the backseat so she could peek at Christian's profile under his hat brim, and the inner melody swelled to angels' harps.

When Christian stopped in front of Miriam's house, Lizzie jerked her gaze away. She didn't want him to catch her staring. After taking out the wheelchair, he once again lifted Miriam tenderly and arranged her blankets. Then he held the front seat forward so Lizzie could scramble out of the back. When he held out a hand to help her down, rapid drumbeats accompanied the heavenly music in her heart.

Her throat tightened. No one had ever treated her as delicate and precious. Mamm had been too busy working overtime at the diner, and she'd left Lizzie alone for hours to fend for herself. Lizzie blinked to hold back the tears gathering behind her eyes.

If only she could cling to Christian's hand as she went through life. When they were young, he'd take her hand to help her down from precarious perches or assist her over rough ground. Back then, his touch had been sweet and innocent. Now, it stirred a longing for something deeper.

After he let go, the loss of his touch left Lizzie bereft. Her childhood longing for him flooded back, and she didn't want him to leave. "Would you like to stay for supper?"

He'd grasped the wheelchair handles to push Miriam into the house, but stopped to gaze deeply into her eyes. "I would, but I need to get back to Johanna."

She read regret on his face. Had he been as affected as she was by their shared childhood?

He broke their intense stare. "I'd better get your *aenti* into the house before she freezes." He shivered. "I wish I could eat with you. I'm sure it would be better than hospital cafeteria food." He grimaced.

Lizzie unlocked the door, and Christian lifted Miriam's chair over the threshold. "Where to?" he asked.

Miriam stared up at him with pleading eyes but didn't answer.

"The kitchen, I guess," Lizzie said behind him. She moved in front of them to show him the way and rolled the propane light into the room.

The soft, warm light made a halo around her head. She took his breath away. For a brief moment, a vision flashed before his eyes. Lizzie cooking in this kitchen. Johanna well, her hair grown out and in a bob. Miriam's eyes lively and focused. And . . . him at the head of the table, Lizzie beside him, their heads bowed for prayer, while steam rose from their plates.

The phone in his pocket buzzed, breaking into his fantasy.

Merle? What did he want? "Excuse me," Christian said to Lizzie. "I need to take this call."

The minute Christian answered, Merle ranted, "The idiot I hired to take your place cut three floor tiles wrong. Three! I'm making him pay for them, but I can't have this kind of incompetence. I want you at the house by six tomorrow installing that tile."

Christian pulled the phone away from his ear and stared at it. He had his job back? Although he needed to make a living, he wasn't sure he wanted to return. And he didn't want to give up his time with Johanna. "I can't—"

"You angling for a raise? Okay. Two dollars more per hour." When Christian didn't answer, Merle's voice turned nervous. "Five?"

Christian tried again. "I can't be there by six."

You don't have to pick me up, Lizzie mouthed.

He shook his head. No way would he let her walk in the snow. Besides, he didn't want to give up the chance to be with her.

"Get there whenever you can. And lay that bathroom tile right." Merle clicked off.

Holding the phone out, Christian stared at it. First, Merle had fired him. Now he'd gotten a five-dollar raise?

"Was that your boss?"

"*Jah*," he said dispiritedly.

"He sounds impatient."

"That's putting it mildly." Leave it to Lizzie to put a positive spin on Merle.

"It must be hard to work for him."

Christian nodded. *Jah,* it was. Did he really want to work for someone like that? He didn't. Once Johanna was out of the hospital, he'd look for another job.

"I'd better go." Reluctantly, he headed for the door. He'd like to stay and explore his budding feelings for this beautiful redhead whose smile charmed him. He wanted to compare the small girl he'd admired and adored to the lovely grown-up woman she'd become. "I'll miss being with Johanna tomorrow. They moved her out of PICU."

"That's a good sign. Please don't pick me up tomorrow. I plan to go in early again. Spend your time with Johanna."

"What time are you going in?" He didn't want to miss her this time.

"Six."

"She'll be asleep." He took a small note from his pocket and pressed it into Lizzie's palm.

Lizzie didn't even glance at it. "Stay with Johanna. I mean it, Christian."

The steely tone of Lizzie's voice reminded him of her commands when they were young. He'd always done her bidding. Now, though, he planned to ignore her wishes. He might get in trouble with her, but it would be worth it.

* * *

Lizzie didn't shut the door until Christian's buggy disappeared from sight. Then, she shivered and closed it. Oddly enough, when they'd been outside, she hadn't noticed the cold. The flames he'd built inside her kept her warm, but now that he'd gone, the chill crept back. Watching him drive off reminded her too much of leaving him years ago.

The paper he'd tucked into her hand earlier crinkled, and Lizzie opened it. At the top, a phone number stood out in bold printing. Underneath, he'd written, *Please call me whenever your work hours change. I missed you this morning.*

He'd missed her? Lizzie hugged the note to her with a long, drawn-out sigh. *He missed me.*

Wait! He hadn't meant that the way she'd taken it. He must have stopped by to pick her up, and she'd gone in early. Lizzie felt terrible. He'd come all this way in ice and snow.

Miriam had no phone, so Lizzie couldn't let him know of changes in plans. If only Mrs. Heise were home. But when Lizzie returned to the kitchen, a note lay on the counter weighted down with a key. She tucked Christian's message into her pocket and picked up the other paper.

> *Sorry for leaving so abruptly. Please take everything in my cupboards, refrigerator, and freezer. I don't want it to go bad. I'll probably stay in California for a few months to help with the babies. Two are a lot more work than one, I expect. Plus, they have three other young'uns. If you wouldn't mind checking on the house from time to time, I'd appreciate it. And, of course, use the phone and anything else you need.*

The scrawled name at the bottom looked like *Tilda*.

Lizzie would go over after she put her *aenti* to bed and clean out the refrigerator. She wouldn't want food to rot and leave a stench behind.

Picking through the cans on the pantry shelf, she found two cans of soup with unexpired dates. The others she slipped into a trash bag. She'd put them in Mrs. Heise's garbage can and pull it out to the curb for pickup so Miriam wouldn't see them and get upset.

They still had a little salad left from Sunday and a few slices of bread. When they sat down to the piping-hot soup, Miriam bowed her head for prayer. Even when her *aenti* seemed to be totally out of it, she always prayed.

Childhood training seemed to be carved indelibly into the heart and mind. So did memories.

"Anna Grace?" Miriam startled Lizzie. "That boy has a good heart. I can't believe you're making him wait so long. Why don't you marry him already?"

Lizzie stared at her *aenti*. That was the longest sentence Miriam had spoken since the accident. Maybe Lizzie should play along. Except for confusing her with Mamm, Miriam seemed to be aware and in present time.

Dipping her spoon into her bowl, Lizzie admitted, "I'd like to marry him, but he hasn't asked me yet." As she said it, longing shot through her. Although it was much too soon to consider it, the words rang true and expressed a desire buried deep inside.

"*Humph*. I'll have to talk to him about that."

"*Neh*, please don't." Panic squeezed Lizzie's insides. What if Miriam actually said something to Christian? Even if Lizzie tried to pass it off as the ramblings of a confused old woman, he might think she'd given her *aenti* the idea.

"Sometimes young fellows need to be prodded."

"Not Christian." *Please, not Christian.*

Miriam frowned. "Who's Christian?" Her eyes took on a faraway, glassy look during the explanation that Christian had just driven them home.

Lizzie exhaled softly when her *aenti* returned to eating her soup mechanically and humming tunelessly under her breath between bites. Although Lizzie had been wishing Christian could have stayed, she was relieved he hadn't. Suppose Miriam had said that in front of him. How would Lizzie ever have explained it?

Chapter 8

Last night after Miriam went to bed, Lizzie had finished cleaning out the pantry and dragged Mrs. Heise's full garbage can to the curb. She'd placed boxes and cans from Mrs. Heise's cupboard on the empty pantry shelves and prayed Miriam wouldn't notice the difference.

Not that her *aenti* seemed inclined to do any cooking or much of anything else. Maybe being in a wheelchair disoriented her, and her energy would return when she could walk again. Lizzie hoped so.

Right now, Miriam silently scooped up the last of her oatmeal as Lizzie wrapped aluminum foil around two huge pot roasts from Mrs. Heise's refrigerator.

Before breakfast, Lizzie had browned the meat and chopped onions, carrots, celery, and potatoes to spread over the top of the roast. She'd dumped one can of cream of mushroom soup over each one and sprinkled packets of onion soup mix, water, and spices on top. After sealing the packages, she set them in baking pans and turned the oven to two hundred. By the time they returned from work, the meal would be done.

Scraping on the front sidewalk startled her. She rushed to the window to find Christian shoveling their sidewalk.

Lizzie opened the front door. "I can do that."

"I'm almost done. I'll be right there to get you."

He'd always been thoughtful when they were young. Not only had he done kind deeds, but he'd also apologized when their pranks had accidentally hurt others. It seemed he hadn't changed.

By the time Christian knocked, Lizzie had washed the breakfast dishes and helped Miriam into her coat.

His smile brightened the early morning grayness. "I salted the walkway, but some spots are still slushy. I'll take Miriam out first and come back for you. I wouldn't want you to slip."

She could walk to the buggy herself, but she waited for Christian to return. He offered her his arm, and she took it. Although she shouldn't cling to his arm this way, being so close to him made her want to cuddle up. At that thought, she stiffened.

"Is something wrong?" He slowed, and in the streetlight, eyes as brown as melted chocolate met hers.

Lizzie's heart galloped like a runaway horse. She had to rein it in. An impossible task with her arm tucked through his. "*N-neh.*"

"I thought you were about to fall."

He was right. But she already had. She'd fallen for him.

The imprint of Christian's arm against hers lingered as Lizzie decorated cupcakes. She hadn't finished yesterday's list, but more order sheets had been pinned to the corkboard in the hallway. She wouldn't even look at those until she finished these. Miriam sat by the counter watching intently as Lizzie created icing Christmas trees on top of each cupcake and added icing dots for colored lights.

"Pretty trees," her *aenti* whispered as Lizzie boxed them up.

"They are, aren't they?"

Her face serious, Miriam looked up. "Trees are for *Englischers*. We don't decorate trees."

"That's right. This is for an *Englisch* Christmas party."

"I see."

Her *aenti* seemed to be carrying on a conversation, and Lizzie rejoiced. But when the bakery opened, Miriam's faraway look had returned. She turned pages of the magazines or stared at the customers, her face blank.

Lizzie's heart sank. Twice now, her *aenti* had started conversations, only to sink back into depressed silence. Lizzie wished she could find a way to cheer her.

A woman muscled her way through the door. "I'm here to pick up a poinsettia cake for my ladies' Christmas tea." Her voice reverberated around the small space. "Name's Anderson."

Lizzie scurried over. "I'll be right back with your order." Running her finger along the wire mesh shelves in the walk-in cooler, she found the *A*'s. *Abbot. Aldinger. Allgyer. Altorfer. Anderson.* With a smile, Lizzie picked the box up gently and headed for the cash register.

"Here you go, Mrs. Anderson."

With a frown, the woman corrected her. "It's Ms. No man in the picture. No need for one."

Lizzie pinched her lips shut before she blurted out, *I'm so sorry*. The woman didn't look as if she'd appreciate pity. And despite Lizzie's fantasies about Christian, she had no one to court her either, so who was she to pity Ms. Anderson?

The woman waved money in Lizzie's face. "Do you intend to give me change?" Her clipped voice snapped Lizzie from daydreaming.

"O–Of course." She took the money and held out change.

Before Ms. Anderson could take it, a dog howled outside. Lizzie swiveled her head toward the noise.

"Oh, the poor thing." Dropping the money on top of Ms. Anderson's cake box and forgetting everything else, including the line of customers waiting to pick up Christmas cakes, Lizzie dashed from behind the counter and out into the snowstorm.

She bent down to pet the bedraggled dog whining outside the bakeshop window. Passing cars splashed slush on the muddy animal, while he strained to get into the store.

"What in the world's going on?" Rebecca hurried from the kitchen, wiping her hands on her apron. "I thought I heard a dog out here."

"Can we let him in out of the rain and slush?" Lizzie begged.

Rebecca sighed. "I wish we could, but what if the health department inspector happens to stop by?"

"I can't let him shiver in the cold."

"Of course not. Take him around to the back and use the outside stairs to my apartment. Bathe him good. Then we'll decide what to do."

"And what about me?" Ms. Anderson huffed as she stalked to the doorway. "That girl just dropped my change here and ran outside. And look at all these people waiting."

"I'm sorry, Ms. Anderson. I'm sure Lizzie didn't mean to be impolite. She has a soft heart. Seeing a lost dog in the snow upset her."

Lizzie couldn't help overhearing as she struggled to keep the dog from darting through the door.

Ms. Anderson sniffed. "Caring more about animals than people." She drew back at the sight of the stray. "Get that animal out of my way, or I'll call animal control and the health department."

That left Lizzie no choice. She scooped up the shivering dog, who tried to kick and squirm out of her arms, and headed around the building. The last thing Rebecca needed was for Ms. Anderson to call the health inspector.

As Lizzie turned the corner, Ms. Anderson yelled after her.

"You'd better not take that dog into the kitchen. That's a health violation."

"I won't." Lizzie tried to keep her retort polite, but her words came out too tart. She hoped she hadn't lost a customer for Rebecca.

After promising herself she'd make no mistakes here at Rebecca's Porch, already she'd broken a plate, spilled coffee on Christian, left early to take her aunt to the hospital, brought her aunt to the bakery, added fifty cake orders to Rebecca's list, and dragged in a stray dog.

And she'd only been working four days.

Lizzie leaned close and whispered to the wriggling puppy. "Sorry, but you need to come with me. I promise I'll soon have you warm and dry and fed." If she had to give him the meat from her lunch sandwich, she'd see the poor thing had something to eat.

As usual, Rebecca came to the rescue. She opened the back door to the kitchen and called out as Lizzie struggled to climb the slippery wooden steps to the apartment, "I have dog food upstairs for Goldie. Take two bowls from the cupboard and fill them with water and food for that little guy. You can bathe him in my tub. You'll find dog shampoo and several old, clean towels in the closet."

A short while later, a dripping white Westie emerged from the tub. Lizzie wrapped him in towels. He nosed at her sleeve, and his yips turned to whines.

His hoarse bark worried her. Did dogs get sore throats? Maybe he'd been barking too much. She wrapped him in a towel and cuddled him close.

After a brisk drying, his fur still stayed damp. The warm air in Rebecca's apartment would dry him.

"Come, Snowflake," Lizzie called as she poured food into a bowl.

The dog skittered after her. He seemed to like the name she'd chosen. When she set down a water bowl, he lapped up half of it.

"You're thirsty, aren't you?" She refilled the bowl.

Goldie stood up from her bed and nosed the little intruder. Snowflake yapped fiercely and jumped up as if to attack, but Goldie only stared at him. Lizzie petted both of them. "You behave now."

Once they'd settled down, Lizzie returned to the kitchen. "I think the dogs will get along. I'll skip my lunch to make up the time."

"Don't be silly," Rebecca said. "Caring for animals counts as work time around here."

For about the millionth time, Lizzie thanked God for her employer. She also realized something. Although she'd given Rebecca plenty to stress over, Lizzie hadn't broken any dishes or spilled anything on customers since that first day. Working in a loving, relaxed atmosphere had cut down on accidents.

Lizzie washed up and put on latex gloves to decorate more cupcakes while the other girls took turns handling the register. About ten minutes later, paws thumped down the inside stairs to the apartment, and a dog whined behind the door. *Snowflake*. He must have finished eating.

She hoped he wasn't going to be a problem. But the plaintive whining continued nonstop.

Rebecca headed for the door. "I'll see if I can interest him in some of Goldie's toys." But the minute she opened her door, Snowflake scooted through the swinging doors. Lizzie and Rebecca both charged after him.

Snowflake dashed straight for Miriam's wheelchair.

"Oh, you precious thing." Miriam bent over to pet Snowflake. And for the first time in almost a week, she smiled.

Snowflake sniffed all around her chair. Then he hopped onto

her lap and nuzzled her arms, her sides, and her face, whining the whole time. Miriam hugged him to her. Soon, he settled into a ball, and, with a blissful smile, she petted the sleeping dog.

Rebecca, who'd followed Lizzie out to help catch the escaped puppy, had tears in her eyes. "We can't take the dog from her."

Aden had run out after them, and he smiled down at Rebecca. "Can we say he's a service dog?"

"What a great idea!" Rebecca grinned at Lizzie. "He's helping your *aenti*, isn't he?"

"*Jah,* he is." Miriam had perked up at the sight of the dog. No longer slumped in her chair, she glanced around eagerly when she wasn't gazing at Snowflake.

"Look at my puppy, Lizzie," she called.

Lizzie's eyes misted. That was the first time her *aenti* had called her by the right name.

Christian stood, pressed his hands into his aching back and then rubbed his knees. He'd finished tiling the bathroom a little earlier than he'd expected. Maybe he'd treat himself to coffee at Rebecca's Porch while he waited for Lizzie to finish her shift.

He cleaned up as best he could. "I'll be back tomorrow to grout," he told Pete.

"I'll tell Merle when he stops by. How's your daughter doing?"

"The surgeon thinks he got all of the tumor, but he wants her to have chemo."

"That sucks, but I'm glad she's okay."

"Thanks." Christian shifted from foot to foot. He didn't want to be rude, especially after Pete had helped out with the roofing job.

"I can see you're itching to leave. Go on." Pete nodded toward the door. "I'm sure you're eager to see her."

Jah, he was, but Christian had another female in mind at the moment. Of course, Christian couldn't wait to see Johanna. But first he planned to drive Lizzie home.

When he pulled up outside Rebecca's Porch, she was pouring coffee for two young Amish men. She smiled at both of them, and Christian's stomach clenched. What if one of them was interested in her?

He tied his horse to a hitching post and strode inside. He pushed so hard, the door slammed behind him. He hadn't meant to announce his entrance that way.

Everyone, including Lizzie, turned to stare at him.

"Sorry," he muttered.

"I'll be done soon." Lizzie headed over with a cup and the coffee pot. "Don't worry," she said as she filled his cup two-thirds full. "I'll be back with your cream and sugar." She returned with the right amount.

"You remembered?"

"How could I forget?"

From her inflection, she sounded as if she couldn't forget him, not how he fixed his coffee. Or was that only his imagination?

Rebecca stepped out of the kitchen. "If your ride's here, Lizzie, you can go."

"What about the puppy? Should I take him with me?"

"*Neh,* Aden's walking both dogs right now. This evening, he and his brothers will ask around the neighborhood."

Outside two dogs barked. One loud, and the other quieter and hoarser.

A door banged overhead, and one dog bounded down the inside steps and scratched at the first-floor entrance door from Rebecca's apartment to the bakery.

Christian moved to the counter to study all the cupcakes Lizzie had decorated. She was so talented.

The dog whined and slammed against a nearby door.

"Come here," Aden called, but the dog went crazy. He yapped and leaped at the door into the hallway.

Lizzie stared wide-eyed as the door bulged outward from the impact of the dog's body. "*Ach,* I hope I'm not leaving them with trouble."

Rebecca walked in behind her. "It'll be fine. I'm sure Snowflake will settle down."

"Do you think he misses my *aenti*?"

"Could be," Rebecca said. "I'd send him home with you, but we need to keep him here in case we find his owner."

Lizzie nodded and headed over to her *aenti,* who seemed forlorn.

When Christian followed Lizzie, the dog's frenzied barking settled into whines and moans. "I hope I didn't set off Rebecca's dog."

"*Neh,* it's a stray."

"A stray?" Christian turned to her eagerly, but then he slumped back. "It couldn't be Sampson," he mumbled as he pushed Miriam's wheelchair into the parking lot.

"What?" Lizzie looked up at him with bright, curious eyes.

An expression he remembered so well. An expression that always led to new adventures. And often trouble. He smiled at the memories.

He'd gotten so lost in thought, he'd forgotten to answer her. "The boy who's watching our dog Sampson called to say he'd gotten out last night. After Johanna fell asleep, I went over there to search for him. I looked until three."

"Three in the morning? And you still got up to take me?"

Christian loved the indignant look on her face. "It was no problem. I can catch up on sleep tonight."

"Don't ever do that again."

"What?" he teased. "Search for a dog or pick you up?"

"Oh, you." Another one of her lightweight taps on his arm. This one felt like a love tap. He turned to face front and flicked the reins. He didn't want her to see his response to her touch. Or to the word *love*, even if he hadn't said it aloud.

"You think this stray might be yours?" she asked.

Christian shook his head. "It's too far from Bird-in-Hand."

"Bird-in-Hand?" Her words were almost a screech.

Too late, he realized his mistake.

"You live in Bird-in-Hand?" she demanded.

He couldn't lie. His mumbled *jah* set off her fury.

"Our house is not on the way to Bird-in-Hand. That's in the opposite direction."

Christian fumbled for an excuse. "Not if I take the back roads and stop at Rebecca's Porch."

"I see." Sarcasm colored her words. "There are no other coffee shops or bakeries ten miles closer to the hospital or your house."

"They aren't Rebecca's Porch." *And you don't work there.*

"You. Are. Not. Ever. To. Pick. Me. Up. Again."

Each of her words shot like bullets through his heart. He took a deep breath, hoping to stop the bleeding. But what could he say to make her change her mind?

Miriam shifted in her seat and looked from him to Lizzie and back as if trying to understand the fight.

Danke, Christian whispered silently to Lizzie's aunt. "What about your *aenti*? Are you going to risk her getting pneumonia?"

"*Neh*." Her quiet, almost tearful answer shook him to the core.

He pulled in front of the house and turned to face her. "Lizzie, what's wrong?"

She waved him away, but her eyes shimmered with tears.

"I won't come if it upsets you that much."

Once again, she flicked a hand in the air. "I-it's not that."

"What is it then?"

She only shook her head. "We should get inside." She followed him as he pushed Miriam inside. "I'm so sorry you haven't found Johanna's dog."

"Me too," he said. And he was even more sorry that she wanted to cut him out of her life.

Chapter 9

Lizzie could sense Christian's coldness, his hurt. He'd closed himself off, but he treated Miriam as gently as ever. Lizzie missed holding his arm as she walked behind him and the wheelchair, but after the way she'd just acted, she didn't blame him for staying away from her. She'd been so upset at his driving miles out of his way that she'd overreacted.

While Lizzie opened the front door, he pushed Miriam into the living room, then hurried outside and down the sidewalk without another word. She sniffed. The scent of onions and beef wafted through the room. She'd forgotten about the roasts she'd put in the oven that morning.

"Wait!" she shouted to Christian as he pulled away from the curb.

He drew his horse to a stop but didn't turn to look at her, and she ached inside.

"I have something for Johanna." She hoped he'd wait for something for his daughter. "I'll bring it right out."

Lizzie packed two plates and two sets of silverware into a plastic cooler she'd found on the pantry shelves. She'd washed it out last night. Now she lifted out one baking pan holding a foil-wrapped package, cushioned it with a dish towel and a pot holder, set it into the cooler, covered it with another towel, and snapped the lid down.

Outside, she rounded the buggy and placed the cooler on the passenger seat.

"This is for Johanna?"

Lizzie couldn't look him in the eye. "And for you. I didn't want to say that in case you refused to take anything from me after the way I acted."

"*Ach,* Lizzie, how could you think that?" His wounded expression added to her guilt.

"Christian, will you forgive me for the way I spoke to you?"

"Of course."

"You never held grudges, did you?" No matter how much trouble she got him in, he never once tattled on her, and he never blamed her.

"We're supposed to forgive everyone."

"*Supposed to* is not the same as doing it."

This time, he looked her right in the eye. "Who have you refused to forgive, Lizzie?" His words were gentle, not accusing.

She nibbled on her lip and stared off into the distance. Old memories ran through her mind, one after another, but she couldn't pinpoint anyone she hadn't forgiven. "No one, I guess, except . . ."

"Except who?"

"You. I said I was sorry for how I spoke to you, but I'm not sorry for what I said. I can't believe you drove so far out of your way to pick us up."

"Don't you think you deserve help?"

Lizzie didn't know how to answer that. Nobody had ever gone out of the way to help her before. Mamm had tried, but she'd been so busy working and caring for her parents, she had little time for Lizzie. The Kallises had been kind to let her stay in the apartment, but while she was growing up, they'd always acted as if she were a burden.

"You didn't answer me, Lizzie."

She choked up. "Because I can't. Well, maybe I can, but I know you won't agree with me and then we might get in another fight and I couldn't bear that and—"

He held up his hand to stop her. "I didn't know we had a first fight. When was it? I missed it."

"I guess it was only me who was fighting."

Christian laughed. "I think it takes two to fight. Unless you're fighting with yourself."

"Oh, you."

"I thought we settled this before. I enjoy picking you up. If I didn't get you, I'd be concerned about you—and your *aenti*—getting back and forth safely. If it makes you feel any better, the house I'm working on is only two miles from Rebecca's Porch, so it didn't take me far out of my way."

Now, Lizzie felt even more miserable for yelling at him. "I'm sorry."

He reached out and lifted her chin. "Look at me."

At the touch of his finger on her skin, she sucked in a breath, and when she met his eyes, she drowned in those pools of velvety chocolate.

"Even if I had to drive fifty miles or one hundred miles or more, you are absolutely worth it, Lizzie Bontrager."

She pulled away before she did something foolish, and she averted her eyes so he couldn't see the tears in them. That had been the most beautiful thing anyone had ever said to her.

In her mind, voices clamored, pointing out her faults, criticizing her actions, telling her what she'd done wrong. And Lizzie herself heaped on even more self-reproach. But Christian hadn't believed any of it. He'd gone out of his way to be kind, to treat her as worthwhile.

"You don't know what that means to me," she said in a choked voice.

"Lizzie, I'm going to keep repeating it until you believe it. You treat everyone else as if they're important and special."

"Well, they are." She hoped she didn't sound defensive.

"Exactly. And so are you."

Christian could tell from her expression that Lizzie didn't believe what he'd said. Not really. How could he get it across?

Maybe that wasn't his job. *Dear Lord, please show her the truth.*

"You should go," she said softly. "Johanna must be wondering where you are."

All this week, he'd been torn. For the past five years, his daughter had been number one in his life, but now that he'd found Lizzie again, he wanted to share some of his time with her too.

As much as he disliked leaving, he couldn't wait to find out how Johanna had done today. "I'll see you tomorrow morning."

She shook her head. "*Neh,* you won't."

"Lizzie, please let me drive you to work."

"You can't." She paused for a moment, long enough to deflate him, before saying, "I have the day off."

It surprised Christian how much he'd miss their time together. "Well, Thursday, then."

She didn't acknowledge that. Instead, she asked, "You're working tomorrow, aren't you?"

"*Jah.*" He got his hopes up that maybe she'd invite him for lunch, only to have them dashed.

"I have plans for the day."

"I see." He tried not to show his disappointment. "I'd better go, but I'll see you Thursday."

"Only if you're working near Rebecca's Porch."

"I am."

Her nod set his heart singing. He drove to the hospital, humming a tune from the *Ausbund*.

He carried the cooler up to Johanna's room. His spirits lifted to see her connected to fewer tubes and monitors. The bruises made it hard to tell if she was better, but she kept her eyes open as far as she could despite the swelling.

"You're awake." He settled on the chair beside the bed and took her hand.

"What's that?" She pointed to the cooler on his lap.

"I don't know. Remember Lizzie? She said this was for you. And maybe me."

He opened it and inhaled onion and spices. He lifted the towel and opened the foil. Steam rose from meat covered with gravy and vegetables. His mouth watered at the aroma of onions and beef.

Johanna sniffed. "That smells good."

Delectable was more like it. Christian dished out portions for each of them. The meat melted in his mouth. His first homemade meal in ages tasted divine. Warm and filling, it wrapped him in Lizzie's caring. She disliked people doing kind things for her, but she filled other people's lives with love and light.

Even Johanna, who'd picked at her meals since she'd first been allowed to have food, ate almost half of her supper. She must have noticed how he'd gobbled down the meal. "Want the rest of mine?"

"You need to eat."

"I like it, but I'm too full."

"Want me to save it for later?"

She shook her head. "I ate some of my lion cupcake. That was yummy."

Christian smiled to see she had the lion head facing her, but she'd nibbled from the tail. She passed over the rest of her dinner. He couldn't let good food go to waste.

A voice inside his head taunted, *You're only eating that to clean the plate?*

He had to be honest. Although the meal tasted delicious, its connection to Lizzie made every bite special.

The word he'd used earlier hit him with full force. *Love*. He shied away from it. They hadn't seen each other since they were young. How could a childhood friendship grow into love?

It couldn't. What he felt for her was fondness. Affection. Attraction. After all, Lizzie was a beautiful woman—inside and out. But all those words seemed inadequate. Maybe caring. Yet, once again, he tiptoed around the word *love*.

He pushed it from his mind. It was too much too soon. But the word niggled at the back of his brain. He could come up with no other word to express his feelings, but he wasn't ready to accept the truth.

Christian groaned and stretched. He'd fallen asleep in the chair beside Johanna's bed, still holding her hand. A nurse must have covered him with this blanket sometime during the night.

"You're still here, Daed?" Johanna asked sleepily. "Don't you have to walk Sampson?"

He squirmed. He still hadn't told her the dog was missing. The boy and his father had combed the neighborhood and put up posters. Christian had planned to look last night after Johanna fell asleep. Tonight, he'd search again. Or perhaps someone had responded to the posters.

He didn't like to mislead her, but he didn't want sadness to interfere with her recovery. Surely, they'd find Sampson before Johanna's discharge. Then, after she returned home, well and healthy, they could laugh together about Sampson's adventures.

Chapter 10

"Where's Snowflake?" Miriam asked the minute she woke.

"At the bakery." Unless Aden had found the dog's owner last night.

Tears in her eyes, Miriam looked everywhere as Lizzie wheeled her into the kitchen. "Anna Grace, find my puppy."

"He's at the bakery," Lizzie repeated.

"Let's get him."

"Tomorrow. Today I have a special trip planned."

The light died in Miriam's eyes.

Lizzie wished they'd brought the dog home, but maybe going out would perk up her *aenti*. "After breakfast, we'll do some chores and then ride in a car."

"Tilda's?"

"Mrs. Heise is away. We'll have a different driver."

Lizzie had seen a sticky note labeled *Drivers for Miriam* on Mrs. Heise's refrigerator door. Lizzie planned to run over and call one. Rebecca had insisted on paying Lizzie a percentage of all the specialty cupcake sales yesterday. Along with tips from some of the customers, Lizzie should have enough for their outing.

They finished breakfast, and Lizzie tried to engage Miriam in chores. As Lizzie washed the dishes, she set them on a towel in front of Miriam. Sometimes her *aenti* dried, but other times she stared vacantly.

Every once in a while, Miriam roused and asked about the puppy. Maybe they should think about getting a dog for her, but would she bond with another dog? And would another dog take to Miriam the way Snowflake had?

Lizzie fielded her *aenti*'s plaintive cries to find the dog as she cleaned. She finished all the paperwork in the dining room, cleared out drawers stuffed with junk, and stored the bills and receipts in one of the empty drawers with the checkbook. She still needed to throw out old food in the cupboards, but she'd save that until her *aenti* went to bed.

After Lizzie did some baking and fixed a special lunch to take along, she headed for Mrs. Heise's house to use the phone. "I'll be right back," she told Miriam. "I'm going to call a driver,"

"Get Snowflake." Miriam called after Lizzie.

"You'll see Snowflake tomorrow." She hoped that wasn't a lie. Although she wanted the dog to be reunited with his owner, Lizzie had gotten attached to the little guy when she'd bathed him. She'd felt an instant attraction to him from the moment she'd dashed out to rescue him. Maybe a dog would be good for both of them.

Half an hour later, a driver pulled up out front. Debbie, a large, cheerful woman, helped Lizzie get Miriam in the car. "Where to?" she asked.

"The hospital. Is there a toy store on the way?"

Debbie knitted her brows. "Hmm. Best I can suggest is to go to one of them big stores what sells everything."

"Let's do that." When they stopped, Lizzie asked if Miriam could stay in the car.

"Sure thing." Debbie kept the radio on, playing hymns.

Miriam had tilted her head to one side, as if enjoying the music. She should be fine until Lizzie returned.

Lizzie hurried in, praying they'd have what she wanted. She found a stuffed animal, paid, and headed back to the car. A short while later, Debbie pulled in front of the hospital.

Miriam whimpered and clung to the car's armrest.

"She don't sound like she wants to go in."

Lizzie hadn't thought Miriam might be afraid. "We're not going into the emergency room. We're going to visit a little girl. You'll be all right."

Even after Lizzie and Debbie helped her into her wheelchair, Miriam gripped the arms. She looked as if she'd like to stop Lizzie from moving forward. If only Lizzie had thought this out better.

Whimpering through clenched teeth, Miriam traveled through the lobby. She quieted when they got inside the elevator.

"Have you seen my puppy?" she asked the woman beside her.

The woman shook her head and backed away.

She's not contagious, Lizzie wanted to tell the woman, but the elevator had stopped on the fourth floor. She asked a nurse for the room number and headed down the hall.

By now, Miriam was staring around her, peering into doors with her usual curiosity. Maybe that would keep her mind off Snowflake.

They found Johanna's room, and the little girl smiled at them. Lizzie relaxed. She hadn't been sure if Johanna would welcome a visit.

"I know you," Johanna said to Lizzie. "You made my lion cupcake." She rotated the cupcake so Lizzie could see where she'd taken some bites. "And we had a good dinner last night. Daed said it tasted much better than hospital food."

Lizzie laughed at the underwhelming compliment. "I hope it did."

"*Jah,* it really did. I couldn't eat all of mine, so Daed ate that too."

Perhaps that meant Christian had enjoyed it. Lizzie did a little inner dance. But right now, she'd come to spend time with Johanna. "Your *daed* said he had to work today, so I thought you might be lonely."

"I miss him when he's gone."

When Johanna's eyes filled with tears, Lizzie wanted to hug her. But she wasn't sure about the little girl's fragility, and she didn't want to bump the tubes and cords.

Miriam interrupted. "Have you seen Snowflake?"

At Johanna's puzzled look, Lizzie explained, "We found a stray dog. He's staying at the bakery, and my *aenti* misses him."

"I miss my dog too," Johanna told Miriam. "I wish he could be here at the hospital with me. Daed left late this morning to feed and walk Sampson. I hope my puppy wasn't too hungry."

"But he's—" Lizzie snapped her mouth shut. Christian must not have told Johanna the dog was missing.

"What?" the little girl asked.

Lizzie changed the subject. "You'll be going home soon, won't you?"

"Not for almost a week. I might not be home for Christmas."

If Johanna had to stay in the hospital for Christmas, Lizzie would make sure the little girl had a special day.

"It's lonely here when Daed's gone. Some of my friends come after school, but they can't during the day."

So, Johanna had company in the late afternoon? It relieved Lizzie to know that when Christian picked her up, he hadn't been leaving his daughter alone.

"I'm glad you came to see me," Johanna said shyly.

Lizzie held out the bag she'd brought. "Maybe this will help you on lonely days."

Johanna opened the bag and pulled out the stuffed lion. "Oh, he's cute." She hugged it close. "*Danke.*" Then the joy on her face slipped into embarrassment, and she set the lion on the bed beside her. "I'm too old for stuffed animals. I'm already seven, you know."

"That is very grown-up. You know, when I was ten, we moved away from Lancaster, and I didn't have any friends at my new house, so I was very lonely." *And I really, really missed your* daed. "I slept with a teddy bear to keep me company," Lizzie confessed, "until I turned twelve."

"Twelve?" Johanna's eyes rounded.

Lizzie nodded. "*Jah*. Hugging that stuffed bear close made me feel less lonely while my *mamm* worked long hours."

Johanna flicked a sideways glance at the lion propped up beside her. "I'm not lonely with you here, but when you go, maybe I'll hug him."

"Try it," Lizzie encouraged her. "I think you'll find it helps."

"I'm lonely," Miriam said.

Johanna stared at Miriam with sympathetic eyes. "Would you like to hold my lion?" She held it out to Lizzie. "Can you give this to her?"

Lizzie passed the lion to Miriam, who hugged it close.

"Does it help?" Johanna asked.

Miriam didn't answer. With her cheek resting on the lion's head, she closed her eyes and hummed a lullaby.

Lizzie's heart ached for her *aenti*. All those years of living alone must have been hard. Miriam had never had children to hold and hug. No wonder she'd gotten so attached to Snowflake. Lizzie vowed to hug her *aenti* more. And they definitely needed a dog.

Johanna leaned over and whispered, "She's like my *mammi*, who's in heaven. Mammi used to hug me and hum like that."

Christian finished work by midafternoon. "I'm headed out now."

"You'll be back tomorrow, right?" Pete sounded anxious.

"Jah." Christian wished he didn't have to come back. He wanted to spend more time with Johanna—and Lizzie.

"Only three more bathrooms to go" was Pete's parting shot as Christian left.

Christian shook his head. He'd never understand why this retired *Englisch* couple needed so many bathrooms and bedrooms for only two people. If they had a big family like the Amish did, it might make sense. Even then, it seemed wasteful to have unused bedrooms and bathrooms. They could use their wealth to help others.

He pushed away his judgmental thoughts. This *Englisch* couple was paying his salary. He should be grateful to them and to Merle for his job.

Danke, Lord.

As he drove toward the hospital, Christian's annoyance dissipated. Snow from the blizzard had been plowed into high piles beside the road. A light coating now covered the nearby fields with fresh white. Instead of concentrating on everything that bothered him, he could focus on the beautiful scenery and all the things he loved.

That word again. *Love* brought to mind Lizzie. How he enjoyed her cheerful chatter, her radiant smile, her giving spirit . . .

Christian was still adding to the list of things he loved about Lizzie when he walked into Johanna's hospital room. He stopped short. Had spending so much time thinking about Lizzie made him imagine her standing here?

"Daed!" Johanna squealed.

His daughter's ear-piercing greeting made them all jump. And Christian's heart took an extra leap. Lizzie really was here.

Both the girls he *loved* were in the same room.

He hugged Johanna, avoiding the cords and bruises, and wished he could do the same with Lizzie.

"Christian?" Lizzie's voice was faint. "I didn't expect you so early."

Was she disappointed? Had she been hoping to avoid him?

She must have read the hurt in his eyes, because she stammered, "I didn't mean, um, it's not that I'm not glad to see you. I am, it's only that I thought you'd still be working and—"

"And I surprised you."

"You did," she agreed. "But it's a nice surprise."

Had she tacked that on out of politeness?

"Daed, look." Johanna pointed to Miriam, asleep in the wheelchair, cuddling a stuffed lion. "Lizzie brought me that lion, but when Mammi—I mean, Miriam—said she was lonely, I shared it with her."

"I'm glad you were kind, Johanna."

Behind him, Lizzie said softly, "She has a giving heart like her *daed*."

Christian wanted to turn and look into her eyes, to see if she'd meant that, but he worried if he did, he might not be able to glance away. "I know someone else who has a giving heart."

"*Jah,* me too." Johanna pointed at Lizzie.

Christian winked at his daughter. She'd done what he wished he could do.

"We should go," Lizzie said. "Our ride will be here soon."

This time, Christian turned around. "I could take you."

"I'd like that."

Had he heard her correctly? She'd spoken so quietly, he'd barely heard her. Was she softening toward him? Was she going to allow him to care for her the way he wanted to?

Johanna said wistfully, "I wish I could go too."

"Soon," he promised.

Lizzie's eyes held compassion as she turned to his daughter. "I don't want to take your *daed* away from you. Our driver might already be here, so your *daed* will be staying with you."

Christian's high spirits plunged. He'd gotten his hopes up. Lizzie's words had held out promise and possibility. A chance for a relationship.

Johanna beamed at Lizzie. "Will you come back and visit me? I like you and Miriam."

"We like you too. I can visit on my days off from the bakery."

A jumbled mess of feelings collided inside Christian. He wanted to be with his daughter more than anything, yet he also longed to be with Lizzie. If only he could find a way to keep them both in the same place together.

"You know," Lizzie said, "Rebecca's Porch closes from midday on Christmas Eve until the day after New Year's. If you need someone to stay with Johanna here at the hospital or even once she goes home, I'd be happy to do that. Miriam enjoys being around Johanna too."

"You'd do that for us?"

"Of course." Lizzie said it so matter-of-factly, like it wasn't a sacrifice, like she'd be more than willing to do it.

His heart swelled with appreciation—and love. The word he kept pushing to the back of his mind.

"Lizzie, I don't know what to say."

"I do," Johanna piped up. "Say *jah* and *danke*."

They all laughed.

"You're right, Johanna." But a mere thank-you couldn't contain all Christian's gratitude. No matter what he did, he could never outgive Lizzie.

Chapter 11

Over the next few days, Lizzie and Miriam grew more and more attached to Snowflake. He spent most of the day curled in Miriam's lap until Aden took both dogs for a late afternoon walk. Snowflake, a mild-mannered and laid-back dog during the day, always grew frenzied and wild behind Rebecca's apartment door whenever Christian arrived to get them. Was Snowflake upset that Miriam was leaving?

As Christmas Eve drew near, Lizzie found herself humming as she worked. The only thing to mar her happiness at work was Rebecca's health. Their boss hadn't been feeling well, and everyone worked frantically to make Rebecca's special poinsettia cakes.

Lizzie decorated hundreds of cupcakes while also cutting out piles of poinsettia flowers and spreading the final fancy coats of icing on dozens of cakes and waiting on what seemed like a gazillion customers. She looked forward to the holiday break when the bakery closed. Her other concerns, besides Rebecca's health, were hoping Christian found Sampson and fretting about the unpaid tax bill. She took all three of these troubles to the Lord in prayer.

Her days had fallen into a pattern that thrilled Lizzie. Christian dropped her and Miriam off at the bakery every morning and went to work early at the *Englischer*'s house. Then in the afternoon, he took Lizzie and Miriam to the hospital with him. Lizzie warmed up meals or casseroles in Rebecca's upstairs oven, making enough for Rebecca and Aden to enjoy when they'd closed the bakery. Then Lizzie took their meals to the hospital so they could spend the evenings with Johanna.

Sometimes, Johanna was sleeping when they arrived, her arms wrapped around her stuffed lion. Other times, the lion sat propped on her pillow while Johanna whispered and giggled with school friends. But wherever the lion happened to be when they walked into her room, it ended up in Miriam's arms.

After Johanna fell asleep, Christian tucked the lion into bed with her before driving Lizzie and Miriam home. Then he stayed for several hours to share conversation and hot chocolate with Lizzie.

One night, she discovered he'd been cruising around his neighborhood every night after he left her house. "You've been doing what?" Her voice came out shriller than she wanted. She tried to tone it down. "That means you've only been getting three or four hours of sleep at night."

"Being with you gives me so much extra energy, I could stay up all night," he insisted. "Besides, I need to find Sampson before Johanna comes home."

He gave Lizzie a smile that melted her into a puddle and left her tongue-tied. When she could speak again, she placed a hand over his. "I worry about you."

"I know, and I like it." He turned his hand over, so he could interlace his fingers with hers.

"Be very careful."

"I promise I will."

"You'd better because I've been looking forward to this forever."

His eyebrows quirked. "Forever?"

"All right, for the past week or so." But in her heart, she had been looking for a love like this forever. Christian hadn't said that word, and neither had she, but she'd sensed it.

Lizzie could hardly believe tomorrow was Christmas Eve. When Rebecca's Porch closed at noon, Christian planned to pick up Miriam and Lizzie after Johanna's discharge, and they'd spend the rest of the day together. They'd all be celebrating her getting out of the hospital early. And Lizzie couldn't wait to give Johanna a special surprise. But if Christian didn't find Sampson . . .

Christian interrupted her worries. "Merle offered double pay if I work tomorrow and Christmas Day."

"You said *neh,* didn't you?" Christian wouldn't skip Christmas Day dinner, would he? She'd already bought everything for the meal, and she'd baked rolls and desserts.

"Merle threatened to fire me if I didn't show up."

Lizzie sucked in a breath.

"Don't worry. I told him I'd see him the day after Second Christmas."

"What if he fires you?"

"He tried before, and it only lasted two days. Even if he does, I've been talking to Aden about helping him with his construction work. He wants to spend more time at the bakery."

Lizzie laughed. "I wonder why."

"Probably for the same reason I want to spend all my spare time there."

"You're interested in Rebecca?" Lizzie couldn't resist teasing.

Christian grinned. "Nope. I'm interested in someone else at the bakery." He stood and headed for the door. "I'd better search for Sampson."

"I'll be praying you find him."

Lizzie stood by the window, hugging herself, until Christian drove out of sight. Living in Lancaster had been a dream come true. God had given her so many blessings. With all the love and joy flowing her way, Lizzie's heart expanded until it might explode in fireworks and streamers.

She'd opened her heart to include Miriam, Johanna, Rebecca and Aden, her coworkers, and Snowflake. And best of all, the friend who'd been the most important person in her childhood had now become the most important person in her adult life after God.

On Christmas Eve morning, the staff at Rebecca's Porch gathered for a special breakfast in the early morning before opening. It cheered Lizzie to see Rebecca seated at the head of the long table, eating from the plate Aden had prepared for her from the buffet. Her cheeks were pale and she'd lost weight, but she gave each of them her usual cheerful smile.

After they finished eating, Rebecca tapped her glass to get everyone's attention. "I want to thank all of you for helping with the customers, the baked goods, and especially my poinsettia cakes. I hope you all have a special Christmas with your families. Before we open the store this morning, Aden will hand out paychecks."

Sarah received hers first. She tore it open and stared at the check inside. "You've made a mistake on mine."

"*Neh,* I'm also paying all of you for the holiday week, and I added a bonus." Her eyes damp, Rebecca looked at each one of them. "The business has done very well this year, thanks to all of you. If you hadn't pitched in to get the poinsettia cakes done, my reputation might have been ruined. I couldn't have done it without you." She saved an extra special smile for Aden.

Lizzie opened her check and gasped. "I don't deserve this."

She'd only been here a short while. Everyone else had worked the whole year.

Rebecca turned to her. "Yours also includes extra for all the cupcake business you brought in. People who've seen your cupcakes are already booking cakes and cupcakes through June of next year."

Aden chimed in. "Rebecca claims your cupcakes brought in more business than all of her advertising has in the past two years. I suggested she give you part of her advertising budget for next year."

Lizzie couldn't believe it. This was more than enough to pay Miriam's back taxes. Her throat tightened too much to speak. She hoped her overflowing eyes expressed her gratitude. After all she'd done to mess things up for Rebecca, her employer had been so generous.

"We have one more gift for you, Lizzie. At least we hope it'll be a gift." Rebecca looked doubtfully at Aden.

"Since we haven't found Snowflake's owner," he said, "and Miriam seems to love him, we thought you might like to take him home with you." Then he opened the apartment door, and Snowflake raced out, freshly bathed, with a bright red bow around his neck.

Now the tears did come. "I can't believe it. You've been so generous and kind to me."

Christian's words came back to Lizzie. And suddenly she understood. God, in His mercy, had done the same thing. He'd poured out blessings and even given His only Son when none of them deserved it. But once she'd accepted that gift, He considered her deserving of His love.

"Let's get this food cleaned up and the dining room back in order." Rebecca gathered her dishes. "It looks like the parking lot is full of customers waiting to pick up their poinsettia cakes."

Lizzie moved Miriam's wheelchair to her usual corner, and

Snowflake lay curled on her lap. The next few hours became a flurry of cakes, cupcakes, and customers. And then the door opened, and Christian strode in, one arm around Johanna, supporting her. And Lizzie's heart couldn't possibly be fuller.

Except . . .

Poor Johanna! Her face tear-stained, she gave Lizzie a half-hearted smile.

Then, with a loud yipping, a white whirlwind raced across the floor and jumped on Johanna. Snowflake practically knocked her over.

"Down, Snowflake," Lizzie ordered, but the dog ignored her.

Starry-eyed, Johanna sank to the floor and wrapped her arms around the dog. "Sampson! You found him, Lizzie! *Danke! Danke!*"

Lizzie turned questioning eyes to Christian, who stared from her to the dog and back in astonishment.

"How did you find Johanna's dog?" he asked.

"This is the stray I found, and we've been caring for him. But how did Sampson come more than ten miles?"

An *Englisch* customer waiting in line for her cake turned around. "I've heard stories of dogs traveling great distances to find their owners."

"He was looking for me," Johanna declared.

"I'm sure he was, dear," the lady said. "I'm glad he found you."

"That also explains why Snowflake—I mean, Sampson—sniffed the wheelchair and stayed beside it." Lizzie still couldn't believe it, but some of Snowflake's behaviors made sense. "You've been lifting Miriam and folding the wheelchair and putting it into the buggy. Sampson recognized the smells." It also explained why the dog went crazy whenever Christian came into the shop.

"Well, you invited Johanna to the bakery for a surprise." Christian laughed. "You certainly gave her one."

"That wasn't the surprise I meant. Let me get that one."

Lizzie hurried into the kitchen to get the cake she'd baked using Rebecca's secret recipe.

Several customers *ooh*ed and *ahh*ed as she carried it out. "Can we order one of those?"

Rebecca stood at the register. "They'll be available after the new year. Only with regular vanilla and chocolate batter. The special poinsettia batter is only available at Christmastime."

"Can we put in our orders for next year's poinsettia cakes now?"

"Check back after the new year." Rebecca motioned to the long line of customers waiting to pick up their cakes.

"I'll be right back to help you, Rebecca."

"Take your time. That precious little girl should be celebrating today. I'm so glad she's out of the hospital. Aden and I have been praying for her."

"*Danke*." Christian's eyes shone.

Lizzie bent down to Johanna's eye level and held out the cake.

"Two presents?" Johanna's face lit up with delight. "Oh, it has a lion on it."

Lizzie had figured Johanna would prefer a lion to a poinsettia.

"Let me get Miriam." Christian hurried over and brought Miriam to one of the tables.

Miriam looked almost as excited as Johanna. She clapped when she saw the cake, and she couldn't keep her eyes off Johanna cuddling the dog.

When Johanna held out a hand for a piece of cake, Sampson crawled into Miriam's lap for a petting.

After Lizzie handed the first slice to Johanna, the little girl set the cake in front of Miriam and leaned over to hug her. "*Danke* for taking good care of Sampson. I wish you could be my *mammi*."

Miriam beamed. Johanna sat on a chair beside her, and they

took turns petting the dog. Johanna and Miriam shared smiles and whispered together as they ate their cake.

Lizzie went back to helping hand out poinsettia cakes until the line dwindled to a trickle.

"You can go now, Lizzie." Rebecca smiled at the small group around the table. "So you can spend time at your party."

With joy in her soul, Lizzie headed for the table. Christian met her eyes, and his smile set her heart aflame.

"If you're ready to go, I'll take Johanna and Sampson out to the buggy and get them settled in the backseat. Then I'll come back for you and Miriam. I hope you won't be too squashed back there."

"I'll be fine." She'd endure any hardship to spend time with Christian, but snuggling up with Johanna and Snow–Sampson could hardly be called a hardship.

As Christian, Johanna, and Sampson headed for the door, Miriam started to cry. She held out her arms. "Snowflake, come back, come back."

With distress in her eyes, Johanna watched tears trickle down Miriam's cheeks.

"Don't worry," Lizzie whispered to Johanna. "Miriam got attached to Sampson while you were in the hospital, but she'll be fine." Lizzie wondered if another dog could take Snowflake's place for Miriam.

"I cried like that when Daed told me Sampson was lost." Johanna's eyes filled with tears. "It's hard to lose a dog." She glanced from Sampson to Miriam and back several times. "I don't want to see her cry."

What a caring little girl Johanna was. She'd learned it from her *daed*.

Then taking hold of the bow around Sampson's neck, Johanna walked him over to the wheelchair. "You can have Snowflake." She knelt and hugged the dog. "Be a good dog, and stay here, Sampson." Biting her lip, she stood.

"*Danke.*" Miriam leaned over and hugged Johanna.

Over their heads, Lizzie's and Christian's gazes met. Misty-eyed, Lizzie melted at the love-light shining in his eyes.

Christian cleared his throat. "I have a better idea. Why don't we share Sampson?"

Did he mean what she thought he did? She answered with a joyful *jah*.

Johanna, her eyes damp, glanced from one to the other with a puzzled look. "How would we do that?"

"Well, if we all live in the same house . . ." Christian explained, giving Lizzie a tender, questioning look.

"You mean, Lizzie would be my *mamm*, and Miriam would be my *mammi*?"

More like her great, great aunt, but Lizzie didn't correct her. Miriam wouldn't mind being called Mammi. "*Jah*, I think that's what your *daed* has in mind."

"I do," he confirmed.

Johanna danced around in a circle. "That's the best Christmas present ever." She rushed over, grabbed Lizzie's and Christian's hands, and dragged them closer to the wheelchair for a group hug.

Then while Christian kept his arm around Lizzie and whispered sweet nothings in her ear, Johanna knelt and ruffled the dog's fur. "Did you hear that, Sampson Snowflake? We're all going to be a family."

"We certainly are," Christian agreed. "The very best family ever."

Epilogue

Christmas Eve, one year later

Snow fell softly outside the window as Lizzie braided Johanna's hair before bed. Pine garlands strung over the mantle scented the air, and several candles flickered on the shelf, sending a soft glow across his wife's beautiful face. Christian's heart burst with gratitude for all his blessings.

So much had happened in the past year since he'd met Lizzie. After her chemotherapy, Johanna's hair had grown back, and now it had almost reached shoulder length. He never could have gone through those treatments alone. Lizzie had stayed with him every step of the way. And after they married in the spring, all four of them—well, five counting Sampson Snowflake—had moved into Miriam's larger house and remodeled it.

When Merle refused to let Christian have time off for Johanna's chemo, Aden stepped in and offered Christian work. All the people in town who'd known Aden years ago and trusted his family gave him more remodeling jobs than he could handle. He let Christian set his schedule around Johanna's treatments, and Rebecca had offered Lizzie a job making specialty cupcakes. Lizzie could bake them late at night or early in the morning, so she could care for Johanna while Christian worked.

Sometimes Lizzie substituted for sick bakers or servers. When she did, she brought Miriam, Johanna, and Sampson Snowflake with her.

"Ready?" Lizzie's sweet voice roused him from his reverie.

He nodded. With Johanna between them, they headed upstairs. Miriam had gone to bed an hour ago, so the three of them tiptoed softly up the dark staircase. Christian and Lizzie prayed with Johanna, tucked her in, and kissed her good night.

"Tell me a bedtime story," she begged.

Lizzie lowered herself into the rocker near the bed. "How 'bout Daniel and the lion's den?"

Johanna giggled. "My favorite." She hugged the stuffed lion Lizzie had brought to the hospital. She never slept without it.

Christian's whole being filled with love as Lizzie leaned over and smoothed a few stray locks from Johanna's face. He wanted to do the same to the two soft curls that had sprung loose from Lizzie's bob, but he'd wait until later when they were alone together. He'd pull her close and kiss her and tell her how much she meant to him and . . .

He forced himself back to the room.

With a special smile at him, Lizzie squeezed Johanna's hand. "It's our favorite story too." Then she turned her attention to Johanna. "That's because you braved your own lion."

"I was brave, wasn't I?"

Christian cleared his throat, but his words still came out husky. "You certainly were. You faced every challenge."

"*Jah,* you did." Then Lizzie told the story and kissed Johanna again. "Good night, sweet one."

After they closed the door behind them, Christian took Lizzie in his arms. "You're a sweet one too."

She gazed up at him with adoration. "Can I say the same?"

"Well, I'd rather be the strong one or—" He never finished because Lizzie stood on tiptoe and pressed her lips to his. And he forgot what he'd planned to say.

Then she wove her fingers through his. "I want to give you an early Christmas gift."

He touched a fingertip to his still-warm lips. "You already did."

She laughed. "I have another one. Well, two, actually. But first, I want to put a surprise on Johanna's nightstand for when she wakes tomorrow."

Lizzie tugged on his hand and led him into the kitchen, where she lifted an upside-down cardboard box from the counter. Underneath was one of Rebecca's special poinsettia cakes like the one Lizzie had made him last year for their first Christmas together.

"That's for you." Lizzie gestured toward the cake. "It's to celebrate our first year together. And to remind you that we did things backwards. You asked me to marry you before we dated."

"I know. But I did ask you again in the spring. And you said *jah* both times."

"I'm so glad I did."

"So am I." He bent to kiss her again, but she pressed a hand against his chest to stop him. "I'll get too distracted to take Johanna's gift upstairs. Maybe you could wait in the living room by the fire."

"Don't take long."

"I won't." She removed a lion cupcake from the gas-powered refrigerator and hurried to Johanna's room.

His pulse quickened as her soft footfalls descended the staircase, heading toward him. How could he tell her how happy she made him every time she entered a room? How wonderful she made their life together? How much she meant to him?

Words failed him when she walked into the room. He stood and opened his arms. She came running toward him. Lizzie did everything with exuberance. She flung her arms around him and hugged him tightly.

He lowered his head to meet her lips, but once again she stopped him.

Breathlessly, she whispered, "First, I want to tell you something. Your second Christmas gift is"—she lowered her head and her voice, until he could barely hear her—"we're having a baby."

He could only stare at her.

"In the summer." Then she reached up and drew his mouth down to hers.

His heart full of wonder, Christian responded to her kiss, still dazed by her news and by God's goodness.

A healthy daughter. A beloved wife. A new baby. In addition to the birth of Christ, those had to be the most precious blessings of all. All the best Christmas presents ever.

The Christmas Cupcake

Loree Lough

This story is dedicated to all the teachers out there whose patience and commitment to duty helps students of all ages improve their lives and expand their horizons . . . especially those with reading difficulties.

Acknowledgments

A warm thank-you to Alma Mae Smithson, whose work with functionally illiterate adults has, for decades, inspired numerous "I can finally read!" stories. Thanks, too, to the Kensington editorial staff for inviting me to participate in this collection (with Shelley Shepard Gray and Rachel J. Good), and the talented design team that created the beautiful, reader-pleasing cover. Last, but certainly not least, heartfelt gratitude to God, for providing ideas, reliable equipment, and the time and energy to create this story.

Chapter 1

The cool November breeze riffled Bolt's silky black mane, and Noah finger-combed it back into place.

"Why does he have to wear these dumb blinders?"

Tessa set the brake, then joined her brother on the sidewalk. "Because without them, every bit of trash skittering around on the road would startle him."

"And cars, speeding past the buggy, too." He stroked the Clydesdale's forehead. "But still, they look uncomfortable."

For as long as she could remember, Noah had been more concerned with the feelings of others—even horses—than his own! The trait was proof that he had not inherited their father's meanness, and she thanked God for that every day.

"Know what else I don't understand?"

She grabbed her purse, thinking, *No, but I am sure you will tell me!*

"Why do we come all the way to Lancaster to buy cupcakes for your students when there is a perfectly good bakery at home?"

"Because here at Rebecca's Porch, whether my order is large

or small, I get the same friendly treatment." One hand on the brass doorknob, she said, "Will you come in with me?"

"I would rather keep Bolt company."

"He will appreciate that. How about some coffee for the ride home and a muffin for you to share with him?"

Noah pressed his cheek to the horse's. "Hear that, big fella? Tess is going to bring us a treat!"

The horse nickered and nuzzled Noah's neck.

She understood her brother's need to stand guard. It happened with less frequency lately, but terrifying memories kept them on alert. The young *Engles* seemed particularly fond of spooking horses, then standing back, laughing as terrified animals tore through the streets, destroying Amish buggies and flattening anything in their path. Some years back, Noah had watched helplessly as two horses were shot dead for upending tables and chairs in a sidewalk café and nearly trampling a few diners as well. The horrible scene woke him from deep sleep, even now.

Lord, watch over him and Bolt, she prayed, and stepped inside, where she was greeted by the tastebud-teasing scents of fresh coffee and hot-from-the-oven bread.

Jedediah Miller stood with brothers Asher and Reuben Stuery, each holding a black felt hat.

Three years ago, she'd purchased a storm-damaged buggy from Jed, then spent hours repairing torn seats and painting the body, and two weeks' pay for new wheels and brake and a triangular orange reflector fastened to the rear.

Jed stopped talking and waved her closer. "And how is the *maedel* with her very own buggy!"

His habit of calling all females *girl* frustrated some women—his wife included—but Tessa found it charming. "I am well. What brings you to Lancaster today?"

"Gertie must buy more yarn, which meant a trip to the bank."

Many people his age preferred larger, more established institutions, which meant doing business here in Lancaster rather than in Bird-in-Hand.

She glanced around. "Gertrude stayed home?"

"That woman has a one-track mind these days, cleaning, knitting, sewing to welcome the *kleinkind*. Any day now, I expect tiny quilts and clothes to spill from the windows!"

Asher joined his laughter. For years, Tessa had interacted with the younger Stuery brother at church services and town socials, but she'd never had occasion to hear him laugh this way. *I wouldn't mind hearing it again and again. . . .*

"Every day," Jed continued, "I say 'Gertie, it is one *bobbeli*, not three!' "

For years, it had been believed that Freda, Jed, and Gertie's only child, was barren, so this happy anticipation was a blessing for all to see.

"You could not convince her to join you?" Asher asked.

"Not even with the promise of sticky bread."

"Ah," Asher said, "so you will bring her some?"

"A double order!"

Asher leaned one elbow on the counter and faced Tessa. His left eyebrow lifted. So did the left corner of his mouth. "And what brings *you* here, girl with her very own buggy?"

If the Amish didn't view flirtation as inappropriate, she'd have said that was exactly what he was doing. And the possibility warmed her, toes to bonnet.

"I buy cupcakes every month, to celebrate student birthdays."

"How many in your class?"

"Thirty-eight."

"They *all* get a cupcake?"

"Those celebrating get a candle, but yes, everyone gets a cupcake."

"What about their teacher?"

Tessa was about to tell him that if any were left over, she took them home when Reuben said, "Where were you when *I* was in school?"

"In a cradle, I reckon," Jed put in.

As he snickered, the girl behind the counter said, "Miriam is icing your sticky buns. May I get anything more for you today?"

Jed handed her a ten-dollar bill. "One small *kaffi*, black." He winked at the brothers. "No sense bringing some to Gertie. It would be cold before I got home."

A streak of pink icing on her apron matched the girl's rosy cheeks. Tessa hadn't seen her before and read her nametag. "Are you new, Ruby?"

"I started two weeks ago. Pray for me that I will not grow fat and slow, eating broken cookies and day-old cake!"

"Oh, I am sure that all the work you do burns every calorie."

"God willing!" she said. "Now, how may I help you?"

Tessa gestured toward the brothers. "These gentlemen were here before me."

"We don't mind waiting," Asher said.

"Please," Tessa told Ruby, "take care of them first."

Jed picked up the bakery box and put on his hat. "See you in church!"

When he was gone, Ruby focused on Reuben. "And what may I get for you?"

"What think you, Brother?" He pointed at the menu board. "Sticky buns for the folks' visit with the Beamishes?"

Asher didn't answer right away. Hesitation gave way to confusion as he squinted at the long list of bakery items. Tessa had seen the same expression hundreds of times on her father's face as he attempted to make sense of—

"Well?" Reuben prodded.

Asher stood up straighter. "Streusel cake will go further. If there are any left, that is."

"Oh, yes," Ruby said. "We have apple and peach today."

Reuben nodded. "Good idea. Mamm can send the bishop and his wife home with a few slices, earn some brownie points." He looked at Ruby. "The peach streusel, please. And two chocolate whoopie pies."

While waiting for Ruby to fill his order, the remaining threesome exchanged idle chitchat. The chilly late fall weather. The prospect of snow. A *Budget* article about upcoming Thanksgiving and Christmas gatherings, and another featuring the new industrial plant on Route 30.

"How many men in our community will end up working there, do you think?" Asher asked.

"I saw Williams and Abrams there while filling out my application. They said others were thinking about it, too," Reuben said. "If God blesses me with a job, it will mean steady hours and company benefits. A good thing for Sarah and the boys."

Asher frowned slightly, then slapped a hand to the back of his neck.

Why the frown? Tessa wondered. Facing Reuben again, she asked, "What do they manufacture?"

"Metal railings, gates, horse stalls, stairs, and the like."

Asher's voice grew quieter, deeper, the way her father's did as slow anger churned in him. "You applied for a job there?" he grated. "This is news to me."

Reuben, arms crossed, said, "Since when do I need to run such things past you?" Asher's frown intensified, and Reuben continued with, "Take it easy. I will help in the woodshop, every chance I get. It is the least I can do, considering all you have done for Mamm and Daed."

"I can handle the workload alone. My concern is that you won't like factory work."

"If that is the case—and I hope it is not—I will quit."

That seemed to diffuse Asher's annoyance. *Good,* Tessa

thought, because she hadn't liked seeing the brothers at odds, even for a moment. Hadn't liked thinking that Asher, like her father, had a hair-trigger temper.

The girl boxed up the streusel and, while dropping two whoopie pies into a white paper bag, stated the amount due. Asher, Tessa noticed, not Reuben, paid the tab, and added the change to the tip jar beside the cash register.

"*Danke,*" Ruby said, then faced Tessa. "You are picking up cupcakes?"

"I am. Four dozen. I'd also like two raisin muffins and two cups of coffee."

Ruby disappeared into the back as the brothers made their way to the exit. Reuben was half in, half out the door when Asher said, "Will we see you on Sunday, Tessa?"

"How would it look for the teacher to miss services!"

"*Goed,*" he said. "And the gathering after?"

His expectant expression reminded her of the way the boys in her class looked, asking how much longer until the lunch recess.

"That is my plan."

"*Goed,*" he said again. "*Ik zie je daar.*"

Over the years, Tessa had likely heard "I will see you there" a hundred times, but the words had never sounded better.

She paid for the cupcakes, stacked the cartons, and shouldered her way outside.

"Warm in there, eh?" Noah said, relieving her of the packages.

"No, not especially." She helped him slide the containers onto the back seat. "Why?"

"Your cheeks are as pink as these boxes, that is why." He wiggled his eyebrows. "If not the heat of the oven, it must be because of something Asher said."

Denying it would be a lie. Admitting it would open her to a barrage of brotherly taunts.

"I need to go back inside to get our coffee and muffins. Are you and Bolt ready for the road?" Hopefully, the time gap would provide a much-needed distraction, because how could she explain her dreamy feelings about Asher when she didn't understand them, herself!

Five minutes later, as they rolled east on Old Philadelphia Road, Noah held the reins with one hand. "While you were inside, something odd happened. An *Englisher* wanted to peek into our buggy."

"Why?"

"He heard that some Amish buggies have battery-operated headlights, taillights, and turn signals, and wanted to see for himself."

She looked at the buttons, switches, levers, and retractable dual cup holder, designed, built, and installed by her brother. And he'd done it all while monitoring the massive wood-fired kiln that had, for generations, helped make Beachy Pottery a sought-after commodity.

"He was impressed, yes?"

Though Noah stared straight ahead, she could see his smile. "I believe so."

She broke off a chunk of her muffin and handed it to him.

Noah popped it into his mouth. "*Some* people thought the system would fail."

More than a year had passed since Noah had added the upgrades. He'd been so excited, showing their father what he'd accomplished, and so disheartened when Gideon had called the improvements a colossal waste of time, money, and materials.

"And some people should keep their opinions to themselves. These enhancements make night driving safer," she reminded him, "for us and for others on the road. I know of no one else who could have turned a bizarre collection of scraps into something so useful!"

Noah harrumphed, just as he had on the first anniversary of

their mother's death, when they'd gone to the cemetery to clear weeds from around the cold gray stone that said IDA BEACHY and the dates of her birth and death. "It looks clean and tidy," she had said. "Mamm would approve." He'd responded with an angry snort, and growled, "She would still be with us if not for *him*." That had been their one and only visit to the graveyard, and they'd never again discussed the cause of her death.

"So," Noah said, interrupting the dour memory, "Asher wants to see you on Sunday, eh?"

She gave him another piece of the muffin. "Have you taken up mind reading?"

"The bakery door was open just far enough for me to hear." He flashed a mischievous grin. "If you ask me, he is interested in you. A good sign."

I did not ask you. But the idea that Noah might be right piqued her curiosity. "A good sign? How so?"

"You have devoted your life to me and . . . *him*. You deserve to be happy, with someone who will love and protect you."

Noah's words took her back to a recent visit to this same Lancaster bakery, when a woman's melancholy voice had filtered down from the overhead speakers: ". . . *I hope he turns out to be, someone to watch over me* . . ." The lyrics and music should have soothed her. Instead, they'd conjured an image of her father, fists doubled menacingly at his sides, raging because she'd forgotten to stoke the kiln fire and nearly ruined an entire pottery order. Though Gideon hadn't hit her—yet—she'd wondered how long before he *would,* and asked herself if God would ever see fit to bless her with someone to watch over her.

She cleared her throat. "Asher asked me a simple question. Let's not read anything more into it."

"A man his age, still living with his *moeder en vader*?"

"But I thought he turned the unused barn on the property into a house of his own."

"He did. I have seen it. A good, solid place that keeps out the wind and rain, but it is a stone's throw from the Stuerys' house, so . . ." He chuckled. "Plus, it sorely needs a woman's touch."

From the corner of her eye, she saw him looking at her.

"*Your* touch, maybe."

"Noah, honestly." She smoothed her apron. "What kind of silly talk is this? I barely know the man."

"What's to know? He treats his family well. Earns an honest wage. Why, he is even kind to his horses. And his face would not exactly stop a clock."

The handsome face, the way Asher carried himself—straight back, chin up, eyes ahead as he focused on his destination—were but outward traits. Her father, even in his sixties, was a fine-looking man. *But when something—or some*one*—sounds too good to be true . . .*

"Street angel," she heard herself say, "house devil?"

"Like Daed, you mean." Noah sipped his coffee. "All the more reason to spend time with Asher, find out for yourself which controls him."

The angel or the devil . . .

"Mamm met Daed more than a year before they married. Do you think she saw signs that he could be brutal before the wedding?"

"Could be." Noah returned the cup to its holder.

"Then why would she have married him?"

"Maybe because, like so many women, she thought her love had the power to change him."

Solid advice, disguised as an opinion? In the bakery, Reuben had mentioned how much his brother had done for their parents. Added to what Noah had just said, and things she'd heard in passing—how he'd maintained the Stuerys' home, rebuilt the family business, taken the helm when a back injury forced their father's early retirement—were the good deeds a smokescreen that hid a sadistic streak?

Noah steered the buggy onto Route 23. "You have been lost in thought for a long time. What is on your mind?"

She sidestepped the question. "You still have not explained how Asher's simple question means he is . . . interested."

"Just a hunch." Noah shrugged. "But what if I'm right? What could it hurt to watch him, see how he behaves when things don't go his way?"

Their father's flare-ups most often happened under those very circumstances.

"Do you feel he is interested, then?" When Noah didn't respond right away, Tessa added, "Or that *I* am attracted to him?"

Ordinarily, her brother's laughter soothed her. Today, it did not.

"What I feel is irrelevant. What matters is that, one way or the other, you need answers to your questions."

Questions? Like the one that had surfaced in the bakery earlier, when Asher's barely concealed confusion seemed eerily similar to the way her father acted when asked to read anything?

"We will be home in a minute, Tess, and you have not even touched your muffin. Or your coffee."

"You can have them."

He patted his flat stomach. "Had my fill, but thanks."

"Then I will give them to Daed."

"To sweeten the sour mood he will be in when we get back later than expected?"

Every month when she announced her plans to buy cupcakes for her students, her father kicked up a fuss: Why waste money on spoiled children who should be home, working to help their parents? His outbursts were the main reason Tessa preferred Rebecca's Porch to the Bird-in-Hand bakery; what he didn't know couldn't hurt her *or* her impressionable pupils.

Now, as the *BEACHY POTTERY* sign came into view, she braced herself for another tirade. Yet again, the lovely song came to mind, and she wondered if the Almighty had inspired Asher's sudden interest in her.

Few things would make her happier, because oh how ready she was to have someone to watch over her!

Chapter 2

Asher gave each ratchet strap a hefty tug.

"Keep that up," Reuben said, "and those belts will leave permanent indentations in your boards."

"Better that than risk losing one."

"At those prices, I hear that!" Reuben climbed onto the wagon seat. "Plus, we have enough trouble with the *Englishers* without scattering two-by-fours along the road."

Asher joined him and gave the reins a gentle snap, setting the horses into motion.

After they'd gone a mile or so, Reuben took his whoopie pie from the white bakery bag. "How long before you will finish Mamm's chicken coop?"

"Now that I have all the materials, a day, maybe two."

"Need a hand?"

"You have enough to do at your place." Asher grinned. "Unless you are looking for an excuse to get away from home?"

"You know me too well. What time should I be there tomorrow?"

"It will be at least ten o'clock by the time I've finished my regular chores."

"Good. Time enough to complete mine and have breakfast with Sarah and the boys."

Since marrying Sarah, Reuben's typical good-natured demeanor had become even more evident, making Asher wonder if he'd ever feel as content with his own life.

"What is next on Mamm's list?" Reuben asked.

Lists required reading and writing, things Asher had spent a lifetime trying to avoid. "I hope there isn't one."

Snickering, Reuben elbowed Asher's ribs. "You know better than that. Day before yesterday, she brought cookies for the boys, told us to take care when we visit, because—"

"—there is a loose board on the front steps. I promised to fix it this week."

"Our mother has many good virtues, but patience is not one of them." Reuben used the whoopie pie as a pointer. "New shoes on your team?"

"Put them on last week."

"With everything else on your plate, why not let Moses do it? He is a farrier, after all."

"I enjoy the work. Plus, it saves money."

"I once heard Daed say that you pinch pennies so hard, Lincoln cries."

"Only once? I hear it every other day!"

They rode in companionable silence for a moment or two, and then Reuben said, "Looks like Salt and Pepper settled in quickly."

This past June, Asher had taken the train to Baltimore's Pimlico racetrack to meet with a well-known breeder of racehorses. The man introduced him to two purebred Arabians. Neither had won a race in more than a year, making them unsuitable as milers or studs, and the owner let both go for less than Asher had paid for the American Saddlebred that pulled his parents' buggy.

"One would think thoroughbreds would be high strung, but these are downright docile."

"No screaming crowds, no dusty racetracks. I think they are enjoying retirement," Asher said.

"Will you change their names?"

"To what?"

"Something less spicy," Reuben suggested.

"My brother the comedian," Asher kidded. "But no, they respond well to Salt and Pepper. I see no reason to confuse things."

Reuben polished off the last of his chocolate treat and dusted his hands together. "If that's how you feel, why did you flirt with Tessa Beachy?"

"What?" Asher turned slightly, studied his brother's face. "What are you talking about?"

Lips pursed, Reuben deepened his voice. " 'Will we see you on Sunday, Tessa, and the gathering after?' " he said, mimicking Asher's earlier questions.

"It was a simple, neighborly inquiry, nothing more," he grumbled.

"A good match, if you ask me."

I did not ask you, Asher thought. And yet curiosity made him ask, "A good match?"

"You have to admit, she is easy on the eyes. Hard-working, caring, and smart, too. What more could a man ask for?"

Asher's brain locked onto the word *smart,* and he asked himself what a woman like Tessa would see in a man who'd never learned—

"On Sunday, invite her to take a walk with you."

Many times before they announced their intention to marry, Asher had seen Reuben and Sarah hurry toward the path that encircled the churchyard. Visible to anyone who chose to look, the walkway was close enough to satisfy those who believed in proper chaperoning, yet far enough to guarantee couples the privacy to discuss just about anything.

"There are at least two places where you can disappear from view. You know, in case you've a mind to sneak a quick kiss."

One glance at Reuben's wistful expression made it clear . . . his brother's thoughts had taken him back to the days when *he'd* taken full advantage of those places. It also sparked an image of Tessa: tiny, trim, acorn-colored hair and eyes that couldn't decide if they were brown or green, with a smile that lit every dark corner of his heart. Under the right circumstances, Asher would consider himself blessed to sneak a quick kiss!

"Just do it."

"Do what?" Asher moved the reins from his right hand to the left.

"Spend time in her company. Get to know her. And if you still want her in your life, pray about it. And then, should it be God's will . . ."

"What gives you the impression I want her in my life?"

"Could it be that you barely took your eyes off her while we were in the bakery, looking like a lost pup, might I add?"

Asher sat back. "No, I didn't." He removed his hat, ran a hand through his hair. "Did I?"

" 'Fraid so, li'l brother."

Asher jammed the hat back onto his head. "Then I guess it is a good thing the bakery wasn't busy this morning."

"Relax, Ash. I noticed that Tessa was too busy watching Noah through the window to notice where you were looking."

"Come to think of it, I noticed that, too."

"What did you make of it?"

"Just being cautious, I suppose. Not that I blame her. Those scars are still visible on his face."

About this time last year, a group of *Englisher* teens had attacked Noah, stealing the cash he'd just withdrawn from the bank. The officers who'd responded to the teller's frantic phone call put a stop to the attack, but not before one of the boys had shoved Noah through the plate glass window. He'd refused to press charges, which only emboldened the teens, who'd stepped up their bullying of the Amish who visited Lancaster. If not for a council mandate, making such harassment illegal, the assaults might be taking place still.

"Never saw rowdy young'uns in Bird-in-Hand," Reuben said, "or I might have blamed them for Ida Beachy's welts."

It had long been suspected that Ida's husband had caused her cuts and welts, but there wasn't much anyone could do—not even the bishop or church elders—when Ida persistently blamed her own clumsiness for the injuries.

"Think he ever strikes at Tessa?" Asher quickly added, "Or Noah?"

"Who?"

"Your feet don't fit a limb," Asher kidded. "Gideon Beachy, that's *who.*"

"If he has, this wise old owl hasn't seen evidence of it." One shoulder lifted. "But then, long sleeves, trousers, and skirts can hide a lot."

Asher reflected on that for a few minutes, and Reuben broke the ensuing silence with, "What is going on in that head of yours?"

"Can't think of a reason Gideon would strike Ida. She was never anything but pleasant."

"Closed doors and windows can hide a lot, too."

"Especially in houses that sit far from the road, as the Beachy's does."

"Careful, Brother."

"Careful? Why?"

"If anything improper is going on over there, *that*"—using

his chin as a pointer, Reuben indicated Asher's fist, doubled-up on his knee—"will solve nothing."

Asher followed Reuben's gaze and relaxed the hand—not an easy feat, because the very thought of anyone harming Tessa—

"Most you can do is pray."

"Yes, that is the neighborly thing to do."

Reuben's burst of laughter surprised him. "Gideon could be abusing Tessa, and you find it *humorous*?"

"Of course not, but your overprotective reaction is. What do you know about her?"

He thought she was lovely, but beyond that, Asher knew very little about Tessa Beachy.

"My advice stands, Ash: Get to know her. Who knows? The *wife* you save may be your own!"

This time, the laughter was anything but quiet.

"I believe something has addled your brain." Asher couldn't help smiling as he said it, because imagining himself married to Tessa was a pretty picture indeed.

The windup alarm on Tessa's bedside table clanged, and woke her with a start. "Some mornings, I would like to throw you against the wall," she told it, and pushed the Off button. Four thirty never felt less pleasant than on frosty autumn mornings, when the cold nights clung tight to the house, sneaking through windows and stealing every degree of warmth.

She hit her knees, shivering as she said her morning prayers, then hurried downstairs to stoke the parlor's woodstove fire. In the kitchen, she hopped from one foot to the other while preparing the percolator. "Should have put on your slippers. This floor is like ice!"

"Talking to yourself again?"

"Good grief, Noah, you scared me half to death!"

"Didn't mean to." Stretching, he hid an expansive yawn behind a big hand. "Did you sleep well?"

"If you call tossing and turning half the night sleeping well, yes." Tessa laughed. "My own fault. I stayed up far too late, reading about the history of Bird-in-Hand."

"Ah, a lesson for your scholars, eh? I remember writing a long, boring paragraph about it, even drew a picture of the ramshackle inn that inspired its name."

"As if I could forget!" Tessa slid the napkin holder aside and exposed the impression of his heavy-handed drawing of William McNabb's crude hut, still visible on the table's surface.

He rubbed his backside. "And I'll never forget the paddling I got when Mamm saw it!"

"Yes, but seeing your talent, she suggested Daed put you to work, painting designs on the pottery."

Wincing, Noah flexed his right hand. "I must find a way to earn my own living."

"Oh? Thinking of taking a wife, are you?"

Both eyebrows rose toward his hairline. "You must be joking!"

"Why would you need your own money, except to support a family?"

"So I could retire."

"At age twenty? Now who is joking!"

He pretended to hold a paintbrush. "How will I work if arthritis cripples me before I turn thirty?"

"I had not thought of it that way." She hugged him. "Poor Noah."

"*Veel verdriet, zuster*," he said, stepping back. "The floor isn't the only thing that is cold as ice."

She hugged herself to fend off the chill. "Would you be a dear and check the fire while I get dressed?"

Hands on her shoulders, he turned Tessa to face the kitchen doorway. "Gladly. Now go, get warm."

"Pancakes for breakfast?"

"With berries?"

"If I can find any in the freezer."

"I will look. Which reminds me, I need to check the propane gauge. With all the baking you have been doing lately, the tank is probably close to empty."

Tessa wasted no time slipping into her dress, winding her hair into a snug bun, and putting on her shoes. "One day soon," she muttered, grabbing one of two black caps from the shelf in her closet, "I hope to trade you for a white one!"

Of course, that meant getting married, and, at twenty-five, the prospect looked less and less likely.

As she stepped into the hall, she thought of Noah's claim that Asher was interested in her.

"Less likely, unless . . ."

"Unless what?" Gideon asked, joining her at the top of the stairs.

An honest answer would invite a stern lecture. *Why spoil a perfectly good morning?* she thought.

"*Goedemorgen*, Daed. You slept well, I hope?"

He rotated his left shoulder. "As well as can be expected."

She started down the stairs. *For a man who beat his wife to death, you mean?* On the landing, she said, "I am making pancakes for breakfast, with blueberries, if Noah found any in the freezer."

"Make mine plain."

"Why are you rubbing your chest?"

"Should have closed the window. The cold air left me stiff and sore."

"Warm up by the woodstove. I will call you when your plain pancakes are ready."

"Bring me coffee."

And as she entered the kitchen, Tessa prayed that God would hide her look of displeasure when he found it too strong, or too weak.

Mercifully, he didn't complain. Didn't eat, either, and left the house without a word.

"What's his problem this morning?" Noah asked.

"He said the breeze from his open window made him achy."

Her brother carried his plate to the sink. "Need a hand with these?"

"Your timing is impeccable," she teased as his plate disappeared into the sudsy water. "The rest of the dishes are already washed."

"Now, be nice, and I might help with the supper dishes." He slipped into his jacket. "I'm going to town to order feed for the critters. Want me to drop you off on my way in?"

"Definitely!" The ride would cut ten minutes from her trip to the schoolhouse. Ten minutes she could spend firing up the woodstove, and filling both six by eight-feet chalkboards with age-appropriate lessons.

After stowing her schoolbag at her desk, Tessa lit all three lanterns. It took three back-and-forth trips from the woodpile to the inside bin to stack enough logs to last the day. Weeks-old, crinkled copies of *The Budget* went into the stove's belly, followed by bark chips and twigs, topped off with small branches. One strike of a kitchen match was enough then to start it roaring. Then she opened the partition that separated grades one through four from five through eight. Halfway through her first year as the community's teacher, she'd installed it in the hope of cutting down on visual distractions. A thick wire, strung near the ceiling, became a makeshift curtain rod, and stitched-together white bedsheets were turned into a curtain. And if she did say so herself, it had more than served its purpose.

Tessa rolled up the shades, and, just like every morning for nearly four years, she marveled as the sun's first rays sparked over the horizon, painting a shimmering backdrop for crimson barns and silvery silos that nestled in lush valleys. Iddo Roltz's dairy cows plodded along at a leisurely pace, seeking fertile pastures, while Collin Albrecht's colts frolicked among contented stallions and mares. If only the children were here to see God's majesty, displayed like fine artwork!

But, why couldn't they! An idea was spawned, and she could hardly wait for them to arrive so that she could put it into play. . . .

The grandfather clock in the corner pealed, filling the room with seven gentle, mellow notes. Tessa crossed the room to wind it for the day, and thought of the morning when Silas Driscoll had delivered the gift. He'd held the children captive with his Tale of Time: "If you lose money," he'd said, "you can make more. When one meal ends, there is always another. Land and houses and horses can be bought and sold, over and over again, but time? Time is a gift from God, and once it's gone, it can never be recovered." Silas had made eye contact with each child before concluding the lecture with, "So be sure to spend it wisely!"

Right about now, some of those wide-eyed students were hurrying to finish their homework assignment—a paragraph describing the perfect Thanksgiving—while others completed household chores. They were honest and good, respectful and hardworking, from the first to the last. Before they knew it, they'd grow into steadfast, God-fearing men and women, and Tessa was as proud as if they'd been her own flesh and blood.

She dropped onto the squeaking seat of her wooden desk chair and opened her schoolbag. Her Bible, right on top, fell open to an oft-read passage: " 'And whenever you stand praying, forgive, if you have anything against anyone, so that your Father in heaven may forgive you your trespasses.' "

It is a marvel that you haven't worn the print from the page, she thought, tracing the tearstained words. God promised mercy, even to those like her, who harbored bitter suspicion in their hearts. How long, she wondered, before the burden of resentment was lifted, so that she could forgive her father for his part in her mother's death?

But this was no lesson for children. Tessa flipped the nearly transparent pages, and found the perfect verse. She always enjoyed her students, but thanks to her idea, she had a new reason to look forward to their appearance.

Soon, Sam Müller would pull up out front. His offer to pick up children who lived on the outskirts of town saved them a three-mile walk, and gave Sam an opportunity to show off the horse and buggy he'd paid for with his own earnings. Something told Tessa the resourceful boy would go far!

Thirty minutes before the bell rang, the double doors opened with a *whoosh,* and in walked Hamm Tobias and his son Daniel. She didn't know which one looked most upset.

"*Goedemorgen,* Tessa. I have come to talk with you about Dan'l, here."

His son's puffy, red-rimmed eyes told her he'd been crying.

"Daniel is one of my best scholars, a good example to the others, turning his work in on time, returning every borrowed book, never speaking out of turn, and willingly helping the younger students." She smiled at the boy. "Why, I would not be the least bit surprised if someday he became a teacher himself!"

But the more she talked, the harder Hamm frowned. "Just came to tell you face to face: he is finished with school."

Daniel hung his head. It happened all too often, and, although Tessa prayed for a way to stop it, the practice of putting children to work continued. Parents were sensible, though, allowing children to remain in school long enough to learn to read, write, add, and subtract. Those skills, they reasoned, were beneficial in any line of work. Unfortunately, many thought science, history, geography, and literature were not. So Tessa lost no fewer than five students a year—boys, mostly—to the community's shops, factories, and fields.

"What if I bring books and classwork to your house a few

times a week and work with Daniel there, so he will not fall behind?"

"Nah. He will be too busy, earning a living."

"If I promise the lessons will not interfere with his job, may I—"

"His *job,*" Hamm interrupted, "is adding to the family coffers." He softened his tone slightly to add, "Your motives are pure; I realize this. But *you* must realize that if his mother and I did not need him, we would not have made this decision."

She wanted to say something to comfort Daniel and reassure Hamm, but feared adding fuel to an already fiery situation.

Hamm cleared his throat. "The rest of the children will arrive soon, so we must go. Thank you for all you have done for my son." He gave the boy a gentle shove.

"Thank you, Miss Beachy."

"It was my privilege, getting to know you these past four years. I look forward to seeing you in town and at church." Oh, how she wanted to add that he could stop by, any time, to borrow a book, ask a question, or just talk!

A faint smile brightened his face, and he nodded. She followed them to the door, and, as they rode away, saw Daniel throw another half-hearted smile over his shoulder.

If there had been time, Tessa might have sat down and wept for the boy who never missed school. But when the rest of the children showed up, they'd wonder why Daniel had been forced by necessity to end his education. Somehow, she had to help them understand and accept that even disappointment like this was God's will.

If she could do that, perhaps she could then apply that same perspective to her own life, and cope with the fact that Asher might never be more than a neighbor.

Chapter 3

With the holy kisses and hand shaking finished, the Stuery men sat shoulder to shoulder, fifth bench from the front, as they had for as long as Asher could remember. Facing them on the other side of the church sat the Stuery women and Reuben's youngest son. After a brief opening prayer, the preachers filed out to seek God's counsel, and the rest of them sang.

Some held copies of the *Ausbund,* and others sang the German hymns from memory. The blend of voices, old and young, high and low, created a pleasing, harmonic resonance that pulsed within the little church. Only the *vorsinger*'s notes stood out, but just for the few seconds it took to begin each line.

Asher sneaked a peek at Tessa, two rows from the back. It took self-control to suppress a smile at the way she looked, chin up and eyes closed, lips barely moving as she sang. It took even greater self-control to look away. *If we held services in one another's homes,* he thought, *I could* hear *her sing, too.*

Nearly three hours had passed before the congregants filed into the basement, talking and laughing as the women set out colorful tablecloths and piled-high bowls of food. What a relief it was that the community had set aside the rule that put men and boys on one side of the space, women and children on the other. It did Asher's heart good to see whole families crowded around the long folding tables, nourished as much by one another as the eats.

He scanned the room, disappointed when he didn't see her. Since she'd been the main reason he'd agreed to attend the after-worship gathering, Asher said a quick good-bye to his family and climbed the concrete steps that led up to the parking lot . . .

. . . and nearly ran smack-dab into her.

"Tessa! How good to see you."

Ducking into the collar of her coat, she smiled self-consciously. "I forgot my contribution," she said, showing him the napkin-covered pies balanced on each palm, "and had to go home to get them." She stood on tiptoe to peer over his shoulder. "They haven't started eating yet, I hope."

"The blessing has been said, but the food line has barely formed."

A cold gust slipped under one blue and white-checked cover, causing its corners to flutter, exposing a fork-pricked *A* in the crust. Causing her to shiver, too.

"Let me help with those, so you can get out of the wind. Are they both apple?"

"This one is," she said, handing it to him, "and this is peach."

Asher held the door. "Peach," he repeated. "My second favorite."

Tessa led the way and didn't stop until she reached the dessert table, and placed hers among chocolate- and white-frosted cakes, pans of brownies, plates of fudge and cookies, and berry cobblers.

"I am tempted to start my meal right here," she said.

"If you do, I will, too."

A tiny sigh escaped her lips. "Ah, but a schoolteacher must set a good example for her scholars."

He scanned the room, looking for the boys and girls she'd taught to add and subtract, and read and write. He envied them a little, but put it aside as she helped herself to a napkin, paper plate, and plastic flatware.

"Where is your family?" she asked, and served herself a portion of green beans.

"Over near the windows. Yours?"

Tessa had just scooped up a serving spoon of potato salad, and paused before dropping it onto her plate. "Noah and my father, they . . . they could not make it."

He hadn't seen them in church, but then, he'd been too busy sneaking peeks at her to really notice. But with her family strangely absent, where would she sit?

"Why don't you join us for the meal? I know my mother and sister-in-law would love spending time with a woman, surrounded by men and boys as they so often are."

"You know, I have always wanted to get to know them better, so thank you, I will take you up on the offer." Tessa moved down the table, adding ham, a chicken thigh, a golden biscuit to her plate. "You aren't eating, Asher?"

He quickly grabbed a plate and a fork. "What do you think of all these throwaway items?"

She looked up at him. "Well, I suppose they save time. Save the ladies' stoneware from chips. Saves them having to wash tablecloths and napkins. And lessens the chance that silverware will accidentally end up in the trash. So I suppose they are all right."

"But . . ."

Tessa looked left, right, took a step closer, and whispered, "But I miss the clink of forks on plates and the clank of spoons, stirring sugar into coffee mugs."

"You know, I feel the same way. But then, I have never been expected to clean up afterward."

"Believe it or not, I miss that, too. There was something comforting about being with the women, collecting the plates and flatware, then standing side by side to wash and dry them, and giggling as we tried to decide who brought what."

He tried to imagine her that way: Tessa, giggling. But if his heart beat quicker just envisioning it, maybe it was best he couldn't see the real thing.

They squeezed between the tables, and, when he reached his family, Asher announced, "Look who I found, filling a plate. Her father and brother could not attend, so I asked her to join us."

Reuben got to his feet, picked up his plate and fork, and stepped into the aisle. "Sit here, Tessa, so that you and Mamm and Sarah won't have to cross-talk."

"Yes, please do," his mother agreed, clearing the space of biscuit crumbs.

"And this gives me a chance to talk with you," Sarah said, "to find out what Paul needs before going to school next fall."

While the women laughed and chatted, Reuben and Asher sat on either side of their father and exchanged a quick but concerned glance. Not quick enough to escape Adam's notice, however.

"Something I ought to know about, boys?"

Stuery & Sons Contracting had, for generations, been a family-only business, and their father had been none too pleased when he'd learned that his eldest son might soon leave it to work at the new factory. But they'd covered that ground and didn't want to go over it again, here.

"Nothing that can't wait," Reuben said, and, with a nod toward the rest of the family, hinted that he didn't want to discuss the subject now.

Their father's voice was little more than a whisper when he

said, "So it is not about Asher's interest in the pretty young lady over there?"

Relief relaxed Reuben's serious expression. Asher, on the other hand, didn't feel much like talking about his feelings for *the pretty young lady over there*.

His nephew stepped up to ask if he planned to attend the baseball game.

"What game?"

Peter's eyebrows rose. "Didn't you see the signs we put up? There must be a million of 'em, all over town!"

Yes, Asher had seen a few posters, tacked to porch posts and bulletin boards, but as usual, he'd walked right past them. Why stop, pretend to read, and risk someone asking his opinion on the subject?

"It begins as soon as the social ends," the boy said, "and I hope to be the starting pitcher!"

"Just . . . hope?"

Peter pouted. "I am not as tall as the rest, not as strong, either. But I have been throwing a ball into a bushel basket that I nailed to the back side of the shed. I get it in nearly every time, so if they give me a chance, I will show them."

"But, Son," Reuben said, "you are the youngest boy. Most of the others are eight or ten. It's nothing personal."

It seemed plenty personal to Peter, as evidenced by his frown. Then, suddenly, he grinned. "Say, I have an idea!"

Oh, this should be interesting, Asher thought.

"Will you fill in for Thomas's father, Ash?"

"Fill in?" Asher pictured John Plank, tall and loud and big around as a barrel. "Doing what?"

"He is our umpire. Without him, it won't be a game; it will just be practice. There are enough of us to split into two teams, and Sam's father promised ice cream for all of us, with sprinkles for the winners. There can be no winners if there is not an actual *game!*"

"That is quite a dilemma. But why can't John do it?"

"Hurt his back, baling hay."

"That is a shame." Asher leaned forward to better see Reuben. "And *your* father cannot step in because . . ."

Thanks, Reuben mouthed, *thanks a lot.*

Before Reuben could think up an excuse, Tessa said, "Oh, you should do it, Asher. I love baseball, don't you?"

Was it sunlight, pouring through the tall, narrow windows that made her eyes glitter like diamond dust, or had he completely lost his mind?

"You will be there?"

"Many of the boys are in my class, so . . ."

Another image formed in his mind: Tessa, on the sidelines, rosy-cheeked and clapping mittened hands, exhaling vapor into the cold air as she cheered for her boys. *How will you concentrate on the game, looking at* that *sight*!

"Why are you staring at Miss Beachy that way?"

"What way?"

"Like, well, I cannot explain it. But she will be my teacher soon, you know."

In other words, *stop staring at Miss Beachy!* He could count on one hand the number of children he knew who were as bright and well-spoken as his nephew, and have fingers left over. Sarah and Reuben spent countless hours with their children, talking, answering questions, reading, and it showed in the way they communicated. *If only he was less perceptive,* Asher thought.

"The game starts soon, you say?"

Peter did a little dance. "Does that mean you will do it?"

Asher drew his nephew into a sideways hug. "How can I say no with you standing there, looking like a boy who just got a new pony?"

From the corner of his eye, he saw Tessa's smile of approval.

And how could I say no, knowing how much she wanted to hear yes?

"Thanks, Ash. You are the best uncle in all of Bird-in-Hand!" Peter darted off, ran backward a few steps while adding, "Just wait 'til I tell the others that *I* got us an umpire. They will *have* to let me pitch now!"

As Peter joined the other boys at the dessert table, Asher looked across at Tessa, who was laughing at something his mother had said, laughing again at Sarah's response to it. *You must be losing your mind,* he thought, because in this latest vision, he pictured her sharing birthdays and holidays with his family, not as a Beachy, but as one of them.

Tessa stood, and his mother said, "Oh, you are not leaving already, are you?"

"Yes, but only for a while. I have some reading to do."

"Good, because I think Peter would like you to watch his game." She caught Asher's attention and, wiggling her eyebrows, said, "I think my son would like that, too."

Tessa blinked a few times before meeting his eyes. "Thank you for inviting me to join your family. I can't remember when I have enjoyed a social more."

She hadn't been gone more than a few minutes when Adam said, "My son, the umpire."

"*Humph.* Just this once."

"My son, the *naïve* umpire."

Asher didn't get it, and said so.

"You are on the list."

"What list?"

Reuben snickered. "The one that marks you available for who knows what."

Not a problem, he thought. If someone asked him to volunteer for something he didn't want to do, he'd politely decline.

"*You should do it, Asher,*" she'd said.

Oh yeah, he'd politely decline, all right, unless that someone was Tessa.

Tessa stood at the sink, staring out the window and absent-mindedly washing pie pans.

She saw that Noah had mowed this afternoon, and the cut grass now spread out from the house to the tree line like a shaggy blanket. The row of arborvitae separating the yard from the animal pens had grown to fifteen feet tall. *Big difference from when you taught me how to plant them, isn't it, Mamm?*

Oak, maple, and birch leaves—each its own vibrant shade of yellow, orange, or red—nestled between the blades of grass. The trees released still more, some turning in lazy somersaults as they sailed toward the ground, while others, like one-winged butterflies, flitted left and fluttered right before silently coming to rest.

Autumn, her mother's favorite time of year. Oh, how she'd loved watching as trees' branches went from fat and green to brown and bare. "They are teaching us," she'd say, "how lovely it can be to let go."

But letting go isn't *lovely, Mamm,* Tessa thought. *Not when you miss someone the way I miss you.*

If Ida had lived, what advice would she have given her only daughter, who found herself hopelessly enamored of Asher Stuery?

"You keep scrubbing that pan, you will wear a hole in it."

Tessa flinched. "Do I need to put a bell around your neck, Noah Beachy?"

"Sorry if I startled you again. Thought sure you heard the door close behind me."

"We missed you at the social."

"We?"

She nodded at the plastic-wrapped plates and bowls on the

table. "Sarah and Rose Stuery sent a few things for you and Daed, and I saved you some pie."

"How fortunate, because I'm famished." He slid a plate from the stack in the cupboard. "I trust you had a good time?"

"I sat with the Stuery family, got better acquainted with them." She rinsed the pan. "Funny how you can live among people for years and not really know them."

"And now that you do, what is your verdict?"

"Brother dear, if you had been born an *Englisher,*" she joked, "I think you might be a lawyer. But yes, I like them."

"One in particular. Admit it. I am right."

"Where is Daed?" With any luck, the question would side-track Noah. "I have not seen him since breakfast."

"Out walking, I suppose. Or embarking on another of his secret adventures." Noah smirked, helped himself to a forkful of ham. "Why? Do you miss him, too?"

Facing the sink again, she rinsed the second pan. *Shouldn't you feel guilty for* not *missing him?* Over the years, Gideon had often lit out for places unknown, staying away from home as long as a week at a time, putting his workload on her mother, Noah, and herself. During his first disappearances, she'd stayed up night after night, pacing and praying. Unnecessarily, as it turned out, for God had brought her father home, disheveled and bleary-eyed, but safe.

Noah bit into a buttered biscuit.

"If he stays away for more than a few days, I can lend a hand in the shop."

"Thanks, Tess, but I should be fine."

He recovered the food, put the plates and bowls into the fridge. "By the way, I checked the propane levels. We won't need a refill for at least two weeks."

"Good. That means I can restock the freezer. Is there plenty of gasoline for the generator, too, just in case?"

"Now, now, have I ever *not* watched over you properly?"

Someone to watch over me . . .

Tessa stacked the pie plates and carried them to the sideboard. While putting them away, she noticed her mother's serving platter. Tessa hugged it to her bosom.

"What is that?" Noah wanted to know.

"Mamm's favorite platter."

"Favorite?" he echoed. "Then why did she never use it?"

Tessa explained how the platter and matching soup tureen had been part of the first dinnerware set fired by Beachy Pottery. She turned it over, so he could see the familiar hallmark . . . a curlicue *BP* inside an imperfect circle, and, beneath it, numbers that identified color and style codes and date of manufacture: 1921.

"Where is the rest of the set?"

"Daed's tantrums."

"He destroyed everything, except for the platter?"

Tessa returned it to the cabinet. "And the soup tureen. Mamm hid them."

"Makes no sense, does it, that she cared more about protecting the Beachy name than Daed?"

"We will never understand him, not if we live to the age of Methuselah."

He shook his head. "Peaceful without him here, isn't it?" Noah pulled out a kitchen chair. "Sit, have some pie and coffee with me."

Sensing his need to talk, Tessa sat and listened. It had taken hours, he said, to arrange delivery of enough firewood to power the kiln, and he'd spent hours more feeding the big oven, and monitoring the dampers. He'd processed, packed, and shipped five orders of dinnerware to buyers in nearby states, and, although he much preferred working with the clay and painting designs, completed the bookwork, too.

"The man who presumes the worst about everyone," he said, "trusts me to do all the banking."

"What choice does he have, when he refuses to learn to read or write?"

A dry chuckle prefaced Noah's comeback: "Thanks for the vote of confidence!"

"You know I didn't mean it that way. I only meant—"

"It was a joke, Tess." He sipped the coffee. "Cold," he said, grimacing. "Bleh."

"Let me make another pot."

Noah carried their plates and mugs to the sink. "Instead, tell me about your time with Asher."

"Oh, we talked some."

"So, no walk around the path?"

"The only walking we did took us from the food table to his family's table."

"Too bad. But there is time."

"For what?"

"To get acquainted with him. And just so you know? I don't think he has anything in common with Daed." Noah worked the kinks from his neck. "If you need me, I will be at the shop."

"But I thought you finished this week's orders!"

"I will be reading, not working."

"The good book?"

"The ledger book, which—if I find Daed's bookkeeping error—will hopefully allow us to give generously next time the church asks for a donation." He started out the door. "What will you do with the rest of your day?"

"I promised to watch the boys play baseball."

"Sounds like fun. I might join you later." He winked. "Unless my being there will cramp your style."

"Noah! Is that any way to talk!" She wagged a finger at him. "See what happens when you skip Sunday services?"

Laughing, he made his way outside, leaving her with a jumble of thoughts. Of Asher and his apparent struggle to read posters about the ball game. The annoyance he'd exhibited at Rebecca's Porch. Too much like her father?

Much as she yearned for a loving marriage and a home of her own, filled with children—the gifts of that love—she'd rather spend the rest of her days alone than chained to a bully like her father.

Chapter 4

Guilt, Tessa decided, had motivated her to make her father's preferred breakfast: sausage gravy and biscuits. He'd returned the evening before, but his delight did little to blot the bitter memories of the way he'd mistreated her mother, which had kept her up half the night.

The meal happened to be a favorite of Noah's, too, and watching him devour every bite sweetened the bitterness, just a little.

"Tasted good," he said. "How was the ball game?"

"Oh, you should have been there. Peter's teammates let him pitch the last inning, and they won by one run."

"That li'l pipsqueak pitched a winning inning? Well, I'll be." Noah turned a page in *The Budget.* "And how did ol' Asher fare in his umpire role?"

She pictured him, crouching behind home plate, elbow resting on a knee, straightening only to call "Safe!" or "Out!" It was such a delightful image that she barely noticed her father's scowl.

"He did well. So well that I fear he will be asked to do the job again."

"Good man," Noah said, turning another page.

"You know how I feel about having that thing on the table," Gideon snarled.

"Between work at the shop and work around here, this is the only time I have to read it."

"I will not stand for excuses. Besides, why fill your mind with that drivel? Nothing in the thing but gossip and recipes and photographs of women, bragging about their latest quilt. Not even an obituary, so friends can send condolences."

Noah carried his dishes to the sink. "They print obituaries," he said under his breath, "which you'd know if you could read."

Tessa cringed, hoping their father hadn't heard the snide remark.

Gideon crumpled the paper. "Gibberish," he said, and threw it into the trash, "good for nothing but cleaning fish."

"But Daed," Noah said, "it provides a means of communication for us. We have chosen to live Plain. No television, no computers, no Internet, and telephones only if absolutely necessary for business purposes."

"Who are you to question centuries of tradition!"

"I was not questioning it, Daed, merely pointing out that the paper serves a useful purpose."

"Wasting time is not the Amish way."

"Oh, but years of bullying your wife *is*?"

Dear Lord, Tessa prayed, *for his own sake, silence him, please!*

Gideon got up so fast that his chair crashed to the floor. He crossed the room in five heavy steps and stood, trembling with rage, nose to nose with his only son. Despite the fury burning in their father's eyes, Noah continued his rant.

"The Bible says 'Husbands, love your wives, and do not be harsh with them.' And 'Live with your wives in an understanding way.' And yet you beat Mamm bloody on a regular basis, caused the internal bleeding that killed her. So spare me your talk about tradition and the Amish way."

"I am your father," Gideon roared, "and you will *not* speak to me that way!" His fist connected, and Noah staggered, regained his balance as the arm was raised again.

Tessa moved between them. "Stop, Daed. No more of this, please."

But the blow landed hard on her cheek, would have knocked her to the floor if Noah hadn't caught her.

Stunned by the sight of his children battered by his own hand, Gideon turned on his heel and walked away.

"Noah, you are bleeding." Tessa led him to the sink, hands shaking as she pressed a clean, cool cloth to his upper lip, then took him back to the table, where they sat, inspecting each other's injuries.

"How will you explain a black eye to the children?" he asked, voice muffled by the towel.

"And how will you explain a fat lip to the workers?"

He shook his head. "I have to leave."

"They can get along without you for a few more minutes. You need time to settle your nerves, wash the blood from your face, and change your shirt."

Noah looked down, and, seeing the red spatters on his shirt, said it again: "I have to leave, to find someplace else to live."

"What! Where would you go?"

"I can stay at the shop until I figure it out."

She exhaled a relieved sigh. "You will stay here in Bird-in-Hand, then?"

"Yes. I have to. I can't leave you here alone with him."

Noah got up, started pacing, pounding his right fist into his left palm. "He does not know that I heard, but several large companies have offered to buy Beachy Pottery. When Daed returned from that last disappearance and put the company in my name, he said . . ." He scrubbed a hand over his face. "I could sell it. Bank enough money so that he could take care of himself, use the rest to give us a new start. Ohio. Indiana. Anywhere but here."

Leave her students? The only home she'd ever known? *And* Asher?

Who but a fool falls boots over bonnet for a man she barely knows! Things had been bad in the past, but never this bad. Like it or not—and she did not—Noah might be right about leaving Bird-in-Hand.

"Once the school board members see my face, they will jump to conclusions—the worst conclusions—and assume this will happen again. What choice will they have but to replace me?"

She'd never been one to give in to tears of self-pity, but Tessa gave in to them now.

"Aw, now, please stop that." Noah unfolded the cloth, found a clean, blood-free corner, and dabbed at her tears.

"Ouch."

"Sorry. The eye hurts, huh?"

"I will live."

"This is all my fault. I knew better than to speak to him that way, but I, just, things . . ." Jaw clenched tight, he shook his head and started over. "I don't want you to worry. I made the mess; I will clean it up. When he comes back, I will apologize. Grovel, if need be. That should smooth his ruffled feathers. Then we will steer clear of him until we figure things out."

"I have a feeling we will ask God's forgiveness a lot in the next few days."

"What? Why?"

"When people ask what happened, we will have to lie."

"Good thing for us, then, that He understands how weak and stupid we humans can sometimes be."

Tessa exhaled a shaky breath, and prayed for strength. For endurance and patience. And forgiveness for any untruths she and Noah might utter in the next days to protect themselves.

"As long as you will be in town to pick up lumber . . ."

Asher tensed, because every time his mother started a sentence that way, it meant she was about to ask him to do something he'd rather not, like hanging curtains or rearranging furniture.

"Stop by the market on your way home, will you? I am nearly out of sugar and flour. Cinnamon and vanilla, too."

He relaxed. Picking up a few kitchen staples was preferable to sweeping cobwebs from the root cellar or swabbing the outhouse!

After hitching the wagon alongside the store, Asher checked the straps that held the lumber in place, and, satisfied it wouldn't shift, made his way straight to the baking aisle. What a pleasant surprise, seeing Tessa there, reaching for a can of cocoa on a high shelf.

"Let me get that for you," he said, handing it to her.

"Thanks," she said, and added it to the shopping cart that overflowed with noodles, rice, honey, and baking supplies.

"Stocking up for the winter?"

"Something like that."

Admittedly, he didn't know her well, but it seemed out of character that she wouldn't look at him. Her voice sounded slightly gravelly, and he thought it odd that she'd worn a black bonnet, the kind with a deep brim, such as widows often wore. Asher leaned down a bit, hoping to peek around it, but she quickly looked away.

Asher hurriedly tossed his mother's requests into his basket, and stood behind Tessa at the checkout counter. He could tell that she was working hard to conceal her face from the cashier, too. His purchases, all totaled, might have cost twelve dollars, but, to speed things up, he bagged them himself and slapped a twenty on the counter. He needed to get outside, fast, and catch up with her if he hoped to find out what she was trying to hide.

Outside, she stood beside her buggy, struggling to heft overstuffed sacks into the back seat. Asher placed his package on the ground.

"Let me do that for you," he said, relieving her of the bags.

She had to turn—only for a second—to thank him, and instantly he saw what she'd been hiding: a bruise, deep blue and purple, that spread from her cheek to her temple. Her eye was swollen, too. This was not the result of a fall, or an accidental collision with a door. Nothing but a fist could have left four almost-black circles inside the bruise.

Fear and fury filled him—fear that she'd been harmed, fury at the man who'd hurt her. Grasping her upper arms, he forced her to face him.

"Tessa," he whispered, "*what happened?*"

She stiffened. Recoiled. Utter panic glinted in her eyes, and, realizing she'd seen his gesture as an act of aggression, he let go.

Her lower lip quivered. "It's . . . nothing." She climbed into the buggy, settled onto the seat, and grasped the reins. "I am fine."

Asher prayed for self-control, gentled his voice, and said, "Are you sure?"

She held his gaze for a lingering moment, and a myriad of emotions rolled over him: Protectiveness. Helplessness. Overwhelming affection. "You can talk to me, you know."

"I, I can't talk about it."

Can't? Or, fearing retribution, won't?

The tenets of the *Regeln eines Gottseligen Leben Sido* came to mind: "Do nothing in anger. . . ." said the *Rules of a Godly Life*. Believers were expected to exercise faith and courage, take time to pray, consider every word and action, give anger time to cool, and ensure that each reaction would be Godly.

You must have no faith or courage, he told himself, because he didn't want to think and pray his anger away. He wanted to give her abuser a dose of his own medicine.

Against his better judgment, he latched the buggy's passenger door. Was he sending her home, alone, to face more of the same? "If you change your mind, you know where to find me."

Tessa smiled, barely. "I appreciate the offer, but I do not want you to get involved."

I am already involved, he thought as she snapped the reins and set the horse into motion.

If a stray cat hadn't yowled from the alleyway, Asher didn't know how long he might have stood, watching the buggy grow smaller as it rolled up the road.

All the way home, he thought about that bruise. Saw it as he off-loaded boards, as he stacked them in the barn-turned-warehouse. Her sad, scared look lingered in his mind as he unhitched the team, while he hung the harnesses in the barn. With every stroke of the grooming brush, he considered his options: mind his own business and hope for the best, seek the bishop's advice, or seek Gideon Beachy out and—

"Easy there, or you'll swipe the hair clean off the poor beast."

He stopped brushing, stroked the animal's gleaming coat. "What brings you here, Brother?"

"Bad news, I'm afraid."

Boots crunching over the hay-strewn floor, Asher returned the grooming brush to its place on the tack bench.

"I didn't get the job at the factory."

The news came as a relief to Asher, who hadn't been looking forward to training Reuben's replacement. But his brother *had* been looking forward to working a nine-to-five job. What could he say but, "You are disappointed, I'm sure."

Reuben explained how the company's representative, sent ahead to round up suitable employees, hadn't been enthusiastic about the Amish applicants. "Said we are overqualified for the work, that we will grow bored and quit, wasting the time and money the company would spend training us. It's bunkum, plain and simple."

"Isn't that a prime example of what *Englishers* call discrimination?"

"Maybe, but I do not care. The more I thought about it, the more I realized that we want for nothing, Sarah and the kids and me. We have good health, a solid house, food and clothes, wood to keep us warm, I'm two minutes from work, and my coworkers are all Stuerys. I don't need a nine-to-five job. So the rejection is a blessing."

"It's good to hear you say that," Asher admitted. "I was not looking forward to replacing you with a non-Stuery."

"You know how I hate clichés, but God works in mysterious ways."

Asher grabbed a handful of oats, held it under Pepper's nose. "Sorry if I was a bit rough on you, boy."

The horse's partner nickered and bobbed its head.

"You will get some, too, Salt."

"Why *were* you going at the brushing like a madman?"

"I saw Tessa in town earlier with a bruise on her face, big as my fist."

Reuben frowned. "Let me guess. She did not say who hit her."

"From the little I know of Noah, I doubt it was him."

"The two are like best friends. Together all the time. Swapping jokes. So that leaves just one person."

"Gideon," they said together.

"Before Ida died, I remember seeing bruises on her, too."

"And the poor woman limped as often as not."

Other than the crunch of oats between the horses' teeth, there wasn't a sound in the barn.

"Things like wife abuse go against everything we believe in," Reuben said.

"And he should be held accountable."

"What happened to Ida—to any woman whose husband beats her—infuriates me. I do not know Tessa as well as you do, but hearing that she has been the victim of such abuse makes me angry, too. But Ash, it is not your place to hold Gideon accountable. That obligation falls to the bishop. So if you are thinking of getting him involved in this, well, it is a big step, and a big risk."

"A risk for Gideon!"

"And for you, too, when shunning could be the result."

Asher secured Salt's stall gate, checked Pepper's latch, and stood near Ginger's enclosure.

"You have always been the contemplative type," he said, stroking her nose, "and at the risk of exposing you to yet another cliché, you know better than most that I tend to shoot first and ask questions later." The horse nuzzled his neck, prompting a smile. "But I *have* considered the gravity of the situation." He took a few steps closer to Reuben. "The bishop and elders don't take shunning lightly, either. If that is their verdict, who am I to argue with it?"

"That is all I need to hear." Reuben paused, held up a finger. "I'll tell you who might know more about what Ida's marriage to Gideon was like . . ."

"Mamm," they said together.

"I don't know about you, but I could go for a cup of coffee right about now."

Reuben grinned. "And a slice of cake."

They entered the kitchen, one after the other, and found their mother at the sink.

"Well, well, well, look what the wind blew in."

"Is the coffee still hot?" Reuben wanted to know.

"Is it ever *not*?"

Asher grabbed three mugs and placed them on the table. "Where is Daed?"

"Upstairs, resting." She filled the mugs and said, "He threw his back out after breakfast, pushing in his chair."

Adam's original injury, sustained when he fell from a ladder, had put him on bed rest for months. Although he'd recovered enough to get around, the injury had never completely healed, and now a seemingly inconsequential movement might lay him up for days.

"If only he would see a doctor."

"From your lips to God's ear."

Reuben cringed slightly at the use of yet another cliché, and it made Asher grin.

Rose sat between them, wrapped her hands around the mug. "All right, why are you here?"

"We can't visit our mother without a reason?"

"You *can,*" she said, "but you *don't.* So out with it."

Her sons exchanged an "oh well" glance, and Reuben began with, "You were close friends with Ida Beachy. Do you think Gideon abused her?"

Rose's lips formed a thin line. She frowned. Shook her head, then said, "You are right, we were close friends. She told me things in confidence. I would not feel right disclosing them."

Asher nodded. "We respect that, but here is the nut of it, Mamm. I have reason to believe Gideon struck Tessa. Reuben and I often saw Ida limping or bruised—or both—and neither of us believes awkwardness was the reason. Now that she is gone, might Gideon have turned his anger on Tessa?"

For what seemed like a full minute, Rose stared into her mug. "I will not violate her confidence just because she is dead."

"Not even if it spares her only daughter from suffering the same abuse?"

Rose held Asher's gaze for another moment. "If I say what you want to hear, you will bring the information to the bishop?"

"I will."

"Have you considered the consequences?"

"I have." He had no way of knowing whether or not the elders had met with Gideon about the issue in the past, but if they had, shunning was undeniably a possibility.

"Shunning is one of the worst things that can happen to a person, and to everyone whose life he or she touches. If that shame should befall the Beachys, how do you think Tessa will feel about *you* for having set it in motion?"

Rose gave the question a moment to sink in, then added, "What if the elders decide Gideon should be shunned, and Tessa resents you for it?"

Asher took a page from Reuben's think-then-act book and turned the idea over in his mind a few times. Tessa impressed him as a feet-on-the-ground woman who wasn't likely to hold him accountable if his visit with the bishop started the ball rolling toward the shunning of her father. Admittedly, he was attracted to Tessa, and, if she allowed it, he'd pursue a long-term relationship with her. But given the choice between her future safety and their future together . . .

"I will do what is best for her, no matter the cost."

"My advice, brother, is to talk with her before you take such an extreme step."

"Reuben is right," Rose said. "She is smart and articulate, and, under other circumstances, could speak for herself. But fear . . ." She waved a hand in front of her face. "Fear is the great silencer. If you did not already know that, you would not be considering this. But, Son, this is about *Tessa,* not you. In her place, if someone was mistreating me and I was afraid to talk about it, I don't know how I might feel about the person responsible for bringing it into the open."

"But Mamm, by beating her, *Gideon* is responsible, not me!"

"That may be true, but if you care about her, you must respect what *she* wants."

"Reuben, do you agree?"

"Yes, Ash, I do."

Rose stood and said, "I baked a chocolate cake this morning. Who wants a slice!"

"Have I ever *not*?" Reuben kidded.

Saying no would hurt her feelings, so Asher said, "Just a thin slice for me."

Eating it quickly would accomplish two things: compliment his mother's baking skills, and give him time to formulate the questions he'd ask Noah when he left the house.

Trust it to God, he thought. *Just trust it to God.*

Chapter 5

Asher rapped on the shop's entrance door. When no one answered, he turned the knob, and, finding the door unlocked, let himself in.

"Noah?"

A door at the back of the shop opened, and Tessa's brother appeared, wearing a clay-streaked apron . . . and a dark, swollen bruise on his jaw. "Asher, hello. What can I do for you?"

Asher held up two bottles of root beer. "If you have a few minutes, might we talk?"

Noah's eyes narrowed slightly as he accepted the drink, then he led the way into the back room. "Try to overlook the mess. I am working up a proposal that I hope will secure a beneficial contract."

He indicated the empty stool near the drawing board, and Asher sat.

"I was approached by a national department store chain," Noah continued, "that wants us to produce a line of dinnerware specific to them."

Under other circumstances, Asher might have been more interested in Noah's good news. But he'd come here looking for answers: was Gideon abusing Tessa or not?

All in good time, he thought, and leaned forward to inspect full-color and black-and-white drawings of fleur-de-lis, wildlife, mountain vistas, a sandy beach strewn with seashells and starfish, and geometric patterns, on round plates as well as square and oblong. Noah was, no doubt, a talented artist, and Asher said so.

"I do not mean to pry," he continued, "but that's some bruise on your face. Did your father cause the one on Tessa's face, as well?"

"She was not the intended target. Tess tried to stop him from landing another blow."

In other words, this wasn't the first time Noah had been on the receiving end of his father's temper. Both he and Tessa had inherited their mother's slender physique, and stood little chance against a man who stood six inches taller and outweighed them by seventy-five pounds.

"Do you think censure would get him under control?"

"The elders?" An angry frown creased Noah's brow. "Please." His eyes darkened as he ground out, "Last time that bunch tried to help, my mother paid the ultimate price."

The emphasis on *ultimate price* made Asher rethink things. When his mother had told him about her friend's passing, Asher had thought it odd that the doctor had cited internal bleeding as the cause of death. But Noah's unspoken message had been clear: Gideon, not some unspecified internal bleeding, had killed her . . . and if the bishop got involved again, Noah or Tessa might pay a similar price.

"So your hands are tied. There is nothing you can do to protect yourselves."

Noah bristled slightly before saying, "I have written relatives in Indiana and Ohio to investigate work opportunities in Nappanee and Sugarcreek. And . . ." He shifted uncomfortably in his chair. "Can I trust you to keep a confidence?"

Noah was young, twenty or twenty-one at most, and although he'd played an integral role in the family business, his life experience was, at best, limited. That he'd exercised any caution at all amazed Asher, because when he'd been Noah's age . . .

"You have my word," Asher said. "Nothing we have said will leave this room."

"All right then . . ." Noah took a gulp of the root beer, drew the back of his hand across his lips, and said, "Tessa would move with me if I asked her to, but she loves teaching, loves her students, so I will not ask her. But before I move—if I do—I need to make sure she is safe, physically and financially."

He got up, began to pace the small area between his drawing board and the door. "Several national store chains have offered to buy Beachy Pottery. Tessa has never shown any interest in the business side of the company, and, since it is in my name, I could accept one of the offers and divide the profits."

Asher didn't ask why the company was in Noah's name. Didn't ask where Gideon would go once the sale was final. Tessa was his main concern.

"But the house is on company property, yes?"

"Yes, but far enough from the workshop and the warehouse that I could exclude it and an acre or so around it from the sale so that Tess would always have a home."

Impressive, Asher thought, that Noah had given the matter such detailed thought. He pointed at the drawings that might secure a long-term, lucrative contract.

"This deal adds to the company's value."

"Exactly."

Yes, Noah had given the matter a lot of thought, all right. In Asher's opinion, Gideon Beachy was a sorry excuse for a human being! Asher was worried about Tessa, and his heart ached for her young brother, forced by his father's violent tendencies to make choices no man should have to make.

"All your life, you have known nothing but Bird-in-Hand and Beachy Pottery. It must be hard, facing the prospect of leaving both."

Noah snorted. "I spent so many hours in one that I barely know the other."

Asher felt a bit uncomfortable at the moment, because Noah's words, the horrible situation he was facing, made Asher appreciate his own life all the more, and he wasn't at all sure he'd shown those closest to him how thankful he was to call them *family*.

On his feet now, he said, "Sorry that I interrupted your work."

"I'm grateful for your concern for Tess. Knowing she has someone looking out for her makes a hard decision easier."

Asher was touched that her younger brother had put so much faith in him. "I will pray there is another way. It would be a shame if you had to sell the family business and leave the community."

"What have they drummed into our heads since we were old enough to walk?"

"All things are God's will," they said at the same time.

Asher felt the weight of Noah's predicament, and moved woodenly toward the door.

"So you will not visit the bishop?" Noah asked.

"If you think it will stir up trouble for you and Tessa, no, I will not."

"Thank you." He placed a brotherly hand on Asher's shoulder. "You know what else is a shame? That I am only now realizing what a good friend you are."

Asher was glad he'd walked to the Beachys, because the trip home would give him time to ponder Noah's parting words: "No wonder Tess feels as she does about you."

As Asher walked toward home, he thought about that. If only he felt more certain about how the pretty young schoolteacher felt about him, without looking like a bumbling, stumbling, lovesick fool.

And then it came to him: He had trouble reading, and she was a teacher. A friendly, helpful, caring teacher. Now, only one question remained: How to ask if she'd teach *him.*

Tessa treasured this time of day, when the world turned dusky as the setting sun's glow sparkled on roadway grit and lit the white fences that led the way home. With not so much as the hint of a breeze to rustle the shrubbery, she listened . . . to the crunch of leaves beneath her boots, birds twittering above as they fled toward warmer climes, the screak of a hawk that had spotted a snack in the underbrush, the hiss of passing bicycle tires, and every now and again, a friendly "Hello, neighbor!"

She cherished the sounds, each a soul-stirring reminder that despite the turmoil simmering in the Beachy house, peace could be found . . . if she chose to look for it.

Father, I know that You never promised an easy life. Instead, You said, "Trust me." So thank you for these things that prove You are always with me.

"Tessa?"

She looked over her shoulder and saw Asher jogging toward her.

"It's nearly dark," he said, falling into step beside her. "Did the teacher keep you after school?"

Mirroring his lighthearted smile, she said, "Yes, she is quite the taskmaster."

He nodded toward the bulging satchel that hung from her shoulder. "Papers to grade?"

She nodded, too. "As well as books to help me prepare tomorrow's lessons."

They walked at a leisurely pace, talking about the steadily dropping temperatures, the pleasant scent of woodstove smoke that puffed from neighbors' chimneys, the *Raber's Almanac* winter predictions.

Without asking permission, he relieved her of the heavy bag, and she thanked him. "I also appreciate that you have not mentioned the, ah, my bruise."

He shrugged. "Not sure I can help in any way, but, as I said before, if you care to talk about it, I am happy to listen."

"That means a lot."

Asher stooped, scooped up a handful of pebbles, rattled them in a closed fist. "I have a favor to ask," he said, lobbing one into a clump of weeds.

"Not sure I can help, but I am happy to listen."

"Touché."

His easy chuckle brought as much comfort as the seasonal sounds and sights.

"I met with your brother a while ago."

"Oh? At the house?"

"In the shop. He was working on a new proposal."

"Ah, the one for the department store chain."

"Yes, that's the one." Another pebble bounced alongside the road. "Is Noah a natural-born artist, or self-taught?"

"A little of both." What, she wondered, had inspired Asher's visit? "Our mother enjoyed sketching and painting, sold most of her artwork in Bird-in-Hand and Lancaster gift shops."

"You say she sold most of her work, meaning you were able to save others?"

"Yes, and I treasure them."

A frosty gust whipped fallen leaves into tiny twisters that skittered around their feet.

Asher flipped up his collar. "I would like to see them someday."

Four shallow boxes hidden under Ida's bed once held prestretched canvases her mother had ordered from a Baltimore art supply house. Now, the cartons held her unfinished and unsold paintings. If Tessa showed them to Asher, she risked her father seeing, and possibly destroying, them. She could not—*would not*—let that happen.

"Was my father there?" she asked, changing the subject.

"I did not see him."

Just as well, Tessa thought.

"Thank you for keeping me company during the walk home."

"It was my pleasure." He handed her the satchel. "I would like to do it again sometime. Soon."

Tessa would like that, too.

He cleared his throat. "So about that favor . . ."

She hiked the bag's strap higher onto her shoulder as he said, "I know you are busy, and I hate to impose."

"How about if you ask, and let me decide if it is an imposition?"

Asher dropped the remaining pebbles at his feet, dusted his palms together. "I'm embarrassed to admit it, but, I, ah, I never, um . . ." He shook his head and started again. "I never mastered the ability to read. Oh, I get by, using a few tricks, and, from time to time, Reuben helps. I think we have managed to keep it under our hats, but sooner or later . . ."

So, she'd been right, comparing his behavior to her father's. "I am happy to help, Asher, any way I can."

He inhaled a deep breath, released it slowly. "Thank you, Tess."

She'd need to evaluate how his tricks had helped him fake it. Hopefully, he hadn't developed too many hard-to-break habits.

"The children have all left the schoolhouse by three o'clock, and I always stay behind for an hour, at least. We can start whenever it is convenient for you."

"Is tomorrow too soon?"

Tessa smiled. "Of course not."

Asher reached out, wrapped long, strong fingers around her upper arm, gaze flicking from her bruise to the back porch. He met her eyes to say, "Will you be all right?"

She nodded and took a step back. "I will see you tomorrow, then."

"Thank you. I am blessed to call you friend."

Had she gone daft? What else explained her desire to be more than a friend, so much more!

She stood on the top porch step as he walked away, head down, shoulders hunched into the wind. After thirty or so steps, he spun around, waved an arm over his head, and smiled. Tessa couldn't explain how he'd known she'd been watching, but one thing was certain: she'd see his happy, handsome face in her dreams.

After hanging her jacket and book bag on wooden pegs behind the door, she washed up, donned a clean apron, and gathered ingredients for tonight's supper. In no time, a mini assembly line of ingredients appeared: Beaten eggs, spiced flour, drumsticks, and thighs. Soon, the windows fogged from the steam of boiling potatoes and baking biscuits, exactly as they had when she and her mother had shared cooking chores while talking about the events of the day.

Noah joined Tessa and stood at the sink. "You made all my favorites!"

"I like fried chicken, too, you know."

He towel dried his hands. "If I set the table, can we eat sooner?"

"Yes, a whole five minutes sooner!"

His bright expression darkened. "Any sign of Daed?"

"None. But you should set a place for him, just in case."

Frowning, he slid three plates from the stack in the cupboard.

"I hear your proposal is coming along well."

"Do not take Asher's word for it," he said, winking. "Stop by the shop; see for yourself."

The heat of a blush crept into her cheeks, and, to hide it, Tessa pretended to focus on sliding biscuits into a napkin-lined basket.

"That *is* how you know, right? He told you?"

She placed the basket on the table. "In passing. More or less."

"Did he happen to mention—in passing, more or less—*why* he came to see me?"

"No." Now, she met his eyes. "Care to elaborate?"

"He's worried about your safety."

Instinctively, her fingers touched the bruise. "*My* safety? What about your—"

"What a warm welcome!" Gideon said, and hung his jacket beside Tessa's. Rubbing both palms together, he added, "What is the occasion?"

"Occasion?" Tessa and Noah said together.

"Fried chicken. Mashed potatoes and gravy. Biscuits. Harvard beets. All my favorites!"

He poured himself a glass of milk, carried it to the table. "Ever wonder why they are called that?"

Brother and sister exchanged a confused glance.

"Two stories," he said, taking his seat. "Some think the name came from the color, which is similar to that of the Harvard University football team jerseys." He sipped the milk. "Others believe the recipe originated in a British tavern called Harwood. Seems the name got mispronounced, and after a while . . ." He shrugged. "Leave it to the *Englishers* to slap a pointless name on a thing."

Noah's eyes narrowed. "And what would *you* have called them?"

Gideon gave it a moment's thought. "Beets in sweet sauce." He used his fork to write it in the air.

The action reminded Tessa of Asher, and his awkward request for help.

"Keep it simple, I always say," Gideon tacked on, laughing.

Had he forgotten about punching Noah, and her, too? Shouldn't their cuts and bruises be enough to deflate his buoyant mood?

Tessa scraped mashed potatoes into one bowl, poured gravy into another. No sooner had she placed the chicken platter between them than Gideon stuffed half a buttered biscuit into his mouth.

"M-m-m. Light and fluffy, just the way I like 'em," he mumbled around it. "Pass the potatoes, Son."

Silent and scowling, Noah did as asked. Resentment roiled within her, too. Eyes closed, she forced herself to thank the Almighty for the food, the protection of their house, her father's sudden cheerful demeanor, and Asher. . . . In an instant, her ire diminished as she pictured him, sitting down to eat. Would there come a time when he'd share meals with *her*?

"You are a good cook, Tess," Gideon said. "I do not say it enough, but I appreciate everything you do around here."

"Just doing my job," she said without looking up.

"You work hard, and it shows in all that you do."

She didn't need to look up to know that Noah was just as surprised by Gideon's words.

"Mamm deserves the credit," Tessa said, putting down her fork, "for teaching me so well."

"Yes, and the house, the gardens, meals are proof of it. Any man would be proud to call you his wife, any child blessed to call you Mamm."

He'd plied her mother with compliments, too. Half the time, Ida's meek thank-yous inspired kindness, but he was just as likely to rebuke her for not showing enough appreciation, or for committing the sin of pride by exhibiting too much. Afraid he might be setting her up, Tessa hurried to the sink, began filling it with sudsy water.

"That can wait," he said. "You barely touched your supper."

"I just want to soak the pots and pans and cooking utensils," she fibbed. "Once the mashed potatoes harden, they are like cement."

"Oh. Yes. I forgot."

The water hissed, the kitchen clock ticked, and the tines of forks against crockery competed with the quiet.

"Have you ever considered a husband?"

The suddenness of his voice made her jump.

"Every girl dreams of marriage," she said, choosing her words carefully.

In truth, she'd thought about it more than most girls, because most girls didn't want to escape from their own fathers!

"Is there a particular young man in your dreams?"

An innocent question? Or a trap?

Noah must have wondered the same thing, because he rose slowly and gathered his plate and flatware. "Thank you, Tess," he said, sliding them into the sudsy water. "Supper was delicious."

"There is pie. . . ." She hoped he'd read the silent plea in her eyes: *Please don't leave me alone with him. . . .*

He handed her a dish towel. "Daed is right. The dishes can wait. I want to show you my latest designs."

"I have not seen them, either," Gideon said, getting to his feet. Standing between them, he slid arms across their shoulders. "We will go together, and, afterward, we will have pie together!"

Three hundred footsteps separated the back porch from the workshop. She knew, because on many occasions, little-girl Tess had counted, to make the trip more interesting. Now, instead of counting, she prayed.

Prayed that her father would approve of Noah's designs.

Prayed that nothing would rile him.

That the pie would be to his liking.

And his current mood might become permanent.

Chapter 6

Most school days began with whispering, giggling, chair legs scooting across the wood-planked floor, and the thump of books on desktops. Tessa had opened the divider, and even the most mischievous of students quieted at the sound of her yardstick tapping the chalkboard. That, and the promise of fresh-baked cookies for quick cooperation.

Today though, thanks to unrelenting winds that rattled the windows and rain that had soaked hair, shirt collars, and shoes, they seemed uncharacteristically restless. She couldn't comfort them with a group hug, but she could do the next best thing. . . .

"Take off your shoes, and line them up by the woodstove to dry," she told them. "Then pull your chairs up close, too." She handed each a cookie. "While you get warm, I will read. Who would like to choose the book?"

Six-year-old Martha was the first to raise her hand, and, with Tessa's permission, ran to the low bookshelf along the back wall. "This one," she said, returning to her seat. "There is *fire* on the cover, and the boy and girl look very scared, so it must be a good story!"

Smiling as the boys and girls leaned in to see for themselves, Tessa led them in a recitation of the Lord's Prayer and a verse from "Now Thank We All Our God." Few things were more pleasing to her ears than the way their young voices came together in an almost harmonic chant.

"Now then," she said, picking up the book, "*Fire by Night* begins in Boston's harbor, in the year 1635. . . ." Turning to page one, Tessa read, " 'Phillip Smythe had survived several storms in his thirteen years, but none this bad. The huge crashing waves had driven his raft far from the shore, and now, caught in a riptide, it carried him farther and farther out to sea. He lifted his head, squinted past stinging raindrops that pelted his face and thought, *If I could get a glimpse of Boston's Harbor, perhaps I could steer toward land* . . . Phillip prayed, too. He'd built the raft well, but was it strong enough to withstand a beating like this? If not, he was as good as dead.' "

If only their collective *ooh*s and *ahh*s had the power to drown out the storm. Tessa continued reading for nearly half an hour, and, after closing the book, allowed them a moment of disappointment while pinching a few white-socked toes. "Now that your feet are dry, you need to get back to your desks. I have a surprise for you!"

Martha's older brother Mark muttered, "Gonna take some kinda surprise to make up for leaving us wondering what will happen to Phillip next."

"You will find out on Monday, when I read another chapter." Tessa held up a thick stack of colored paper. "This is the beginning of our Christmas pageant."

Echoes of "Christmas pageant" traveled the room.

"But it is not even Thanksgiving yet," her eldest student said.

"You are right, Tim, but this year, I have something very different in mind, and it will take time."

"Not the Nativity play?" Hannah asked.

"You will just have to wait and see." Tessa put the paper back into her satchel. "So tell me. Who will attend the fall Harvest Days this weekend?"

"No 'rithmetic?" Jonah whispered.

"Or sentence diagrams?" Tim whispered back.

Jonah shook his head. "I think maybe all this rain has turned her teacher brain moldy."

Moldy brain, indeed, she thought, and hid a grin by stoking the fire.

Hannah joined the boys' speculations. "Maybe she has fallen in lo-o-ove."

"Love?" Tim echoed, and wrinkled his nose. "Not Miss Beachy."

"Why not?" the girl demanded. "She is pretty. And still young enough to get married."

"Yeah, but she'd need a man for that, and I have not seen her with anyone but her father and brother."

Tessa needed a moment to compose herself, and rearranged the shoes that formed a tidy semicircle around the woodstove. Should she start the younger children practicing their ABCs? The mid-graders working on fractions? The oldest students reciting the Gettysburg Address? Perhaps her brain *had* grown moldy, because she couldn't concentrate on anything but what Hannah had said . . . and how Tim had responded.

She could name three men who'd shown mild interest in her, and, although they were respected around town, none had ever looked at her as if he thought she'd helped the good Lord hang the moon. None of them made her heart beat faster, or inspired daydreams—and night dreams—of welcoming him with a warm kiss at the end of a hard day's work. If they'd noticed her bruise, they hadn't seemed concerned for her safety or well-being. Nor had they shown an interest in improving themselves.

Only one man had done any of that.

No maybe *about it, sweet Hannah. I* have *fallen in love . . .*

. . . with Asher Stuery.

The Stuery brothers sat in their workshop's back room, washing peanut butter crackers down with coffee poured from gray-metal thermoses. Reuben propped his bootheels on a nearby chair while Asher looked over his reading assignment.

"Is it true? You and Tessa have been meeting alone at the schoolhouse?"

Asher looked up from his reading homework. "Where did you hear that?"

"Here and there." Reuben paused, stroked his dark beard. "It is true, then?"

"It is."

"With no chaperone."

Asher didn't like the turn this conversation had taken. "Tess teaches; I learn. Nothing more."

"Easy, Brother. I'm just looking out for your reputation. Hers, too. You know how people talk."

He wanted to say, *"People like you?"* but thought better of it.

Reuben picked up the book, flipped through the pages. "Is it interesting?"

Asher answered with a distracted shrug, and thought of his first session with Tessa. "I did not want to risk insulting your intelligence, so instead of a McGuffey reader or one of the *Dick and Jane* books . . . ," she'd said, and handed him the how-to manual and explaining that since it contained repetitive words and phrases, and subject matter of interest to him, he'd learn faster. He'd recognized right off that *Marketing Your Business* wasn't part of her usual curriculum, and it touched him that she'd put so much thought—and her own money—into helping him.

Reuben returned the book. "Learned anything?"

"I can read the title."

Reuben joined in his laughter. "Daily, hour-long lessons, and that is all?"

The happy squeals of children heading home from school drifted into the workshop. The door slammed, and Peter ran up to his father.

"Homework, Son?"

"Miss Beachy said we didn't have any. And then she sent us home early!"

Reuben aimed a slanted grin in Asher's direction. "Hmm. I wonder why."

"'Cause she is the best teacher in the whole world!" The boy looked up at his uncle. "You goin' to see her again today?"

"Wh-what . . . what are you talking about?"

"Me an' Sam was playin' hide an' seek, saw you go in the schoolhouse."

Asher grabbed his jacket. "The woodpile was low, and I promised to restock it." Not the whole truth, but not exactly a lie, either. He'd delivered enough wood to last for weeks, unless the weather turned foul.

"Teachers are not allowed to be married, and none of us wants a new teacher. Please do not marry her, Asher!"

What had Peter seen to make him say such a thing! "Not to worry. Your old uncle is not the marrying kind." He chuckled, but his heart wasn't in it. This time, he *had* lied.

"Oh, I almost forgot," Peter told Reuben. "I am here because Mamm wanted me to remind you that Groosmammi is coming to supper."

"Not to worry," he said, echoing Asher's earlier comment. "I will not be late."

The boy backpedaled out the door, shouting "See you at home, Daed!"

"Some kid," Asher said. "You are blessed."

"Blessed?" Reuben snorted. "You heard what the boy said. Sarah's mother is coming to supper."

Asher buttoned his jacket. "Yes, blessed." *I would gladly put up with a mother-in-law like yours if it meant—*

"So where are you off to?" Reuben winked. "As if I didn't know."

"Firewood does not deliver itself you know."

Asher jogged all the way to the schoolhouse. He'd forgotten the book, but it didn't matter. She'd taught him well, and, because she had, he could pick out certain words in any book. On cereal boxes and milk cartons. He couldn't wait to show her, see her beautiful, almost-brown eyes light up as she said something like, "See? I knew you could do it!"

Asher entered the schoolhouse and saw Tessa at her desk, brow furrowed with concentration and red pencil poised to write something on a student's assignment. A shaft of sunlight slanted through the window, draping her shoulders, capping her golden-brown hair like a halo. It was a good thing his cliché-hating brother wasn't here to spoil the truth found in his thoughts: *Beautiful enough to stop a clock.*

When she looked up, he saw the fading traces of her father's attack.

"My goodness," she said, rising. "Why the long face?"

Rather than admit the truth, that his heart pounded with anger at Gideon—as well as anger and frustration that he couldn't protect her from the man—he took off his coat and hat and made himself smile. "Cold out there."

"Well, it is plenty warm in here," she said, gesturing toward the tidy stack of logs beside the woodstove, "thanks to your hard work and generosity."

"After our lesson, I will haul in a few more armloads."

"No need for that. One of the bigger boys can do it tomorrow."

Asher moved closer, gave in to the impulse to touch her cheek, and it nearly broke his heart when she flinched.

"Didn't mean to startle you," he said, tucking the offending hand behind a suspender. "I just wondered . . . does it hurt?"

Tessa touched the bruise. "No, not anymore." She pulled a chair up to the desk. "Shall we get started?"

Asher turned the chair around, straddled the seat, and rested both forearms on its top rail. "I, ah, I was with Reuben earlier. Forgot my book." Leaning to the left, he slid a McGuffey reader from the low shelf against the wall, turned to an opening page, and prayed that what he was about to do wouldn't make him look like a colossal fool. "I want to show you something." Turning to the first page, he read haltingly, " 'Here is John,' " then, " 'Ann has a new book. Ann must keep it nice and clean.' "

Her tiny gasp of approval silenced him, and he put the book back where he'd found it.

"I can hardly believe it," Tessa said, laying her hand atop his. "But . . . *how?*"

"By reading the book you gave me. From start to finish. Twice. Learned a few things about marketing our business in the process, but, more important than that, I began to recognize some of the words. On flyers tacked to telephone poles. Sales tags in the stores. Street signs. Just about everywhere I looked."

Tears glistened in her eyes, but she was smiling. Happy tears, his mother called them. Seeing them lifted his spirits and buoyed his courage. Asher sandwiched her hand between his. "Thanks to you, I can *read.*"

"No," she said, forefinger ticking like a metronome, "it is thanks to your own hard work."

Overcome with gratitude, Asher stood, and, grasping her shoulders, brought her to her feet. "I am a practical man and know that I have a long way to go. Others offered to help me, but . . . I knew I could trust you to keep it to yourself if I failed."

"We will not speak of failure, Asher Stuery!"

She looked so determined that he was inspired to say, "All right . . ."

"But . . . ?"

"If only I could show you how much I appreciate you."

"Oh, that will be easy."

He waited, wondering what she'd ask in return.

Tessa smiled up at him, head tilted slightly, and said, "Just keep reading."

She was close enough to kiss, and he might have done it if a crow's shadow hadn't glided past the windows—windows that overlooked the road, where anyone taller than a toddler could look inside. He was reminded of what he'd said to Reuben: "*Tess teaches, I learn. Nothing more. . . .*" Feeling duty-bound to protect her reputation, Asher took a half-step back.

Tessa faced the board. "Would you like to *write* some of the words you read?"

"Will you grade my penmanship?"

"Not on your first try." She held out the chalk.

Asher took it, printed his name and address, and, for good measure, added STUERY & SONS CONSTRUCTION. When he finished, Tessa inspected his work.

"Good job." She propped a fist on her hip. "Now try something you have *not* been writing most of your life."

She had him, dead to rights. "Touché," he said.

Squinting, he visualized the words he'd just read aloud, then tried to duplicate them. ANN, he wrote, followed by JOHN. Then, BOOK.

"I have to say, I am impressed." A grin crinkled the corners of her eyes. And then her lower lip jutted out in a playful pout. "You are learning fast. So fast that I fear our lessons will end soon."

"That disappoints you?"

Tessa said, "You must have noticed, Asher, how much I look forward to our time—"

The old grandfather clock counted out the hours.

Saved by the gong? he thought as she continued with, "Well, I have a mountain of laundry waiting for me at home. And ironing." Tessa hurriedly stuffed books and papers into her satchel. "Good thing I made soup last night. A little thickener when I get home and, voilà, stew! The only question now is, biscuits or dumplings?" Snickering, she grabbed her jacket, handed him his, and donned her cap. "Care to join us?"

The image popped into his head: Tessa, sitting across from him, passing bowls to Noah, refilling mugs, talking and laughing. A warm, happy-family picture . . . until it dawned on Asher that Gideon would be at the table, too, eating that stew. Another picture flashed in his mind: Her father, drawing back his fist and—

"Asher?" Tessa let go of the bow she'd just tied under her chin. "What is wrong?"

"Nothing." He shook his head, summoning self-control. "I . . ." If he thought for a minute he could keep a civil tongue in his head during the meal, Asher would gladly accept her invitation. "I, ah, I need to get home." He laughed nervously. "Just so happens I have a mountain of laundry, too."

"Very funny." She hoisted the satchel onto one shoulder. "Not a fan of stew?"

He followed her outside and relieved her of the satchel, and again pictured Gideon in ready-to-strike mode. He hid his fury by raising the bag. "What's in this thing? Bricks?"

Tessa laughed again and locked the door.

"Seems a shame you have to do that." Using his thumb, he straightened the thermometer that hung beside the door. Thirty-four degrees, it said. "When I was a boy, no one needed to bolt anything. Not windows or doors. Not barns or shops."

She dropped the big key into her purse, pulled the drawstring, and wrapped it around her wrist. "Pity that not all visitors to Bird-in-Hand are tourists, isn't it?"

Asher fell into step beside her. "Do you miss those days? When things were slower, safer?"

After a moment of thought, Tessa said, "I suppose less privacy and security is the price we pay for the extra income brought in by outsiders."

"Outsiders. The annual festival starts next weekend, and always lures a passel of *Englishers* to town. Are you planning to go?"

"I have been saving up for months. I would not miss it!"

Did she realize what she was doing to him, looking so enthusiastic, so *happy?*

"Planning to buy a new quilt?"

"No," she answered. "Apple butter and jam, soaps, and candles are more in my price range."

Seemed a shame, he thought, that a woman who so freely gave of her time couldn't splurge on something pretty.

"What is your favorite color?"

For a moment she looked baffled, then she collected herself. "I like the colors of nature. A clear blue summer sky. Red petals on a rose. Every hue of the rainbow. The zigzag of white on Bolt's forehead. The velvety green of fresh-mown grass . . ." She paused, exhaled a dainty sigh. "And you?"

"Me, what?"

"What is *your* favorite?"

"Hmm . . . Might need help answering that one."

"Help?" She laughed. "Why?!"

"Don't know what to call your hair color, or eyes like yours that change in the light."

She lifted her chin a notch and said, "My eyes are hazel and my hair, plain brown."

"Sorry to disagree, but there is nothing plain about you, Tessa Beachy."

When she blushed, Asher added two more items to his mental Reasons to Love Tess list: she was plain-spoken and modest. And while he wondered why she didn't realize how beautiful she was, Tessa stopped walking.

It only took a second to figure out why: they'd reached the end of her drive. She opened the mailbox, withdrew a stack of envelopes, a catalog, the latest edition of *The Budget*, and extended a hand, fingertips wiggling in a silent request to return her school bag. By his best guess, the driveway that ribboned from the road to the house measured half a mile.

"Mind if I go a bit farther with you?"

An uneasy glance over her shoulder told him she'd rather he didn't. He hated seeing the uncertainty—or was it fear of Gideon—that glinted in her eyes. A Bible verse came to mind. *Anyone who claims to be in the light but hates a brother or sister is still in the darkness.* Until he figured out how to control his temper, he'd best keep his distance.

"Sorry. Didn't mean to put you on the spot." Asher handed her the bag. "Any homework for me, Miss Beachy?"

"I think you have earned an assignment-free night." She slung the satchel's straps over one shoulder. "But you have inspired me . . ."

"*I* inspired *you?*" He laughed at that.

". . . to find another book. Something a little more challenging."

The wind puffed under her cap, blew it to the back of her head, and loosened its ties. If he'd been a tick slower, it would have fluttered away. For the second time that evening, he found himself standing close enough to kiss her. As if she could read his mind, Tessa licked her lips.

Better get hold of yourself, man. . . .

She took a step forward. *For a good-bye kiss?* he wondered. Just in case, Asher licked his lips, too.

Much to his disappointment, Tessa reached up, pressed a palm to his cheek. "Thanks for walking me home and for carrying this bag of bricks."

Her hand lingered there for a moment, and he covered it with his own.

"Your fingers are like ice. Better get inside, where you can warm up."

She nodded, dropped her hand, and walked backward a few steps. "See you tomorrow?"

"Sure. Of course. Yeah."

Asher hoped Gideon wasn't in there, working himself into a foul mood.

Another Bible verse came to mind. Ungodly wrath, he'd learned, was excessive and abusive; with God, a man could express anger without losing control.

Walking away from the Beachys, Asher prayed. Prayed with every step that the Almighty would take control of his temper. Because if Gideon ever hurt Tessa again, Asher wouldn't waste time asking for the bishop's guidance.

He'd take the matter up with the man directly.

Chapter 7

The Friday before Thanksgiving, Tessa made a special trip to the bakery and bought four dozen cupcakes. During her first trip to Lancaster, she'd picked up the usual November birthday treats. This, her second order of the month, was to celebrate how much the children had accomplished, preparing for the annual Christmas pageant. Keeping them fresh overnight would be easy, thanks to the large plastic Rebecca's Porch bag.

She arrived at school earlier than normal, and hid the pink boxes under her desk, where they'd stay until lunchtime. Did they realize that she looked forward to watching them devour the sweet treats every bit as much as they enjoyed eating them?

Time dragged as she led the scholars through morning prayers and scripture readings, and Tessa felt a little guilty about that. *You can make up for it tomorrow, by getting up a little earlier than usual to say a few extra private prayers.* They had earned this special treat by working hard, and, to her knowledge, they'd kept the project a secret.

Only Asher knew what they'd been working on, and that was just because she hadn't quite finished tucking the materials back into the arts and crafts tub when he had arrived for yesterday's reading lesson.

"Leave it to you to come up with a two-birds-with-one-stone idea," he'd said after hearing the details. It had been his proud-papa look that had inspired another two-for-one idea.

Although it was Saturday—her one day to sleep late—she set the clock for four thirty. After feeding Bolt and the chickens and gathering eggs, Tessa did her household chores, and baked a double batch of snickerdoodles. Wouldn't Asher be surprised that not only had she been paying attention when he'd mentioned they were his favorite cookies, but also that she'd baked a batch, just for him!

"It is not Sunday," Noah said as he drizzled syrup on his pancakes.

"I know that."

"Then why are you wearing your best dress?"

She could have told him that the others were in the wash. That she hadn't yet had a chance to iron them. But why fib to Noah, who was as much best friend as brother?

"I am leaving for Asher's soon, to bring him a gift to thank him for chopping and delivering so much wood to the schoolhouse."

"I had a feeling you hadn't baked those," he said, gesturing toward the cookies, still cooling on the counter, "just for me."

"You are wrong, Brother. *Those* are for you. And Daed, of course."

He reached across the table to pat her hand. "Warms my heart, knowing you two are getting along so well." Noah glanced at the clock. "But Tess, it's not even eight o'clock. On a Saturday morning. Ash is a builder, remember, not a farmer. He can sleep late on weekends."

"Oh, but he doesn't. He told me that he never sleeps past six. That on weekends, he works on his house. And only goes into town if he runs out of nails. Or boards. Or whatever."

Noah narrowed one eye. "When did he tell you all this?"

"When . . . when he delivered wood."

"Uh-huh."

She frowned at the impish grin that said what words needn't: *Something is going on between you two.* "For your information, we are friends."

"Who is friends?" Gideon wanted to know. He sat at the table and helped himself to a pancake.

Tessa went to the stove, and, while filling a coffee mug, said, "Asher Stuery."

"Decent fellow." Gideon speared a sausage link. "You could do worse."

Noah rolled his eyes, and Tessa said a quick prayer that their father hadn't seen it. For the last day or two, Gideon's attitude had been almost pleasant. But since neither she nor Noah—nor their mother, for that matter—had ever known what might set Gideon off . . .

He used his fork as a pointer. "What is that in your mother's tin?"

"Cookies. For Asher. To thank him for delivering wood to the schoolhouse."

"How much did he charge you?"

"Nothing." She held her breath. Would this be the *something* that would rile her father?

Gideon gave a nod of approval. "Decent fellow," he repeated. Turning to Noah, he said, "How are things going with the new proposal?"

She could almost read her brother's mind: *You would know if you ever showed up at the shop. . . .*

"The contract has been signed and delivered," Noah said instead, "and I deposited the advance payment."

"And the work?"

"The men will have fifty sets ready for shipment by the end of the month."

"Seems I made the right decision, after all."

More than a year ago, Gideon had put Noah in charge of production, and transferred full ownership to him, as well. That, Tessa thought, was the smartest thing their father had done in many years. Because if something should happen to him while he was off gallivanting, Beachy Pottery employees' jobs and the company's longstanding reputation would remain safe. In her opinion, there was no "after all" about it.

"Think I might spend a few hours in the shop today." Gideon got to his feet. "Need to run a few errands first, but I ought to be there by lunchtime. And Tessa? Tell Asher that when the cookies are gone, we want that tin returned."

Again, Noah rolled his eyes, and, again, Tessa hoped their father hadn't noticed. *Times like these*, Tessa thought, *I wish your face wasn't so easy to read, Brother!*

Once the door closed behind him, Noah said, "Where do you suppose he's *really* going?"

"Who knows." She began clearing the table. "Are the men working today?"

"Yep." Standing, he said, "Overtime, and they are grateful for the extra hours. And speaking of working, I need to get over there, make sure everything is tip-top . . . in case Daed decides to grace us with his presence." Noah shook his head. "Last thing the guys need is to see him fly into another rage."

"See you at suppertime?"

"Definitely. Fourteen-hour days, six days a week . . . I am ready for a long winter's nap." He slipped into his coat. "What is on the menu?"

"Roast chicken, I think."

"Enjoy your visit with Asher." Winking, he touched a finger to the brim of his hat and walked out the door.

Their mother would be proud of the man he'd become, and, first chance she got, Tessa intended to tell him so.

* * *

Tessa decided against hitching Bolt to the buggy and saddled him instead. According to the weather report, the temperature would reach forty-five degrees by lunchtime, warm enough for an easy canter, but since they both enjoyed a good long gallop, she'd need her mother's calf-length wool coat, mittens, and scarf, and, since no one would see her on the seldom-used trail, a thick, knitted hat instead of her poly-cotton cap. She donned the coat and tucked everything else into a large tote bag, saving the cookie tin for last.

The minute she and Bolt made the turn into the Stuerys' drive, Asher's pup raced toward them. She reined in the horse and dismounted, then stooped to pet the dog. "Aren't you a pretty pup! I'd like you to meet Bolt."

The animals nosed each another for a moment, then walked behind her. It only took a minute or so to spot Asher's place, nestled half an acre or so behind the main house. Pale yellow with white trim, the former barn now boasted a wraparound porch and tall, narrow windows, even in the front door.

Tessa tied Bolt's reins to a tree as the dog darted around the corner. She fished the cookie tin from the bag and hung its straps around the saddle horn.

The dog barked three times, and Asher's voice could be heard, asking, "What has you so riled up all of a sudden?"

She saw a ladder, leaning against the fascia. Near the top of the ladder, Asher was squinting into the morning sun, a ten-penny nail poking out from between his lips as he hammered another to hold the gutter in place.

"Good morning," she called up to him.

Asher lurched, then cursed under his breath. After moving the nails from his mouth to his jacket pocket, he climbed down.

"Sorry if I startled you."

"If?" He laughed. "What brings you here?"

She held up the tin. "I made you snickerdoodles, to show my appreciation for all you've done around the schoolhouse."

"My favorite? You shouldn't have." He accepted the cookies. "But I am glad you did."

Tessa laughed, too.

"The house is beautiful."

"Come inside. I will show you around while I taste test them."

He led her into the foyer, down a long hall, and to the kitchen.

"Such a bright, sunny room. Did you make all these cabinets?"

"Made the table and chairs, and the ones in the dining room, too."

What did a bachelor need with a house this big? she wondered.

"Would you like to see the rest of the place?"

"Yes, but . . ."

Instantly, he understood her hesitation.

"I get it. We are alone."

"I know it seems silly, considering how much time we spend on your lessons, unchaperoned. But your parents live so close, and a customer could stop by."

"Tell you what. I will stand on the porch with the door open, hollering directions as you walk from room to room. That way, you can see the place and protect your reputation . . . and mine."

Tessa laughed again, imagining it. "You know, that sounds like fun. Let's do it!"

She climbed the stairs, and he shouted, "First room on your right is mine. Two more smaller bedrooms on the left. And at the end of the hall, the future bathroom."

The rooms were sparsely furnished, but clean and bright, and he'd paid a lot of attention to details, like perfectly mitered window and door frames, and low-gloss hardwood floors. She thought of the occasion or two when, for no apparent reason, he'd fallen silent, looking furious. But seeing all the love he'd put into this place eased her concerns that, like her father, Asher might have a hair-trigger temper that could result in damage to whatever—or whomever—was nearby.

By the time she joined him again, Asher had heated up two mugs of coffee and carried them onto the porch. He'd spread a dinner napkin on the low table that sat between two oversized rocking chairs, and placed the mugs near a sugar bowl and cream pitcher. He'd even remembered the stirring spoons. And beside that, a small plate of snickerdoodles.

"Your work?" she asked, sitting on the nearest rocker.

"It is." He joined her, picked up a cookie. "I had a good teacher."

He spent the next ten minutes talking about lessons learned at his father's knee. How to choose the best wood, the right tool, the proper fasteners for each project. Seeing real sadness dim his eyes when he talked about the accident that had forced the man's early retirement gave her more reason to believe that the only things Asher and her father had in common were gender and a lack of reading skill. Soon, there'd be one less similarity.

"These are delicious," Asher said, dusting sugar from his fingertips. "Old family recipe?"

"You could say that. Passed down from my great-great-grandmother. She was Swiss-German and brought hundreds of recipes from the old country. As well as this cookie tin."

"What do you think it means . . . *snickerdoodle*?"

"No one knows for sure, but I think my mother is right that the name is a corruption of the German word *schneckennudeln.*"

"Crinkly noodles? Are you serious?"

"It is as good an explanation as I have heard." Tessa picked up their mugs. "More for you, too?"

"Sure. Why not?"

It surprised her to see Noah's notebook on the kitchen counter. When she went back to the porch, she brought it with her, tucked under one arm.

"My brother never mentioned that you two had discussed his invention."

"That buggy dash of his is fascinating."

"Will you build one for your buggy?"

"I'm thinking about it."

Tessa flipped through the book, reading tabs that said things like PIECES and PARTS. "What is this?" she asked, showing him something Noah had scribbled in a margin.

"I have to be honest, I am going by his sketches, not the words. Near as I can figure, it has something to do with a manual hydraulic pressure piston pump."

"Goodness! What is *that*?"

"It converts mechanical energy into hydraulic energy by delivering hydraulic fluid, under pressure, through manual effort." He leaned closer, pointed at Noah's drawing. "See how he uses the simple principle of a handle that provides leverage to the internal piston?"

"No, I do not see." Tessa sat back. "But you and Noah do, and I am very happy for you both!"

Asher's laughter echoed through the porch.

"I need to get home, finish grading some papers." She stood, picked up the mugs, thinking to rinse them in the kitchen sink.

"Leave them. Even a crusty old bachelor like me can take care of that job. Do you really have to leave already?"

"Yes, I am afraid so. Daed will join Noah in the shop soon, and I want to be nearby in case . . ." *Hush, you nincompoop. He does not want to hear about your father's prickly personality.* "What is your next project?" she asked.

"The railing. Just need to decide between pickets and spindles."

"Oh, pickets." She started down the steps. "They do not collect as much dust, and are so much easier to paint."

He walked with her. "You know this because . . ."

"My mother chose spindles for the porches and also for the railing that leads upstairs, and guess who was in charge of keeping them clean and chip-free?"

"Good advice. Pickets it is, then."

She smoothed Bolt's mane, and he nuzzled her neck. "Did you hear that, Bolt? Silly me, telling the carpenter why pickets are better than spindles!"

The horse nickered, bobbed its head.

"I know the difference between the two," Asher said, "and can make either from any type of wood you can name. But the dust and paint chips aspect?" He shook his head. "Entirely new to me. So thanks for the tips. For those delicious cookies. And for listening closely enough when I babble to know they are my favorites."

Tessa retrieved her cold weather gear from the tote bag hanging from Bolt's saddle, wound the scarf around her neck, slipped her fingers into the mittens, and swapped caps.

"Funny," Asher said good-naturedly, "but I did not hear about a blizzard in the forecast."

"This good boy," she replied, patting the horse's neck, "deserves a nice, long ride. I could use some time on the trail, too. It will get cold once he gets going."

"Aha. Muddy Run or Groff Creek?"

"Muddy Run, if I had time, but I have done nothing yet to prepare for Thanksgiving dinner."

"Why not join us? My mother and Sarah would love seeing you again."

Tessa pictured the Stuery table, draped in Rose's best tablecloth and covered with heaping bowls and platters being passed by his parents, Reuben and Sarah, and their boys. "It is sweet of you to ask, but it wouldn't be fair, leaving Noah alone." Almost as an afterthought, she added, "Or my father."

Asher didn't answer right away. "Then bring them," he said after a while.

She'd spent enough time with him to know he only worked his jaw muscles that way while struggling with a word.

Tessa unfastened Bolt's reins. "Thank you for the invitation, but . . ." She let her voice trail off, and climbed into the saddle.

"Thank *you,* for stopping by, and for the cookies. I enjoyed the visit." Asher rested a hand on her knee. "The more time I spend with you, the more time I *want* to spend with you. Saying good-bye gets harder every time."

Pulse pounding with emotion, she said, "Try 'see you later' instead."

"Yes, Miss Beachy." And then, "Say, what are you doing next Saturday?"

"I had not thought that far ahead."

"I promised to take Reuben's boys to see the wolves at the sanctuary, and to bring them to the Lititz Hometown Christmas. There will be music, crafts, good food, even a gingerbread contest." He gave her knee a squeeze. "Come with us."

"Isn't it odd that, even though we live so close, I have never visited either place. So yes, I would love to go with you." She turned Bolt around, pulled back on the reins slightly to hold him still for a moment longer. "Well, I do not want to overstay my welcome." She urged Bolt forward, called over her shoulder, "Tell your family I hope to see them soon."

As she rode away, Tessa heard him say, "Impossible for you to overstay your welcome."

The horse, sensing that she'd soon let him run full-out, broke into a trot. "Easy, boy," she soothed, stroking his thick, silky winter coat of hair. "Soon as we clear the hard roads and neighborhoods, you can remind me how you got your name."

Bolt nickered, shook his head, ears swiveling as he waited for her signal.

Tessa leaned forward, pressed into him as trees and boulders blurred past. From neck to withers to ribs, lean muscles tightened. Long, lean legs stretched out, digging into the wind and kicking the town farther behind them. Hoofbeats drummed the mossy ground; heartbeats thrummed against her thighs, reminding her how good it felt to absorb his raw, unrestrained power. Maturity had cured her fear of heights, the dark, spiders and snakes, and stinging insects. But the ever-reliable Bolt had not only cured her fear of speed, but taught her to revel in it.

"Let's not overdo it, old friend," she said, and eased up on the reins. As always, he responded instantly.

Tessa dismounted and, still a bit breathless, pressed her palms to his cheeks. His eyes closed, and a deep, fluttering breath exited his nostrils.

"You have every right to feel satisfied," she said, stroking his glossy forehead. "That was some ride. Just what I needed to clear my head. Now, how about if we go home, so I can give you a good brushing. Some oats and apple slices, too. You earned them, wouldn't you say?"

Bolt bobbed his head, as if to say, "You bet I did!"

Tessa gave him a final pat, then threaded the toe of her boot into the stirrup and hoisted herself into the saddle. The supple leather responded with a low, satisfying creak. The wind had died down, and she could hear Bolt's steady breaths, the crunch of gravel beneath his iron shoes, the piercing shrieks of blue jays. She liked feeling serene and safe—and wondered why life couldn't be this serene all the time.

Tessa hoped Asher's day would leave him feeling as calm.

She'd read lots of romance novels in her teens. The authors' word pictures of heroes—tall, broad-shouldered, muscular—had been intriguing. How would they have described Asher?

Tall. Burly. Dark-haired and green-eyed. Muscular. With a heart-stopping smile and a faint scar that zigzagged across his chin . . .

A childhood injury, she wondered, or something more recent? Next time there was a lull in their conversation, she'd ask about it. The problem with that idea: next time implied there had been lulls. Tessa laughed to herself as her mind returned to descriptions of male romance novel characters. . . .

Strong, bold, disciplined men willing to risk everything to protect the ladies who'd captured their hearts. The stories had been entertaining and enjoyable, but even as a dreamy-eyed girl, she hadn't believed any of it.

Although she'd grown and matured, Tessa didn't feel that way anymore . . .

. . . because Asher Stuery had come into her life, and proved that such men *did* exist.

Chapter 8

Asher stacked the remaining snickerdoodles on a paper plate. *What better excuse for another quick visit?* he thought, rinsing the cookie tin.

No one answered when he knocked on the Beachys' front door, so he made his way to the shop at the back of the property.

"Surprised to see you," Noah said, looking up from the big ledger book. "Tessa must have changed her mind."

"About what?"

"She left for your place early this morning, to bring you . . ." Confusion furrowed his brow when he noticed the tin. "I know they're delicious, but you ate them all? Already?"

Laughing, Asher said, "Not all of them. But I felt guilty holding on to the tin, knowing how much it means to Tessa." He slid it onto the corner of the desk. "Stopped by the house to return it, but no one is home."

"Saw Tessa ride past here a couple hours ago. She ought to be back soon." Noah motioned toward one of two chairs against the wall. "There's an article about the festival in *The Budget.* Have a seat and—"

Slow-paced hoof beats interrupted Noah, who said, "See there? Told you she wouldn't be gone long."

Asher followed Noah's gaze and saw Tessa ride into the barn, just across the way. "That saddle is almost as big as she is. Think I will help her with it."

"Trust me, she needs no help. That girl could lift me with one hand tied behind her back." Noah winked, and, as Asher grasped the door handle, he said, "But I think she will appreciate the offer." He tapped the cookie tin. "Don't forget this."

By the time he reached the barn, Tessa had already loosened the saddle's back cinch, and stood inches from the horse's withers, working on the breast collar.

She gave Asher a quick once-over. "Goodness, Bolt," she said, tying up the latigo, "I think the man is here for a refill!"

Asher held up the empty tin. "I haven't eaten them all. Yet. I just thought, since this tin is a family heirloom, I should return it as soon as possible."

Tessa hung the cinches and dragged a wooden box up close. At barely more than five feet tall, she'd need it if she hoped to remove the heavy saddle. He placed the tin on the tack bench.

"Let me do that for you," he said, and stepped up beside her.

"I have been doing this for years."

"But why, if I'm willing to do it for you?" He slid the makeshift stool aside, lifted the saddle, and deposited it on the nearest rack. He reached past her and grabbed the hoof pick from the tack bench, and, while he dug mud and blades of grass from Bolt's shoes, she palmed the curry comb.

"He seems to enjoy the massage," he told her.

"He likes the dandy brush even better, and so do I. It makes his coat shine so. But do you know what he likes best?"

Having an owner who takes such good care of him, an owner as sweet-tempered and pretty as you? Asher thought.

"When I wash his face. You should see him. He closes his eyes and sighs. Sometimes, he even kisses me!"

Whoever thought you'd be jealous of a horse!

He noticed a spritz bottle on the bench. "What's that?"

"Fly spray. When I saw all the harmful ingredients in the store-bought stuff, I decided to make my own. Cheaper. Healthier. Smells good, too, not all . . . chemically."

"Chemically." He chuckled. "I love the way you make up words." He loved a whole lot more than that, but this was neither the time nor the place to admit it.

Tessa blushed, tried to hide it by pretending to concentrate on combing Bolt's mane.

"So tell me. What's in your spray?"

"Raw apple cider vinegar, essential oils, some mineral oil, dish soap . . ."

"Interesting."

She traded the curry comb for the dandy brush. "I am happy to make some for you."

"How about teaching me to make it instead."

"All right . . ."

They finished up in companionable silence, and, after backing Bolt into his stall, Tessa checked his feed and water buckets.

"Do not worry, Cirrus," she said, stroking his brother's wispy white mane. "You will get a refill, just like Bolt."

"He is the smaller of the two," Asher observed, "but I would guess he pulls more than his own weight."

"And you would be right."

"Did you buy them during a storm?"

She laughed again. "No, my mother is responsible for their names."

"I get calling him Bolt, because of the marking on his forehead. But Cirrus?"

"His forelock hair is white and wispy. . . ."

"I see."

Tessa, dusting her palms together, said, "I am going to clean up and start lunch. I'm making sloppy joes. Will you join us?"

If he said no, he might not see her until Monday, two long days from now. Saying yes meant sitting across from the man who'd hurt her. Asher sent a quick prayer for self-control heavenward, and said yes. When he found out she needed to leave him alone in the kitchen while she washed up after her long ride, he prayed Gideon wouldn't show up while she was gone.

For the first few minutes, he sat at the table, sipping the milk she'd poured before going upstairs. That got old fast, and Asher got up, walked into the parlor, and looked around. Clean and orderly, just like the kitchen, where dinnerware sat in tidy stacks and tumblers sparkled on the open shelves. He scanned the room, from the roll-up window blinds to the afghan on the sofa to the muted blues of the braided rug. How many of the items, artfully arranged on the unadorned side tables—books, clocks, lamps—had been put into place by her mother, and how many were Tessa's idea?

"Sorry to keep you waiting," she said, descending the stairs.

Tessa had changed into a pale blue dress and a white apron that covered most of it. Asher said another prayer, this time to thank God that living Plain didn't require women to wear hats indoors. Unbraided, her hair likely cloaked her shoulders like an acorn-colored cape, and oh what he wouldn't give to see that!

"How can I help?" he asked when she led the way into the kitchen.

"No need, but thank you. It is an easy meal to prepare. Ground beef. Onions. Tomato sauce. Brown sugar. A few secret spices . . . I am happy for the company, though, while I work. Care for some coffee?"

"No thanks." He held up the half-full glass of milk. "This will do."

She wrinkled her nose. "Never cared for the stuff, myself."

"Really?"

"No matter how fresh, it always tastes sour to me."

"Never met a milk hater before."

"Guess you cannot say that anymore, can you?"

Oh, but she was a delight. How could anyone deliberately harm her?

"Where is Gideon?"

"Oh, he is around somewhere."

She didn't sound too enthusiastic. And who could blame her?

"Noah is still in the shop?"

"More than likely. He is rarely late for supper, though." A silly grin lit her face. "Have we spent too much time together today?"

"No such thing as too much time with you." *If you'd have me, I would spend the rest of my life at your side.* "How about if I set the table for you?"

"Firewood, grooming Bolt, now this? How will I ever repay you?"

"Repay me?" Asher moved to her side. "Tessa. If I live a hundred years, I can never repay *you* for—"

Her father joined them in the kitchen, aimed a tense smile in Asher's direction. "What brings you here, Stuery?"

Tessa answered in his stead. "Asher returned my cookie tin, then helped me groom Bolt. I asked him to join us, to show my appreciation."

Had she seen something in her father's face to inspire her to run interference for him? Asher watched as Gideon poured himself a glass of milk, and wondered about the dark circles under the man's eyes.

"Noah told me about the department store deal." Much as he disliked idle chitchat, Asher decided that discussing business might help him feign respect. "You must be pleased."

Gideon sat at the head of the table. "You can say that again."

The back door slammed. "Ah," Noah said, hanging up his coat, "a guest for supper, eh?"

"Have you balanced the checkbook?" Gideon asked.

"That is an end-of-month job, Daed."

"It *is* the end of the month."

"Not for five days yet."

Father and son went back and forth until Tessa stopped the argument with one question:

"Asher, would you do me one more favor and set the table?"

"Happy to," he said. Both Beachy men sat in stony silence while Asher performed the chore. They managed to remain civil throughout the meal, thanks to Tessa's constant chatter . . . about her ride, and the likelihood of snow, preparations for the annual Christmas pageant . . . and Asher got the impression that his presence had a lot to do with the men's cooperation.

Half an hour or so later, Noah got to his feet. "That was delicious, Tess."

"No dessert?"

"After I tie up a few loose ends in the shop."

Gideon stood, too, and tightly gripped his chair's back. "Think I will turn in early." Facing Asher, he said, "It was good to see you, Asher. Give your parents my best. Reuben and his family, too."

Now that they were alone, Asher helped carry dishes to the sink. As she filled it with hot water, he asked, "Do you feel safe, Tessa?"

She added liquid dish soap, and gave the container a squeeze, laughing as tiny bubbles floated between them.

"What a question. I have always felt safe with you."

He outweighed her by at least seventy-five pounds, stood a foot taller. Easy to see why she'd misunderstood the question.

"I am glad to hear it. But what I meant was . . . do you feel safe, here in your father's house, after . . . ?"

Asher sank the stack of plates into the foamy water, then slowly, so as not to startle her, touched the bruise beside her eye. "I hate that he did this to you."

"I hate it too," she whispered, then wiped the suds from her temple with a tentative smile. "I know I sometimes behave like a bubblehead, but until now, it has been figurative," she said.

"Oh. Sorry." He dried his hand, used the corner of the towel to daub suds from her face. "In my opinion, you are perfect." He tossed the cloth aside, cupped her chin in a palm. "Never diminish yourself, not even as a joke."

Tessa searched his face for a lingering moment, then slid her arms around him and rested her cheek on his chest.

"Your heart is pounding like a drum," she whispered.

Asher stood back, just enough to search *her* face. "That is your fault," he said, and, when she smiled, he kissed her. Kept kissing her, until a loud thump from the room above interrupted them.

"Daed . . ."

The worry on her face was reflected in her voice. Asher followed her up the stairs, into Gideon's room, where they found him facedown on the floor.

"Such a shame," Asher's mother said, "that Tessa and Noah must deal with this, right at Thanksgiving time."

His father nodded. "Not easy to give thanks when your father has passed on, but . . . God's will . . ."

"I remember losing my own father," Sarah said. "How are they holding up, Asher?"

"I wish I knew."

After he and Tessa had found Gideon, she'd dropped to her knees, stayed there for a long, long time, then took his lifeless hand in hers, then aimed those big, damp eyes at him and said, "Maybe if I had have loved him better . . ." *You were a doting daughter, and his death isn't your fault,* he'd wanted to say. Instead, he'd harnessed Bolt, carried Gideon to the buggy, and drove her to the undertaker's. Afterward, Asher had taken her in his arms, offered to stay as long as she needed him to. But there were things to do and plans to make, she'd said, and sent him on his way.

"What is wrong with Asher?" his youngest nephew asked.

His older brother agreed. "Yeah. Looks like he might bust out cryin' any minute."

"He's fine, boys," Reuben assured them. "Just thinking about Miss Beachy."

"No need to look so sad, Son," his mother said. "Tessa is a strong young woman who understands God's will."

He blinked a few times, watched as Reuben ladled gravy onto Paul's mashed potatoes.

"I delivered an end table to Deacon Cook this morning," Reuben said, "who told me that Tessa requested one, rather than two sermons, and no singing during the funeral service."

"Isn't that odd," his mother said.

Reuben shook his head. "Not when you take everything into consideration."

As one of Ida's closest friends, Rose understood. "Yes, well, Tessa and Noah will be fine, just fine. After the funeral service, and the gathering, when they are surrounded by God's love and the church family, they will celebrate that Gideon is at peace in heaven."

Her words seemed to comfort Reuben's bright-eyed boys. But they were children, and didn't realize that Tessa and Noah were not surrounded by loving family. Right about now, they were probably emptying their parlor in preparation for tomorrow's viewing.

The hours passed slowly as Asher paced and prayed, and slept in fits and starts, unable to shake one thought from his mind: If Tessa was his wife, he'd be with her now, providing comfort, helping with the arrangements, making sure she knew that Gideon's death had not been her fault.

Next morning at the Beachys', the Stuery family walked slowly past the coffin, muttered quiet prayers, and exchanged polite words with Tessa and Noah. Asher thought they both looked overly tired and drawn. Had they stayed up all night together? Or spent the hours separately, in private mourning?

At work the next day, Asher felt about as wooden as the bench he'd built for the Millers.

And then spent yet another restless night, wishing he could go to her, *be* with her.

He considered himself blessed to have nephews who, even at their young ages, understood that under the circumstances, their outing would have to be postponed. Seated with his family on their usual bench, surrounded by other dressed-in-black congregants, he tried to pay attention while the preachers took turns reading scripture. Asher felt a twinge of pity for Gideon, because not a tear was shed for him. Not in the church. Not at the cemetery. That alone wasn't unusual in a community where the afterlife held far greater importance than life on earth. And yet . . .

He also considered himself blessed to have own his parents with him still. If the mere thought of losing them could bring tears to his eyes, what were the chances he'd remain dry-eyed when that dreaded day came? If he should burst into tears, he stood to get a long-winded lecture from the bishop for dwelling on his loss instead of praising God, because mourning was useless in the lives of the faithful.

By those standards, Tessa and Noah would earn the man's respect; it wasn't likely that anyone else noticed them, standing stiff-backed and silent through it all. But Asher saw and prayed that, in time, God would reveal the truth: Loving their father more, or differently, would not have changed him. The only human with the power to soften Gideon's heart had been Gideon, himself.

The four friends who'd carried the coffin to the graveyard secured its lid, and unceremoniously grasped the ropes that lowered it into the ground. It hit bottom with a dull *thump* as the bishop recited Gideon's name, birthdate, and the day he'd died, concluding with "We commit our brother to the Lord Jesus."

Solemn. Simple. Respectful. *And cold,* Asher thought, looking across at Tessa. Head down and hands clasped at her waist, she stood shoulder to shoulder with her brother as the men began filling the hole. Eyes closed, Tessa flinched ever so slightly each time a shovelful of black, loamy soil peppered the pale pine lid.

And then, blessedly, the job was done, and the congregants, his family included, started walking away. He took a step forward, thinking to wrap her in his arms, but his mother's hand on his wrist stopped him. "She and Noah need time alone. If you care, you will give it to her."

If I care? he wanted to shout.

"You can check on her tomorrow. Better still, the next day."

He knew nothing about losing a loved one, but his mother had buried her parents. A sibling. A baby that had only lived a month.

"A man never grows too old to take his mother's advice," Asher said and began counting the hours until he visited . . .

. . . to cheer her up with some of her favorite cupcakes.

Chapter 9

Asher and Reuben had been in their early teens when their father first took them hunting. After delivering the usual safety instructions, he'd said, "We'll meet right here at noon, when the sun is high and straight overhead."

That's where it was on Sunday morning, when Asher rode up the Beachys' drive.

He'd never been one to wish his life away, but since leaving the graveyard, time had seemed to crawl.

He dismounted, tied Ginger's reins to the hitching rail, and reached up to get the pink box fastened to the saddle.

He took the back porch steps two at a time, peered through the window beside the door, and saw her at the sink. Turning, she quickly crossed the room and let him in.

"Thought you might enjoy these," he announced.

Tessa untied the white ribbon that had secured the box. "You went all the way to Lancaster?" She met his eyes. "And bought these, for me?"

I would buy you the moon and the sun if I thought they'd make you look this happy.

"I hope Noah likes chocolate as much as you do."

"He would eat a rock if I put salt and butter on it!" She stuck out her forefinger, scooped frosting from one of the treats, and popped it into her mouth. "Will you have one with me?"

"Now?"

"The coffee is hot, so why not?" She filled two mugs and sat across from him. "I am glad you were there," she said, peeling away the cupcake paper, "for . . . everything."

"Had to be."

Her brow furrowed with confusion.

"I only wish I could have been right there beside you, instead of across the way."

Tessa handed him a cupcake. "You were." She pressed a palm to her chest. "Here, as close as it gets."

He wanted to ask her to explain. Wanted to tell her that he'd held her in his heart since before their first reading lesson. But she'd gone through so much, especially this past week, that he couldn't bring himself to put her in such a position.

"I see your woodpile is shrinking." Asher pointed to the corner, where a nearly empty basket of kindling sat beside a nearly empty box of six-inch logs. He got up, put on his coat. "I'll bring some in for you."

"Noah can do that."

"He has a lot on his mind, too," Asher said, and went outside.

Across the way, he noticed the horses, standing nose to nose in the paddock. He jogged close to the gate, and, instantly, they walked up to him. "You didn't hear that there is a snowstorm on the way?" He ruffled their thick manes. "We need to get you inside, where you will stay warm and dry."

They must have understood—and agreed—because both followed him straight to the outbuilding. He topped off their food and water buckets, and latched the stalls. "Don't eat it all at once," he warned, and fastened the slide bolt on the wide entry door.

He gathered an armload of wood and made his way back to the house, adding it to the woodbox.

"Asher, really. You do not need to do this. We are perfectly capable of doing it ourselves."

"It makes me feel good, doing things for you." Grinning, he stood in the open door to add, "Why would you deprive me of that?"

Her quiet laughter grew softer once the door closed behind him. He went for another armload of wood, and, when he returned, it surprised him to find her at the sink, weeping.

Asher dropped the wood into the box and threw his jacket onto the floor.

"Tess," he said, wrapping his arms around her. "What's wrong?"

She leaned into him. "I don't know. Nothing. Everything."

He turned her around, hands bracketing her face, thumbs stroking the tears from her cheeks.

"Sorry. I should not . . ."

"Yes, you should."

"But crying, sadness, it is . . ." She sniffed. "It is disobedient. Proof that I have not accepted God's will . . ."

"It is proof of nothing, except that you are human." He led her to the table, gently sat her down. He sat, too, so that their knees were touching.

"I could have loved him better."

Sensing that she needed to talk, Asher sat back to listen.

"I was afraid of him. Blamed him for my mother's death. I avoided him whenever I could."

"And yet, you took good care of him."

She shook her head, loosening a curl from her bun. Asher tucked it behind her ear, and she pressed her cheek into his palm.

"No, you are wrong. For months, he had seemed tired. Looked so pale. Complained of aches and pains. I did not even think to suggest that he see a doctor. And now . . ."

And now he is gone, Asher finished for her, *and I can't help him.*

Her sobs came from deep inside her. Asher pulled her closer, rested his chin atop her head, and prayed for the words to comfort her. He could quote scripture: "He will wipe every tear from their eyes . . ." Or "Let not your heart be troubled . . ." Instead, he lifted her chin on a bent forefinger, urging her to look into his eyes. "Life is too short to waste time on misplaced blame. God reads your heart," he said, touching his nose to hers, "and knows what I know . . . that nothing but good lives there. He will free you of guilt if you tell Him how you feel."

She blinked, and a tear fell from tear-clumped lashes. Calm now, she nodded, then snuggled closer, so close that he couldn't tell where he ended and she began. In this moment, he understood the *look* that had softened Reuben's expression when he spoke of sweet, stolen moments with Sarah on the church path. It had been hard *not* to envy his brother's life, but in this moment, he understood something more: He could have that life . . . with Tessa.

Tessa returned to school on the Monday after the funeral. "Take another day, maybe two," Noah had advised. But she'd taken Asher's simple, straightforward advice to heart, and, lightened of her burden of guilt, decided he'd been right to trust God. It was time to tell him how she felt.

The children lightened her mood even more by cracking jokes, volunteering to erase the chalkboard, asking permission to read aloud from Laura Ingalls Wilder's *The Long Winter.*

If she could, Tessa would take every one of them home with her, so she could enjoy them all day, every day. *You would not feel this way if you had children of your own.*

Did she dare hope that, someday, that beautiful dream would come true . . . with Asher?

Over supper that night, Noah wanted to know how she managed to look so happy.

"Prayer," she answered, "inspired by some well-meaning advice from a treasured friend."

He snickered. "Friend indeed. He is much more than that, and there is nothing wrong with admitting it." He paused. "How do you feel about him?"

Where should she begin?! "He is kind and caring and helpful, always there for his family, and works hard to please them. He is smart and—"

"You could be describing the family dog. Anyone who knows him feels the same way." He paused. "Do you love him?"

"I do not know. Maybe."

"Could you live without him?"

Tessa laughed. "I live without him now."

Noah scrubbed a hand over his face. "Tess, stick with me here. If Asher moved away, and you never saw him again, could you live with that?"

During the hours they'd worked together, his temperament had always remained steady, even when he was struggling to sound out multisyllable words, which made it easy to help him celebrate each small victory. Added to the genuine affection Asher showered on every Stuery, she recalled the generous spirit that inspired visits to neighbors in need for deliveries of firewood . . . and cupcakes. . . .

"No, I could not."

"If he asked, would you marry him?"

"Yes."

Noah snickered again. "That was a quick answer!"

It does not take long to tell the truth, she thought.

"Tell him. The sooner, the better."

"I cannot just walk up to him and blurt out, 'I love you, Asher Stuery!' He will think—"

"—that he is blessed beyond measure."

"But . . ." She bit her lower lip. "But what if he does not feel the same?"

"The way he looks at you? Please."

"How does he look at me?"

"As though you are the best thing that ever happened to him." Noah winked. "Same way you look at him, by the way."

The wail of a siren came through the front window, flashing red and white strobes streaking across the kitchen ceiling.

"Oh, Lord," she prayed, "send your protection. . . ."

"The sirens have stopped, but the lights are still flashing, and they look close." Noah ran into the back entryway, hurried into his jacket, and grabbed the doorknob. "Are you coming with me?"

She slipped into her coat and ran beside him. Once they reached the end of the drive, he said, "It's the Bachmans."

Sometime in the summer, the bishop's newly married daughter and her husband had bought the old Schmidt place, and, in the months since, they'd been working to improve the run-down old house. Four years ago when Tessa became the community's teacher, Grace, barely eighteen now, had been one of her first students, and Grace still held a place in her heart. The girl stood beside her young husband, crying and shivering in the cold spray of the firefighters' hose.

Tessa went to her, slid an arm across her shoulders.

"It happened so fast," Grace said.

"Chimney fire," Earl explained. "I knew I should have cleaned it. Put it off to fix the roof, and now the roof is on fire!"

Grace grasped his hand. "This is not your fault, Husband." She faced Tessa. "Tell him, Miss Beachy. Tell him this could have happened to anyone."

If the bishop had been here, he'd have pointed out that all things are God's will. But Tessa couldn't bring herself to say it.

"Chimney fires happen all the time," Noah said.

The firefighters worked nonstop for an hour, bellowing to one another as they finally worked to put out the fire.

"If you need a place to stay, you are welcome to come home with Noah and me."

"Thank you, Miss Beachy, but—"

"You're all grown up and married now. Please, call me Tessa."

Grace used the hem of her apron to dry her eyes. "Thank you for that, too, but when my father hears of this . . ." She looked at the house—or what was left of it—and started to cry again.

"We appreciate the offer," Earl said, "but we can stay with family until . . ." He looked at the house, too, his lower lip trembling as he added, ". . . until we rebuild."

"I will stop by the bishop's house from time to time to see how you are faring."

A deep voice just over Tessa's shoulder said, "And you know the community will help in every way we can."

"Yes, Asher, we are blessed in that way." Earl pulled Grace close in a sideways hug. "Well, nothing more we can do here. We might as well break the news to our folks."

Noah, Tessa, and Asher stood in a row, watching the young couple walk away.

"How sad," Tessa said, "to start their married life with a tragedy."

Asher nodded in the direction they'd gone. "They have each other." He paused, crossed his arms over his chest. "Reminds me of a man I met once. A customer who had ordered a shelf for his collection of pottery. Showed me his favorite piece, a beautiful vase with ripples of gold all through it, and told me a story about Kintsugi, the Japanese art of mixing lacquer with powdered gold as a binding agent to mend broken pottery. Not only does it make the vessel stronger, it also represents strength, by bringing attention to the cracks, rather than hiding them." He looked at Tessa. "The Bachmans seem broken now, but I have faith that as they rebuild, they will experience things that bond them, one to the other, and strengthen their love."

Noah said, "I need to see about adding that to the Beachy Pottery story. If I can find this binding recipe, I might just break a pot on purpose, so I can mend it and display it in the shop." He yawned. "I am going to bed. Try to be quiet when you get home, Sister."

Smiling, Tessa promised to try, and wondered if she ought to invite Asher to join her for coffee, and maybe another cupcake.

"I will walk you home," he said.

"But Asher, you live in the opposite direction."

Arm extended to lead the way, he said, "Being with you makes me feel good. Why would you deprive me of that?"

Almost word for word what he'd said the other night, after he'd put the horses up to spare her having to do it and refilled the woodbox. She wanted to thank him. Again. Wanted to take Noah's advice and tell Asher that she loved him, that if he asked her to, she'd marry him.

She linked her arm through his, adjusted her pace so that every step mirrored his: left, right, left, right. . . .

"You are a good man, Asher Stuery, and I am blessed . . ." She almost said, "*. . . to call you friend.*" But she wanted more than friendship from him. Much more. She finished with ". . . God blessed me when He put you into my life."

Asher stopped walking, faced her head-on. "If you do not want to kiss me right now, this would be a good time to run."

"I appreciate the warning." Standing on tiptoe, Tessa wound her arms around his neck and pressed her lips to his.

She felt a low chuckle rumbling in his chest and took a step back. "What is so funny?" she demanded, hands on hips.

"You are supposed to close your eyes when you kiss a man."

"And you know this because—"

He silenced her with another kiss.

And this time, she closed her eyes.

Chapter 10

"Have you chosen the person who will get our surprise quilt?"

"Actually, Mary," Tessa said as she faced the class, "I have an idea to run past you. . . . I am sure you heard that a fire destroyed Grace and Earl Bachman's house."

"My *daed* called the fire department," Sam said. "He used the phone shanty on Church Road. Ran all the way there without a coat on. My mother threw a fit over that!"

"I could see the glow from my bedroom window," Joel said.

Sam greed. "Me too. Lit up the whole sky. For miles and miles!"

Tessa clapped twice, and, once she had their attention again, said, "Yes, it was a horrible thing. But something good will come of it."

"How do you figure that?"

Oh, Thomas, she thought, *you were well-named!*

"They will experience the kindness of their church family," she said, "and in time, they will rebuild."

Samuel spoke up again. "My *daed* says they will have to start over."

"And good things can come from that, too," Tessa pointed out. "But here is my idea. . . .

We only need two more squares to complete our Christmas quilt." She looked at each child and added, "I think we should make one that represents their wedding day, and another that shows them together, with a blank line that they can fill in with a date once they have a new home."

The children were quiet for several seconds, until Lucy hollered, "That is a good idea, Teacher!"

"Is there time," Thomas wanted to know, "to make two more squares *and* stitch the whole thing together?"

"Sewing the squares together will be my contribution," Tessa said. "That way, each of you can walk onto the stage, holding your square and reciting your verse."

"I like it," Joel said.

"It will be the bestest Christmas pageant Bird-in-Hand has ever seen!" Lucy agreed.

And so it was settled. The children got to work, discussing which material scraps they'd use to create the Bachmans' squares.

It was the week before Christmas when, following the Sunday service, the community gathered to watch the performance.

Tessa stood at the front of the church and announced, "Your children have worked long and hard on this year's pageant. I think you will agree it was time well spent."

Stepping aside, she signaled her students, dressed in their Sunday finest and lined up at the rear of the church, awaiting her cue. Standing in place, they sang "It Is Well with My Soul." Then, one by one, they walked forward, holding the design side of their squares against their chests. Lucy turned hers around, then quoted from Genesis to explain her Creation picture. One by one, they recited the verses that related to the Garden of

Eden, Moses parting the Red Sea, Christ on the Cross, shepherds with the star, the manger scene, a bride and groom standing atop the Bachmans' wedding date, and finally, the bride and groom facing a plain white house—with a mailbox that said BACHMAN.

Once again, Tessa faced the congregation to say, "Our quilt was created to represent God's love, and it is our gift to Grace and Earl."

"To keep you warm 'til you get your own house again!" Lucy shouted.

When the laughter died down, Tessa said, "This week, we will stitch the squares together, stuff it with batting, and deliver it to the bishop's house on Christmas morning."

Despite the Amish reputation for keeping their feelings in check, there was hardly a dry eye in the church. When she saw Asher's red-rimmed eyes, Tessa's heart pulsed with gratitude. Because how blessed was she to have fallen in love with a man unafraid to show his emotions!

Asher rose earlier than usual, and, after finishing his chores, saddled Ginger and rode straight to Lancaster. God willing, his order would be ready.

When he walked into the schoolhouse, he saw the graph Tessa had drawn on the chalkboard. Across the top were arranged the words, NOUNS, ADJECTIVES, VERBS, ADVERBS. Oh, how good it felt, being able to decipher those combinations of letters. It felt better, still, knowing what they meant.

From the other side of the curtain between the upper and lower grades, he heard Tessa say, "Share the colored pencils, and make a Christmas card for your parents." Questions went back and forth: Pictures? Words? Both? And she answered, "They will be your cards, so you decide."

When she stepped to this side of the curtain, she said, "Asher. What are you doing here?"

"Uncle Asher?" his nephew said.

"'Mornin', Peter." Hopefully, if his presence embarrassed the boy, cupcakes and cookies would change that.

Peter's classmates turned, staring as Asher held up the stack of boxes he'd carried in. "Brought the children some Christmas treats."

Now, quiet gasps and looks of surprise went back and forth.

"What a nice surprise. Please. Bring them up here, and we will hand them out. Samuel, will you open the curtain, please?"

Asher deposited the cartons on her desk. "I did not think to bring napkins or paper plates."

"That is okay," Peter said. "Miss Beachy keeps some in the supply cupboard."

The boy went from desk to desk, delivering paper products, while Asher opened the boxes. "I got enough for everyone to have two," he said, "so help yourselves. Except . . . this one is for Miss Beachy."

The children filed past her desk in an orderly line and carried treats back to their desks. She accepted the cupcake balanced on Asher's palm.

Tessa tweaked a tiny scroll tucked into the icing. "A message?"

"You might call it that."

She pulled it out, unrolled it, and read silently.

"What does it say, Miss Beachy?" little Lucy wanted to know.

"Bet it's a love note!" Samuel whispered to his seatmate.

"Hey," Thomas said, glaring at Asher. "What did you write that made her cry?"

"These are happy tears," she said, fingertips fluttering beside her eyes.

"Well," Peter said, "are you gonna read it to us or not?"

Tessa searched Asher's face, no doubt wondering why he'd chosen this place and time to profess his love.

"I figured if I did it here, with an audience, you couldn't say no."

"Say no to what?" Lucy asked.

"I am hoping to convince Miss Beachy to change her name."

"Why? What is wrong with the one she's got?" Thomas demanded.

"Nothing. Tessa Beachy is a fine name." He met her eyes. "But Tessa Stuery is even finer, don't you think?"

"I get it," Rachel shouted. "He wants her to marry him!"

The only sound in the classroom was the steady *swish-hiss-swish* of the grandfather clock's pendulum.

Asher took the scroll from Tessa, dropped it on the desktop, then held her hands in his.

"What do you say, Miss Beachy? Will you change your name to Tessa Stuery?"

She bit her lower lip. Blinked. Daubed at her tears with a paper napkin, then said, "I will."

"Hey, my sister said that on her wedding day," Rachel marveled.

"Can we come to the wedding?" Peter asked.

"You are my nephew. Of course you can." Asher scanned the rest of the expectant faces that had been watching intently. "All of you will come, too. It's the Amish way, after all!"

A blend of hoorays and yippees traveled the room.

"Can we have another cupcake?" Thomas asked.

Tessa laughed. "Yes, you can."

Thomas took a big bite of the cupcake. His red frosting-covered lips drew back in a huge smile as he said, "You gonna eat your Christmas cupcake, Miss Beachy?"

"It's rather special, so I think I might save it." She turned her back to the class. "Thank you, Asher," she said . . .

. . . and mouthed *"I love you."*

If you've enjoyed CHRISTMAS AT THE AMISH BAKESHOP,
be sure to read
AMISH CHRISTMAS TWINS,
also by Shelley Shepard Gray, Rachel J. Good, and Loree Lough!

AMISH CHRISTMAS TWINS

In these heartwarming, faith-affirming stories, three Amish families face the joys, and challenges, of the holidays—with fruitful results . . .

THE CHRISTMAS NOT-WISH

New York Times and *USA Today Bestselling Author*
Shelley Shepard Gray

When the foster parents they've cautiously grown to love discover they're expecting, orphaned Roy and Jemima Fisher, ages six and seven, are secretly devastated by the certainty they'll be given up. With Christmas around the corner, their only wish is for new foster parents as nice as Mr. and Mrs. Kurtz. Meanwhile, the Kurtzes have wishes of their own—and with faith, they all may be gifted with twice the blessings . . .

NEW BEGINNINGS

Rachel J. Good

Still grieving the loss of her husband and unborn baby in an accident several months ago, Elizabeth Yoder is oblivious to her neighbor Luke Bontrager's deepening affection for her. But while she bleakly faces Christmas alone, it's Luke who reminds her it's the season for giving. And when Elizabeth donates her handmade baby clothes to New Beginnings, a home for teen moms, she soon finds her gifts repaid beyond measure, with Luke's love—and new beginnings of their own . . .

TWINS TIMES TWO

Loree Lough

What happens when two secretive, stubborn people find themselves thrown together to help four rascally youngsters—twins times two!—create a Christmas surprise for their parents? Mischief and mayhem, and just maybe . . . love!